Stories of

KING ARTHUR

AND HIS KNIGHTS

STORIES OF

KING ARTHUR

AND HIS KNIGHTS

Retold by Barbara Leonie Picard

with wood engravings by
Roy Morgan

HENRY Z. WALCK, INCORPORATED

Library of Congress Catalog Card Number: 66-15657

PRINTED IN T[ ]F AMERICA

CONTENTS

Contents

I

The Sword in the Stone

IN the old days, as it is told, there was a king in Britain named Uther Pendragon. He was a good king and mighty, and much of his strength he owed to his chief counsellor Merlin. For Merlin was an enchanter who could read the stars and hold converse with the fairy world; Merlin knew the secrets of nature and the hearts of men; to him the future was as clear as the past, and of either could he speak when he chose; and he could change his shape at will. So that it was small wonder King Uther prospered with such a counsellor.

Now, at that time, the duke of Tintagel, in Cornwall, made war on his overlord, King Uther, and came against him with an army. In the fighting the duke was slain and his men yielded, all save those in his castle of Tintagel which was held by his lady, Igraine. And because she was a brave and noble lady, King Uther's lords pleaded with him that he would make peace with her, and to this Uther agreed. When he saw the Lady Igraine, how fair she was and of how great dignity, he loved her; and because, though of middle age, he had no queen, he took her for his wife, and there was great rejoicing in the land. At the same time he gave in marriage the two young daughters of Igraine and the dead duke, Margawse and Morgan le Fay. Margawse was wedded to King Lot of Orkney in Scotland; and Morgan le Fay, who, for all her youth, was as skilled in sorcery as any witch of thrice her years, was wedded to good King Uriens of Gore.

Soon after this Merlin came to Uther and said, 'On a certain day, a son will be born to your queen, and because there are things which are hidden from other men yet not from me, I know that it would be well if you were to give me the child when he is born, that I may take him secretly to a good knight whom I know, and so shall he grow up in safety.'

And because he ever trusted Merlin's counsel, King Uther agreed to this.

The months passed and there came a day when a son was born to Uther and Igraine, and the little child was wrapped in cloth of gold and given to Merlin, who carried him swiftly away from the castle of the king to the home of a knight named Sir Ector. And Sir Ector's lady took the babe as her foster-child, and he was christened Arthur and reared as brother to her own son, Kay.

Two years later that which Merlin had foreseen took place, and King Uther fell sick and lay dying, with his good Queen Igraine weeping at his bedside. Then Merlin came to the king at the head of all the nobles of the realm and asked, 'Is it your wish that Arthur, your son, should be king when you are gone?' And before all the great lords gathered there, King Uther said, 'That is my wish and my command.' After that he spoke no more, but died. And soon Queen Igraine was also dead, for she did not long survive her lord. And again as Merlin had foreseen, once the land was without a strong man to rule it, the nobles fell to quarrelling amongst themselves and gathering each of them his own army and marching against his neighbour; and in the heart of each one was the thought,'Wherever he is, what is this child Arthur to me? Surely I myself am more fitted to be a king than any other in the land?' And so it went on for many years with all Britain in great turmoil and distress.

But in the home of Sir Ector, young Arthur grew into a handsome lad, courteous and brave; skilled in horseman-ship and all knightly feats, obeying and honouring those whom he thought his parents, and ever loving his supposed brother, Kay. Often Merlin would come to Ector's house and talk with Arthur, telling him strange and marvellous things and teaching him much that a king should know; though Arthur guessed not why he was thus favoured by one whose wisdom had been respected by a monarch.

When Arthur was some fourteen years old, Merlin caused, by his enchantments, a large stone to appear before the great church in London. Upon this stone was an anvil, and thrust into the anvil was a sword, and on the anvil was written in letters of gold, 'He who draws forth this sword is the rightful king of Britain.'

When the people saw this they all marvelled, and many tried to draw forth the sword, but they all failed. Therefore ten knights were chosen to guard the stone and the anvil day and night, that they might keep watch for him who was to be their king.

Soon after, a great tournament and jousting were proclaimed in London for New Year's day, and knights came from all over the land to try their skill at arms, and there were many among them who hoped also to draw the sword from the anvil.

Now Kay, Sir Ector's son, had but lately been ordained knight, and he was eager to show his skill before strangers and wished to test his courage in the tourneying, so he begged that his father might permit him to travel to London and take part in the great gathering. To this Sir Ector agreed, and one morning he and Kay set forth; and with them went Arthur as squire to the new-made knight, to carry his shield and his lance for him and to look to his horse.

They rode across the wintry fields and along the frosty roads until they were come to London, and there they lodged at an inn, close by the great church. Although he said nothing of it to his father or to Arthur, Kay had determined in his heart to try to draw the sword out from the anvil. 'For,' he thought, 'why might it not be I who shall be king as well as any other man?' But Arthur was too eagerly watching and hearing all the sights and sounds of London to have any other thoughts in his head.

On the first day of the jousting, the three of them rode to the place where the contests were to be held, a wide field beyond the city walls. Arthur carried Kay's lance and his shield which he had polished until it shone; but in his eagerness Kay had forgotten his sword and left it at the inn, and it was not until they were in sight of the gay-coloured pavilions which had been set up in the tourney-field that he missed it, and exclaimed in annoyance.

'What has happened?' asked Arthur.

'I have forgotten my sword,' said Kay. 'Ride back to the inn and fetch it for me.'

Arthur did as he was bidden and Kay called after him impatiently, urging him to make haste. But when Arthur came to the inn he found the door locked and the windows shuttered fast and the hostess and all her servants gone to watch the jousting.

He rode along the streets looking for someone from whom he might borrow a sword, but he saw no one at all, for everyone had gone to the fields beyond the city walls. Just as Arthur was despairing, he saw before him the great church, and there, in front of it, the stone with the anvil and the sword.

'I will try to draw out the sword from the anvil,' he thought, 'for it seems there is no other sword left in all the city, and it shall never be said that my brother Kay lacked a sword at his first jousting.'

Even the ten knights who guarded the stone were gone to the tourneying, so that no one saw Arthur when he dismounted and walked up to the stone. He took hold of the hilt of the sword and made to give it a mighty pull, but to his surprise the sword came out of the anvil easily, as though it had never been held fast. Yet Arthur wasted no time marvelling at this; he mounted his horse and galloped back to where Kay waited for him at the entrance to the tourney-ground. 'Here is a sword for you, brother,' he said.

Kay looked at the sword and knew at once that it was the sword from the anvil, for he had stared long at it the day before, wondering whether he dared try to draw it forth. He glanced at Arthur, but Arthur was tightening the girths of his saddle and did not notice him. On an impulse, Kay went to Sir Ector and held out the sword. 'Here is the sword from the anvil, father. Am I to be king of all Britain?'

With wonder Sir Ector asked him, 'How did you come by it?'

And Kay stared at the ground and said slowly, 'My brother Arthur gave it to me.'

Sir Ector called to Arthur and questioned him, and Arthur said, 'I drew it out from the anvil that my brother might not lack a sword. Have I done wrong?'

The three of them rode back to the church, and there Sir Ector bade Arthur put the sword back in the anvil. Then he tried to draw it forth himself, but it would not move an inch. 'Now do you try, Kay,' he said. But though he too tried with all his strength, neither could Kay release it.

'Now shall Arthur try,' said Sir Ector. And when Arthur set his hand to the hilt of the sword, he drew it forth with no effort.

Marvelling, Sir Ector said, 'You shall be king of Britain, Arthur.'

'For what reason should I be king, father?'

Sir Ector pointed to the letters of gold that were graven on the anvil. 'Because it is so decreed,' he said. And he knelt before Arthur and Kay knelt beside him.

'Do not kneel to me, father,' pleaded Arthur with distress.

'I am not your father, lord,' said Ector. And he told Arthur of how Merlin had brought a little child to him, wrapped in cloth of gold. 'And I thought then, and have thought ever since, that you came of nobler blood than I or mine,' he said.

But when Arthur knew that he was not Sir Ector's son, and that Kay was not his brother, he wept and said, 'You and your lady have ever been kind to me, and I could not have loved you more had you been my own parents, nor could I love Kay more were he truly my brother, and now must I lose you all?'

'You must be king,' said Sir Ector gently, 'for so it is decreed, and only one who was a coward and worthless, would shirk a duty God had set on him.'

Yet Arthur still wept. 'I shall never forget all you have done for me. When I am indeed king, ask what you will of me, and it shall be yours.'

'I am an old man,' said Sir Ector, 'and for myself I ask nothing. But there is Kay. If you would make him seneschal of all your household, then should I be well content.'

'It shall be so,' promised Arthur.

Afterwards, Arthur had to replace the sword in the anvil, and then once again, in full sight of all the people gathered there, he had to draw it forth; and with one accord they called to him as their rightful king. And the lords who were wearied of their quarrelling made peace and swore to follow Arthur, so that all the land was his.

His first deed when he was crowned was to fulfil his

promise to Sir Ector, and make Kay his seneschal, the chief lord of all his household.

Good Sir Ector and his lady died soon after, but Sir Kay the Seneschal grew up to have a bitter tongue which he took no pains to curb. He was quick to anger, and his ungracious ways lost him many a friend; but Arthur always loved him, and for himself, not merely for the remembrance of the childhood they had passed together. And for his part, Kay loved Arthur jealously, serving him with devotion even while he criticized what he chose to regard as folly: the king's rashness in danger, his unfailing generosity, and the trust he showed to all.

II

How Arthur Gained Excalibur

ERLIN the enchanter was a good friend to
Arthur during the first years of his kingship,
for there was much for Arthur to learn about
ruling and the ways of men, since he was young to be a
king. Yet before long his subjects, both rich and poor alike,
had grown to love him for his courage and his eager
adventurous spirit and his friendliness towards all men. As
he grew older he would often ride forth on an adventure,
sometimes alone and sometimes in company, and with his
strength and his skill he soon proved himself a worthy
knight, and one well fitted to be a leader.

When he was no more than twenty years old, he was
riding alone in the forest one day, seeking for such an
adventure as he ever loved: a jousting with a strange unknown knight, a rescue of oppressed folk, or the routing of
a band of robbers, when he saw three rogues fall upon an
old man who was walking along the woodland path as
though they would rob him.

'Have courage, old father,' called Arthur, 'and I will save
you.' And he rode fast upon the thieves. Seeing an armed
knight coming against them, they left their attack and fled.
But when Arthur turned to the old man, he saw that it was
Merlin who had taken the guise of a traveller, as he
often did.

Arthur laughed. 'Well met, Merlin. If I had not come
when I did, you would by now be dead.'

Merlin smiled. 'Not I, my lord king. I have ways of avoiding death which are not known to other men.'

'Nevertheless,' said Arthur, 'for all your craft, I warrant you were near enough to death this time.'

'Not so near as you will be, before so very long.'

'What do you mean by that riddle?' asked Arthur.

'No more than I say. So beware.' And with that Merlin vanished, and Arthur was alone.

Puzzling over Merlin's words, Arthur went on his way; but he forgot them instantly when in a clearing in the forest he saw before him a fountain, and by the fountain the pavilion of a knight, and in a moment the thought came into his mind, 'Here perhaps is an adventure.'

And an adventure indeed it was, for hardly had Arthur come by the fountain when a knight hastened forth from the pavilion and called to him to halt. 'No knight goes by this way unless he fights with me,' he said. 'For such is my custom.'

'I am ready for you,' said Arthur. 'And it is an evil custom.'

The knight mounted his horse and he and Arthur attacked with a will, and so much strength did they put in their first charge that their lances were shattered on each other's shields. Arthur drew his sword.

'No,' said the strange knight, 'let us fight again with lances, for you are as good a jouster as ever I saw.'

'I have no other lance,' said Arthur.

But the knight called to a squire who came running from the pavilion with a bunch of lances to give Arthur his choice. And again they rode at each other and again they broke their lances with the force of their meeting. Again Arthur drew his sword.

'No,' said the knight, 'for the love of knightly skill let us try once more with lances.'

Arthur was very willing, and again he chose a lance. And this time when they rode against each other, Arthur's lance was shattered but the other knight gave him such a mighty blow that he was flung from his horse.

Arthur rose and drew his sword. 'You have been victorious mounted, sir knight, now let us see what you can do on foot.'

The knight alighted from his horse and they fought with their swords, battering on shield and helmet and armour until they were both weary, yet could neither get the advantage of the other, so well matched they were. Then by mishap Arthur's sword broke under a mighty blow from the sword of the other knight, and Arthur was left weaponless.

'The victory is mine,' said the knight. 'Yield to me or make ready to die.'

'Never,' replied Arthur, 'shall I yield to you or to any man. And death can come when it will.' And he leapt upon the knight, and seizing him, threw him to the ground. Yet the knight was well armed and Arthur was not, so it was not long before the advantage lay with the knight, and putting off Arthur's helmet, he raised his sword and made to strike off his head.

And in that moment Arthur remembered Merlin's words; yet even as he remembered them, he heard Merlin's voice saying, 'Strike not, sir knight, for the sake of all Britain.' And Arthur saw Merlin standing there beside them.

'Why should I not strike?' asked the knight. 'He is my prisoner, overcome in fair fight, and he will not yield himself to me, so it is my right to have his life.'

'He is King Arthur,' said Merlin quietly.

Upon that the knight was very much afraid of the king's wrath, and he would almost have slain Arthur in his fear, had not Merlin stretched out his arm, so that his sword fell from his hands and he himself dropped to the ground in a deep sleep.

'Merlin,' cried Arthur, 'what have you done? You have slain this good knight with your enchantments, and I swear that I had not before met with such knightly skill. I would have had him for my friend.'

Merlin smiled. 'He is but sleeping, he will wake in three hours. His name is Pellinore and one day he will be accounted amongst the best of your knights.'

'I am glad of that,' said Arthur, 'for I would not have such a man an enemy.'

So Arthur rode away, with Merlin walking at his side, leaving Sir Pellinore to be tended by his squires.

'My good sword is broken,' said Arthur. 'I must find another.'

'Come with me,' said Merlin, 'and I will show you a sword that shall be better than any man could forge for you.' And he led Arthur to the shore of a lake which lay in a valley below a plain. He raised his hand and pointed. 'See, there is a sword.'

And Arthur looked and saw how an arm, clothed in white silk interwoven with threads of gold, rose up from the water holding a sword, and the jewelled scabbard of the sword and its golden hilt glittered in the sun. And even

while he marvelled at the sight, he saw a fair young damsel rising from the lake. 'It is the Lady of the Lake,' said Merlin. 'Speak to her as a friend, and she will give you the sword.'

Full of wonder, Arthur greeted the Lady of the Lake, and she smiled and greeted him in return. 'Lady,' asked Arthur, 'whose is that sword which is held above the water by that arm? I would it were mine, for my own sword is broken.'

'The sword is mine, King Arthur. It is named Excalibur, and I will give it to you as a gift. Take it and the scabbard also.' And with that she was gone, below the waters of the lake.

Arthur stared long in wonder at the place where she had been, but Merlin roused him from his thoughts. 'There is a boat there, moored among the willows,' he said. 'Row out into the lake and fetch your sword.'

So Arthur took the boat and rowed out to where the hand held the sword, and he laid hold of it, and instantly the hand gave the hilt into his grasp and the arm vanished below the water.

On the shore of the lake Arthur showed his new sword to Merlin. 'I thank you,' he said, 'that you told me of this marvel.'

'Which seems the greater gift to you,' asked Merlin, 'the sword or the scabbard?'

'Why, the sword, there can be no doubt of it. Fine as the scabbard is, it is no more than a scabbard, but the sword is the best I have ever seen.'

Merlin laughed. 'Excalibur may be the best sword in the land, but the scabbard is worth ten such swords.'

'How can that be?'

'So long as you wear the scabbard,' said Merlin, 'however sorely you are wounded, you will lose no blood. So take care always to have the scabbard with you when you would fight.'

And Arthur marvelled at his counsellor's knowledge, and promised ever to treasure the scabbard as much as the sword.

But soon after, thinking it well to do so, yet not thinking to tell Merlin what he had done, Arthur sent Excalibur and its wondrous scabbard for safe keeping to his half-sister, Morgan le Fay, who was the daughter of Igraine and her first lord, the duke of Tintagel, and was married to King Uriens of Gore.

III

The Marriage of Arthur

WHEN Arthur had been king for a few years, his lords urged him to marry. 'For,' they said, 'it is not fitting that the land should be without a queen.'

Arthur told this to Merlin, and the old enchanter said, 'Your lords spoke wisely. Is there any damsel whom you would have as a wife?'

'Of all the damsels that I have seen,' said Arthur, 'there is only one whom I could love, and she is the Lady Guenever, the daughter of King Leodegrance of Cameliard.'

Merlin sighed. 'She is fair, my lord king, and she is nobly born, and I admit that one would have to seek far to find her equal, but if you marry the Lady Guenever it will one day bring great sorrow on you and on all this land. Heed my warning and choose another for your queen.'

'It is Guenever whom I want,' said Arthur. 'And if I may not have her, I shall have no other.'

And Merlin sighed again, and then he smiled a little, sadly. 'It was ever so. Present love cares nothing for future grief. You shall have Guenever, my lord king.'

Merlin went himself to Cameliard to King Leodegrance and told him of Arthur's wish. 'You bring me the best news that ever man has brought me,' said Leodegrance, 'that the first knight of the land and the noblest king in all the world should seek to wed my daughter. Tell King Arthur that he shall have her, and that with her I shall send to him the Round Table which I have kept since his father's day.'

Now the Round Table had been made by Merlin for King Uther Pendragon, for the king and the one hundred and forty best knights in his land, and it was fashioned in a circle so that when the knights were seated at it, no one of them should be lower at the board than another, and there should be no envy or jealousy between them. But because of the troubles of his reign, King Uther had never been able to call all his best knights together at one time for feasting and for joyful fellowship; and when he died, the Round Table had been given to King Leodegrance for safe keeping.

So with Merlin and with her ladies and with a great company of knights, and bringing the Round Table, the Lady Guenever set out for London; and she was in truth the fairest damsel in all the land.

Arthur welcomed Guenever with great joy, and he was glad indeed at the gift of the Round Table, bidding Merlin seek out at once the one hundred and forty best knights in Britain, that they might take their places at the Table. But Merlin could find no more than eight and twenty knights who were considered worthy of the honour. 'In time,' said Arthur, 'there will be others to join them, I do not doubt it.' And so, in later years, there were.

After each knight had taken his place at the Table, through Merlin's enchantments his name appeared on his chair in letters of gold, so that the place was always his alone. But of one place Merlin said, 'This is the Perilous Chair, and here no knight shall sit save only one, and the time for him to be of your company is not yet come, so let you all wait for him.' And Arthur and the others wondered at his words.

King Arthur's half-sister, Margawse, the daughter of Igraine and her first lord the duke of Cornwall, who had been wedded to King Lot of Orkney on the day that King Uther had married her widowed mother, had five sons: Gawaine, Gaheris, Gareth, Agravine, and Mordred. Gareth and Agravine were as yet but children and Mordred was no more than a babe in the cradle, but the two eldest, Gawaine and Gaheris, came at this time to Arthur's court. Gawaine was a courteous, gentle-spoken youth, and though he was Arthur's nephew, he was not many years younger than the king, and Arthur had great love for him.

When Guenever was come to London, Gawaine asked a boon of Arthur. 'On the day that you wed with the Lady Guenever, will you make me a knight, my lord uncle?' And Arthur embraced Gawaine with joy and promised that he would indeed do so.

Arthur took his court to his favourite town of Camelot, which is now called Winchester, and there, on a summer's morning, he was wedded to the lovely Guenever. And after the wedding, in the great church at Camelot, Arthur knighted his nephew Gawaine, touching his shoulder with a sword, buckling on the new knight's golden spurs, and fastening his sword about him.

When the knighting was over, Arthur and Guenever and all the lords and knights and their ladies gathered together for the marriage feast; but just as they had taken their places in the great hall of the castle of Camelot, Merlin rose up among them and called out, 'Be still, my lords, for this moment you shall see an adventure.' And even as he spoke, there ran into the hall a white hart followed by a white brachet, a small bitch hound, and after them came sixty black hounds, baying mightily. Right around the hall ran the hart and the brachet and the hounds, and out again through the door, and everyone wondered at the sight. An instant later there rode through the doorway on a white palfrey a strange damsel whom no one there had seen before, and she was weeping. 'Good king,' she cried, 'that brachet is mine, and now I have lost her.' And she set up such an outcry that it filled the hall.

But even while she was weeping a knight on a charger rode through the doorway, and before anyone had guessed what he would do, he had snatched the damsel off her palfrey and ridden away with her, still wailing and protesting, and struggling in his arms.

'There, my lord king,' said Merlin, 'are three adventures to bring honour to your marriage feast.'

'To whom shall they be given?' asked Arthur.

'Let Sir Gawaine fetch the white hart,' said Merlin. 'For it is fitting that the first adventure should be given to him who has but now been made a knight. Let Sir Tor go seek the brachet, and Sir Pellinore give his aid to the damsel.'

With great joy Gawaine took leave of his uncle and Queen Guenever, and with his brother Gaheris as squire and his six hounds running beside him, he rode off on his first quest. Likewise, Sir Pellinore, who had once fought so long and so well with Arthur by the fountain in the forest, and was now, as Merlin had foretold, the king's good friend, prepared himself to set off after the damsel, pleased at the thought of an adventure.

Yet young Sir Tor, who had but lately been knighted,

was poor and lacked both horse and armour. Though he longed for a quest, he wished that it had not been put on him lest he should be shamed by his poverty. But Arthur, seeing his distress, gave him armour, and good Sir Pellinore lent him an old horse, and happily Sir Tor set off.

Gawaine and Gaheris followed the tracks of hart and hounds until a baying in the distance told them that they would soon have their quarry in sight. And in a very little while, on open ground, they saw the black hounds and, away before them, the hart; but the white brachet was nowhere to be seen. The hounds were weary from their long chase, and many were flagging, so that Gawaine and his brother outrode them, and close after the hart, they came to a river. The hart swam over, but just as Gawaine and Gaheris would have ridden into the water, a voice hailed them from the further bank. 'Not so fast, sir knight, for if you cross this river you must joust with me.' And they saw, over the river, a knight on horseback.

'Willingly,' said Gawaine. And he crossed and fought with the knight and unhorsed him. Then Gawaine dismounted and they fought together on foot, and Gawaine gave the other such a mighty blow that the sword cut right through his helmet into his skull, and he fell dead.

'Brother,' said Gaheris, 'that was a blow such as an older knight might well envy.'

'He fought bravely,' sighed Gawaine. 'It is a pity that he should have died.'

They rode on once more after the hart, and as they gained upon it, in a meadow close by a castle, Gawaine said, 'Unleash the hounds, Gaheris, the quest is almost done.'

Gaheris let slip the six hounds, but the hart ran towards

the castle and through the gates, and the hounds went after it. And there in the courtyard of the castle, they brought down the hart. Gawaine and Gaheris came after, but even as they rode through the gateway, a knight with a sword in his hand came out from the castle and slew two of the hounds. Gawaine cried, 'That was ill done, stranger, to slay a man's hounds. They did but act after the way of hounds. It would have been better had you saved your wrath for me.'

'They killed my hart which was a gift to me from my lady,' said the knight.

'You should have kept your lady's gift more carefully. You have let your hart be hunted from Camelot to here. Is that the way to respect a lady's gift?'

The knight was angry and would have avenged the death of the hart, so Gawaine dismounted and they fought together. But Gawaine, for all his youth, was the stronger fighter of the two, and soon he had the strange knight at his mercy, so that he yielded to him.

'I will give you your life,' said Gawaine, 'if you will go to Camelot, to King Arthur, and say that Gawaine sent you, and tell him all your story.' And this the knight promised to do.

Then Gaheris cut off the head of the hart, and the brothers rode back to Camelot together; and thus was done Sir Gawaine's first quest.

Meanwhile, young Sir Tor in his borrowed armour and upon Sir Pellinore's old horse rode after the white brachet. But it was not easy to follow the tracks of one small hound, so as he went he asked all whom he met whether they had seen the brachet. After a time he came to where two pavilions stood, with a dwarf on horseback close by. 'Not so fast, sir knight,' called the dwarf. 'If you ride this way you must joust with my two masters yonder.'

'I am on a quest,' replied Tor, 'and I have little time to spare. But since no knight refuses a fight, tell your masters that I am ready.'

The dwarf blew a horn that hung around his neck, and immediately a knight came out from one of the pavilions, mounted his horse, and rode at Tor. But with the first blow of his lance, Sir Tor unhorsed him; and the knight fell to his knees and yielded. 'Very easily were you vanquished,' said Tor.

Then the second knight came from the other pavilion, and him also Sir Tor overcame so that he cried mercy. 'Go, both of you,' said Tor, 'to Camelot, to King Arthur, and say that you were sent by Sir Tor.' And he rode hastily on to seek the brachet. But he had not ridden many paces before he was aware that the dwarf was following him. 'Give me a boon, good knight,' said the dwarf.

'If I can, I will,' replied Tor.

'Then let me serve you, for I can no longer serve such cowardly knights as those whom you have met with but now.'

And Tor was glad to think that, poor though he was, he had found a servant, and one who followed him for admiration rather than for gain. 'We will ride together after the white brachet,' he said.

'As for the white brachet, master,' said the dwarf, 'I know where she may be found.' And he led Tor through a forest, until, in a clearing, they came upon a pavilion. 'The brachet is within,' said the dwarf.

Sir Tor dismounted, and since there was none to prevent him, entered the pavilion, and there upon a couch he saw a damsel sleeping, and at her feet lay the white brachet. When she saw Tor, the brachet began to bay, so that the damsel awoke. 'What do you here?' she asked.

'I have come for the brachet that is my quest,' replied Tor. 'And by your leave I will have her.' And he picked up the little hound and took her to where the dwarf waited.

'When my lord hears of this,' cried the damsel, 'you will regret what you have done.'

Tor and the dwarf rode off for Camelot, well pleased at their success, but after a time they heard a great shouting behind them, and when they looked back there was a tall knight, well armed and angry, riding after them. 'Give me back the brachet you took from my lady,' demanded the knight, 'or prepare to fight with me.'

'I am ready to fight,' said Tor, 'for the brachet was my quest and I have ridden from Arthur's court in search of her.'

So Tor and the strange knight fought mightily; and if the two other knights whom Tor had met that day were cowards and poor jousters, this knight was not, and much pain did Tor have to hold his own. But at last the fight was over, and the knight lay dead, and a good deed had Tor done, for the strange knight had been of most evil life, a murderer and a great terror to those weaker than he.

And after that, with no more mischance, Sir Tor and his dwarf came to Camelot, bringing the brachet with them.

When Sir Pellinore rode out after the knight who had carried off the damsel, he saw a poor man along the way, gathering faggots for his fire. 'Have you seen a knight ride by with an unwilling damsel?' asked Pellinore.

'He rode by not a half-hour since, lord,' replied the man. 'And such a wailing as that damsel made I have never heard before. Yet yonder, past those trees, I saw another knight ride out from a pavilion and challenge the first, and they were fighting for the damsel when I saw them last.'

Sir Pellinore thanked the man and rode on at a great pace; and beyond the trees, as the man had said, he saw the pavilion with the two knights fighting on foot with their swords, and the damsel standing with their squires and watching them.

Sir Pellinore rode up to the damsel. 'Lady, I have come from the court of King Arthur, and it is my quest that I should find you and escort you there. Will you come with me?'

But while the damsel hesitated, the two squires spoke to Pellinore. 'Good knight,' they said, 'our masters are fighting as to which of them shall have the lady in his keeping. One is her cousin and the other the knight who took her today from Camelot. We beg of you to part them, or they will slay each other.'

So Pellinore rode up to the knights and parted them. 'Why do you fight?' he asked.

'Sir knight,' replied one, 'the lady yonder is my cousin, and I heard her cry for help as this knight rode by with her. He was taking her away against her will.'

'Sir knight,' replied the other, 'the lady is mine, and today I won her by the skill of my arms at King Arthur's court.'

'That is untrue,' said Pellinore, 'for I was there and I

never saw you strike one blow to win her, but you rode into the great hall and carried her off in spite of her cries. And because of that I have sworn to free her and take her back to Camelot. Therefore both of you must fight with me.'

'We are willing,' they said.

But the knight who had carried off the damsel lifted up his sword and slew Sir Pellinore's horse. 'Now are you on foot, even as we are,' he jeered.

Pellinore was very angry that his good horse had been slain, and he fell upon the knight with no delay; and at his first stroke the knight's head was split open and he fell dead upon the grass. Then Pellinore turned to the damsel's cousin. 'Now do you defend yourself, sir knight.'

But the other shook his head. 'Since you have come to the help of my cousin, I have no quarrel with you. I freely yield myself to you, to do whatever you think fit.'

'Then do you persuade your cousin to go with me to Camelot, and I can promise you that no harm will come to her.'

So after Pellinore and the knight and the damsel, who was now happy and smiling once more, had rested and eaten and drunk together in the pavilion, Pellinore set out on a horse which was a gift from the knight, with the damsel before him, and so he came again to Camelot.

And much pleasure did the king and his knights and Guenever have of the tales that Gawaine and Tor and Pellinore had to tell them of their adventures on Arthur's wedding day.

Yet Merlin only smiled. 'These deeds are as nothing to the deeds these three knights shall one day perform,' he said.

But soon after, Arthur lost the wisdom of Merlin, for the old enchanter withdrew himself from the lives of men, and laid himself in a hollow at the top of a tall hill, and there the Lady of the Lake covered him with a mighty rock, and beneath that rock it is said he sleeps still.

IV

The Treachery of Morgan le Fay

A T a time when Arthur was holding his court at Camelot there came to him for the festivities King Uriens of Gore and his queen, Morgan le Fay, who was Arthur's half-sister. King Uriens and Morgan le Fay had one son, Uwaine, who was of an age with his cousin Gawaine and a good friend to him. Morgan le Fay was skilled in witchcraft, and by her enchantments had kept herself as young and fair as any damsel, for all she had a son who was old enough to be a knight. And though she dissembled and spoke fair words to her brother Arthur, she cared nothing for him, wishing that another might be king in his place.

Among the followers of King Uriens there was a knight named Accolon who loved Queen Morgan le Fay for her beauty, and she loved him in return. And secretly she determined that she would kill Arthur and King Uriens, and then by means of her enchantments she would have Accolon chosen king of all Britain, with herself as his queen and lady.

With this in mind, she rejoiced when Arthur sent her his sword Excalibur and its scabbard, and she determined to use both to Arthur's hurt.

One day it happened that Arthur was out hunting with his guests, and as they rode in pursuit of a fine hart, Arthur, King Uriens, and Sir Accolon, being mounted on swifter steeds than their companions, outstripped the others and found themselves alone at the kill, on the bank of a wide river. They sat down on the grass to rest, but it was growing late, and King Uriens said, 'The sun will soon be setting, we shall not be back at Camelot before nightfall.'

In that moment Arthur saw a barge, all hung with silken cloths and fair brocade, come slowly down the stream. 'See,' he said, 'where a barge approaches. Perchance there will be some friends aboard who will give us hospitality.'

The barge came close in to the river's bank, and Arthur called out, but there was no answer. 'This,' he said, 'may well be an adventure. Come.' And he leapt aboard eagerly, with Uriens and Accolon following him. Immediately twelve damsels, richly dressed, appeared, and bidding the two kings and the knight welcome by their names, led them to a table laid with food and wine. At that moment the sun set, and all around the sides of the barge a hundred torches flamed into light, as though by sorcery.

The food and the wine were good, and the damsels served their guests with silent courtesy; and after the meal was done, led each of them to a small cabin with a comfortable couch, and bade them have good rest. And because they were wearied from their hunting, Arthur and Uriens and Accolon lay down and were immediately asleep.

Now, the barge had been an enchantment of Morgan le Fay, to the intent that she might destroy her brother, and when the three of them awoke in the morning, they were none of them on the barge. King Uriens found himself in bed in his chamber at Camelot, and he wondered greatly to be there; Accolon found himself lying on the grass beside a roadway; while Arthur found himself in a dark prison, with all around him the sighs and groans of other prisoners, and the clank of chains.

When he questioned his fellow captives, they told him, 'We are twenty knights, prisoners in the castle of the false knight Sir Damas, and some of us have lain in his dungeon for more than seven years.'

'For what reason does he hold you here?' asked Arthur.

'He has a younger brother called Ontzlake, a good knight and brave, and one who deplores his brother's evil ways, and from Ontzlake does this Damas keep his inheritance, all save one small manor where he permits him to dwell. And ever does Sir Ontzlake offer to fight with his brother for his rights, but Damas is a cowardly knight and will not take up arms even in his own quarrel, but must needs find a champion to fight for him. And that is why he has brought us here, that one of us may be his champion in his battle with his brother. But there is no one of us who would not rather languish here than strike a blow for such an evil knight.'

'This is a shameful custom, and it shall be for me to destroy it,' thought Arthur.

After a time there came into the dungeon a damsel with a torch, and she spoke to Arthur. 'How are you, sir knight?'

'In an evil plight, lady,' he replied.

'If you would be freed from here,' said the damsel, 'then you must agree to fight for the lord of the castle, Sir Damas, against his brother, Sir Ontzlake. Otherwise you shall never escape.'

'If not only I may be released, but all these twenty knights also, then I will be champion for your lord.'

'I will tell him thus,' she said.

So Arthur was taken before Sir Damas, and found him an ill-favoured, boorish knight, and he promised to fight for him against Sir Ontzlake. And Damas for his part promised to give Arthur armour and a horse, and to release the other twenty prisoners and Arthur himself, after the battle was done. 'And when you fight with my brother,' he said, 'you shall fight to the uttermost, until either you or he is dead.' And Damas smiled, for seeing Arthur, how tall and strong he was, he had great hope of his champion and thought to be rid of his brother at last.

Meanwhile, when Sir Accolon found himself on the edge of the highway, he marvelled at it, and began to blame the treachery of the twelve damsels on the barge. 'May God send the two kings speedy help, wherever they are,' he thought.

Then Accolon looked up and saw a dwarf coming towards him, and he knew him at once for a dwarf who served Morgan le Fay, and hailed him joyfully.

'My mistress greets you, Sir Accolon,' said the dwarf, 'and she bids me tell you that by her enchantments she knows that tomorrow you will do battle with a knight. She asks that you will fight in her honour and to the uttermost, giving no quarter, and to that end she sends you here King Arthur's sword Excalibur, and his scabbard. Wear the scabbard and however you are wounded, you can lose no blood, and the sword is the finest in the land.'

'Tell my lady the queen that I will do as she commands,' said Accolon.

At that moment a knight came by, carried in a horse litter, and he called out to Accolon, asking him what he did alone without horse or armour. 'My name is Ontzlake,' he said, 'and if you would have good cheer for a day or two, I beg you come with me to my manor. I was wounded in the thigh at the jousting some seven days ago and may not ride, so time goes heavily for me and a guest will give me much pleasure.'

So Accolon was lodged with Sir Ontzlake that day, and he was with him when the challenge came from his brother Damas. 'What a misfortune this is,' said Ontzlake. 'For seven years my brother has sought a champion, and now that he has found one, I am in no way to fight.'

Accolon remembered the message of Morgan le Fay, and he marvelled at her foreknowledge. 'If you will permit it,' he said, 'I will take your place tomorrow and fight your brother's champion in your name.' And Sir Ontzlake was overjoyed.

When the next day was come, Accolon, wearing Sir Ontzlake's armour and carrying Excalibur, went to do battle for his host; and Arthur, in armour that belonged to Sir Damas and bearing Sir Damas's shield, went to fight that twenty knights might be set free, and the power of Sir Damas destroyed. And because neither wore his own armour, nor carried his own shield, Arthur and Accolon did not know each other.

At their first charge they unhorsed one another, and instantly they rose to their feet and drew their swords. Though Arthur was among the very best of knights, Accolon was a fighter of no little skill, and he had Excalibur. With every stroke he received from Accolon, Arthur was wounded and he grew weak from bleeding; but for all the wounds that Arthur gave him, Accolon lost no single drop of blood, for he wore Arthur's scabbard slung about him. And while Arthur fought it seemed to him that never had another knight than Ontzlake's champion a sword which seemed so like his own Excalibur, and he wondered at it.

Then with a great blow Accolon broke Arthur's sword in two, and with triumph bade him yield himself.

'I have sworn that I shall fight to the uttermost,' said Arthur. 'While I have life I will not yield.' And with that he thrust at Accolon with the broken sword.

'You are no more than a dead man, if you do not yield,' cried Accolon, and he struck at Arthur once again. And it was such a mighty blow he gave him, that with the impact of it Excalibur was forced from his grasp, and in an instant Arthur snatched it up. He fell upon Accolon and tore the scabbard from about him, and with a great stroke threw him to the ground. 'Now had you best ask mercy, sir knight,' he said.

'I too have sworn to do battle to the uttermost,' said Accolon. 'So make an end of me, if you will.'

Arthur put aside Accolon's helmet, that he might strike off his head, and he knew him at once, and stayed his hand. 'Sir Accolon,' he asked, 'how came you by this sword?'

'Much ill has that sword brought me,' said Accolon, 'for by it I shall die. It is King Arthur's sword and was sent me by my love, Queen Morgan le Fay, who knew by her enchantments that today I should have need of it, for she foretold that I should meet in battle with a strange knight, and she bade me fight to the uttermost and give no quarter. Now tell me, before you kill me, how you knew my name, and who you are.'

32

Arthur laid down Excalibur upon the grass. 'I am Arthur, whom my sister would have slain.'

'Forgive me, lord king,' said Accolon, 'for I did not know you.' Then he called aloud to all those gathered there, 'It is even our own lord King Arthur with whom I have fought today. May he have mercy on us all.'

And Sir Damas and Sir Ontzlake and all their followers fell upon their knees and besought the king's forgiveness, and Arthur said, 'How could any of you have known me since I told no one my name? But I have seen too much of the evil ways of Sir Damas, and they must cease.' And he ordered Damas to give up his castle and his lands to his brother and oppress no more unhappy knights; and to Ontzlake he said, 'You will always be welcome at my court, so come to me whenever you will.'

Arthur went to a near by nunnery to be healed of his hurts, taking Accolon with him. But though Arthur recovered, after four days Accolon was dead. Arthur had his body laid on a bier and he ordered six knights to carry it to Queen Morgan le Fay. 'Tell her,' he said, 'that I have my sword and its scabbard once again.'

But before the tidings were brought to her of Accolon's death, Morgan le Fay determined to kill her husband, that so soon as Arthur was slain she might at once marry Sir Accolon.

She rose early in the morning while King Uriens was sleeping and called to her one of her ladies. 'Go, fetch me my lord's sword,' she said. The damsel looked into her eyes and knew what she was about to do, and she fell on her knees and pleaded with her. 'Good mistress, there can be no escape for you if you kill our lord King Uriens.'

But Morgan le Fay grew angry. 'Do as I bid you,' she said.

The damsel ran from the room and fetched the sword, but as she returned with it she went to the bedchamber where young Sir Uwaine slept and woke him. 'The queen your mother seeks to kill the king. I beg of you come to his aid.' Yet for fear of Morgan le Fay's enchantments, she took the sword and gave it to her, trembling. And Morgan le Fay drew the sword from its scabbard and went to the bed. But even as she raised the sword to strike, Uwaine ran into the room and snatched it from her hands. 'Mother,' he cried, 'would you kill my father?'

She did not answer him, but looked down at the sleeping king. 'Will you tell him?' she asked.

'You are my mother,' said Uwaine, 'and I could not see you burnt as one who would have slain her lord. Give me your word not to attempt his life again, and I will not speak of it.'

'I give you my word,' said Morgan le Fay, and she smiled.

Uwaine laid the sword down beside his father and, shuddering, left her.

But a few hours later, when the sun was high, came the six knights bearing the body of Accolon. They gave the bier to Morgan le Fay and with it Arthur's message, so that she knew how her brother had learnt of all her treachery. Her grief for the death of Sir Accolon she concealed as well as she might; but she was certain that when Arthur came to Camelot he would not be as ready to forgive her as her son Uwaine had been. So she sent for one of the knights who had carried the bier and asked where Arthur

34

was, and the man told her the name of the nunnery. 'Will he come soon to Camelot?' she asked.

'Lady, he is even now recovered, and will be here before three days are passed.'

Morgan le Fay knew that she had no time to lose. She called to her forty of her knights and bade them arm and make ready to ride with her, and at their head, on a white horse, she rode from Camelot. All that day she rode and throughout all the night, and soon after dawn she came to the nunnery. 'I am Queen Morgan le Fay,' she said to the portress, and she was admitted. 'Where is my brother the king?' she asked of the nuns.

'He is sleeping,' they answered.

'Then show me his room,' she demanded; and they led her to it. She went to the bed where Arthur slept and saw that he held Excalibur in his hand, and she was angry that she might not take the sword from him without wakening him. But the scabbard lay on the floor beside the bed; so she took the scabbard, and rode away.

When Arthur awoke, he found the scabbard gone. 'Who has done this thing?' he asked.

'Good king, it was your sister, Queen Morgan le Fay, who was here at dawn,' said the nuns. 'She is your sister, so we thought no harm to let her in.'

'Saddle me the best horse you have,' said Arthur, 'and let Sir Ontzlake ride with me, for I must have my scabbard again.'

Arthur and Ontzlake rode out from the nunnery together, and in the fields they saw a cowherd. 'Have you seen a lady and a company of knights ride by this way?' they asked.

'Not above an hour since, lords, a lady rode by at the head of a band of knights. Young she was and more beautiful than any lady I have seen, and she rode towards the forest.'

'That is my sister,' said Arthur. And he and Ontzlake rode at a gallop through the forest until in the distance, in a clearing, they caught sight of Morgan le Fay.

When she knew that she was followed, Morgan le Fay went to a lake that lay in the forest. 'Whatever becomes of me,' she thought, 'Arthur shall not have the scabbard.' And she flung it into the water, so that it was lost for ever. Then she rode fast to an open plain and there, by her enchantments, she changed her knights and herself and their horses to rocks and stones, so that by the time Arthur and Ontzlake came out of the woodland to the open ground, there were no other riders in sight. 'They must have ridden like the wind,' said Arthur. 'Come, let us follow over the plain.' And he and Ontzlake rode right by the rocks and stones, and never guessed what they were.

When they were well past, Morgan le Fay changed herself and her knights and their horses back to their own shapes, and rode for her husband's own land of Gore. And there, in the farthest part of the kingdom, she made strong a castle, so that no man might take it, neither King Uriens nor Arthur; and there she dwelt secure, ever wishing evil to Arthur and the knights of the Round Table.

But King Uriens remained a good friend to Arthur, while Sir Uwaine was one of his noblest knights.

V

Uwaine and the Lady of the Fountain

ONE day King Arthur was taking his ease after a day's hunting, sitting talking of one thing and another with Sir Uwaine his nephew, Sir Kay the Seneschal, and a young knight named Cynon. With them were Queen Guenever and her damsels, working at a tapestry. 'There is yet an hour before the evening meal,' said Arthur. 'Let one of us tell a tale.'

'Not I,' objected Kay. 'Let it be one of the others.'

'Cynon,' said Uwaine, 'you shall tell us a story, for you are the stranger here. Tell us of the most marvellous thing that has ever befallen you.'

Cynon thought for a moment and then he began his tale. 'Some few years ago, when I was very young,' he said, 'indeed little more than a lad, because I was tall and strong and brave enough, I thought myself of consequence. In my father's house and in all his lands, I considered that I had no equal, so I set forth to seek an adventure wherein I might win glory. I travelled a long distance from home until I came to a valley. A river flowed through this valley and beside the river wound a path, and along this path I rode until I saw before me a tall castle. And between me and the castle I saw two fair-haired youths with circlets of gold about their heads, and both clad in yellow brocade with fastenings of gold. They were shooting with peacock feather-tipped arrows from bows of ivory; and watching them was a fair-haired man, clothed as they were in yellow brocade ornamented with much gold. Truly, I had seen such rich garments nowhere before. This man came towards me and greeted me right courteously, and led me into the castle. In the hall were four and twenty damsels sitting sewing yellow brocade, and the least lovely of them was lovelier by far than any other damsel in Britain.'

Here one of Guenever's damsels broke in, 'Shame on you for an uncourteous knight!'

'But I assure you, lady,' protested Cynon, 'that I speak no more than the truth. Indeed, the loveliest there was all but as lovely as Queen Guenever herself, if she will pardon my saying it.' He stopped, abashed, and would not have gone on, had not Guenever looked up from the tapestry and smiled. 'Tell us the rest of your story, Sir Cynon, I vow I cannot wait to hear more of these peerless damsels. It is long since I have been so eager for a tale.'

Encouraged by her courtesy, Cynon went on with his story. 'Six of the damsels took my horse, six of them took my arms and polished them mirror-bright, six of them spread white cloths upon the tables and fetched food and wine on golden plates, and six brought me clothes to wear made of yellow brocade. Then we sat down to supper, and not the smallest dish upon that table but was fashioned of gold, and all the cups were gold and ivory. And as for the meat and drink, never in my life have I tasted better, and never shall, I doubt not. When we had eaten, the fair-haired man asked me whither I journeyed, and why; and in the arrogance of my inexperience I answered him that I was looking for an adventure that was worthy of me, since at home there was no one my equal. He smiled when he heard my answer and said, "If I thought it would be of profit to you, I could tell you where an adventure was to be found." "Tell me," I demanded. "If no good comes of it to you," he said, "remember that you were warned." But I would not heed him, and only asked that he should tell me of the adventure. He said, "Tomorrow, go on through the valley until you reach a forest. Ride through the forest until you come to a wide clearing. In the midst of this clearing there is a little mound and upon this mound sits a man as tall as two men. He has no more than one foot, and one eye in the centre of his brow, and he carries an iron club. Ask him to direct you and he will send you on an adventure which you may consider worthy of your skill."

'The next morning I set off, and by midday I came to the mound in the clearing, and there sat the man with one eye and one leg. And even bigger he seemed to me than my host had said. I asked this great grim man the way out of the clearing and he threatened me with his club and sought to frighten me with words, but I would not leave him until he had answered my question. "Follow that path," he said, pointing, "and it will lead you to a valley. In the midst of that valley stands a great fir-tree. Under the tree is a fountain and beside the fountain a marble slab with a silver bowl chained to it. Fill the bowl with water and throw the water over the slab. If that does not bring you an adventure, then nothing else will." And the monster laughed most horribly.

'I hastened along the way he had pointed out, and sure enough, in time I came to the fir-tree with the fountain. I filled the silver bowl with water and flung it rashly over the marble slab, and immediately there was a sound as of the greatest thunderstorm I ever have heard. The thunder was followed by hail so heavy that in a moment man or beast might have been killed by it, had they no shelter. I was protected by my armour, yet my horse would have been lost had I not held my shield over its head. Then, as suddenly as it had started, the hailstorm ceased and the sun came forth from the clouds once more and the whole valley was filled with the singing of birds. A sweet sound that was, and comforting. Then I saw riding towards me a knight all in black armour, on a black horse, with a black pennon flying from his lance. "What harm have I done you, that you should send such a storm to lay waste my lands?" he called to me. And before I could give him an answer, he lowered his lance and rode at me. I met him with all my skill, and, as I told you, in my own home I was reckoned second to none in combat, but this knight knew more of battles than I could have found time to learn in all my few years, and it was not long before he had me on the ground. I leapt to my feet and prepared to fight on foot, but with never another glance at me, he looped the reins of my horse over his lance and rode away, leaving me to walk back the way I had come; which I did with but little pleasure.

'You may imagine how the one-legged, one-eyed man laughed at me, so that I wished the ground would open and swallow me up. And it was no less shaming to me when the fair-haired man and the two youths and the four and twenty damsels in the castle greeted me with courtesy and gay talk of this and that, but never a word did they mention of how I had fared that day. Yet it must have been plain to them that, battered and footsore, and lacking a horse, I had not fulfilled my boasting. I left the castle early in the morning, and they gave me for my journey a slate-coloured horse with a chestnut mane and tail. I have it still and there is no better horse in my stable. And so I came home, without the glory I had promised myself, but wiser than I had been when I said farewell to my father. And that, my friends, is the strangest thing that ever befell me: how I gained a fine horse and some measure of common sense.' Cynon finished and smiled at the others.

'That is a good tale,' said Arthur.

'Have you never heard since of the fair-haired man or the one-eyed monster or the knight in black armour?' asked Uwaine.

'Not a word,' said Cynon.

'And do you remember the way to that castle in the valley?' Uwaine asked eagerly.

Cynon shook his head. 'Alas, I have forgotten utterly. I came upon it by chance, and by chance I lost the direction again.'

'That is perhaps as well for you,' said Kay drily.

Sir Cynon laughed, but Uwaine said dreamily, 'I should like to find that castle in the valley and meet with the black knight.'

'Words,' said Kay, 'cost nothing.'

'Shame on you, Sir Kay,' said Guenever. 'Sir Uwaine is a brave and noble knight, and one well proved.'

Kay shrugged his shoulders. 'I still maintain, good queen, that it is easy to gain cheap glory by boasting what one would do in straits where one is unlikely to find oneself.'

But the evening meal was ready, so talk of Sir Cynon's adventure ceased, and led by Arthur and Guenever the knights and the ladies went to the great hall to sup.

Yet Sir Uwaine was silent all through the meal, thinking of Cynon's story, and he slept but little that night, tossing and turning on his bed, and by dawn his mind was made up. He rose early and armed himself, and rode out from Arthur's court towards the farthest parts of the land, seeking for the valley with the castle.

And at last, after days of weary searching, he came by chance on that valley, and riding along the pathway by the river, he saw the castle, and there, even as Cynon had said, were two fair-haired youths shooting arrows, and a man watching them, and all of them clad in yellow brocade. Sir Uwaine was given a kindly welcome, even as Cynon had been, and in the castle he saw the four and twenty damsels and the dishes and cups of gold.

And after they had eaten, the fair-haired man said, 'Whither do you journey, sir stranger?'

'I seek the black knight of the fountain,' said Uwaine. 'And I know that you can tell me where I shall find him.'

The fair-haired man told Uwaine, even as he had told Cynon, and Uwaine thanked him.

The next morning Uwaine set out, and at midday he came to the mound in the clearing whereon sat the one-eyed, one-legged man. With jeers and taunts the monster told Uwaine the way that he should go, and in time Uwaine came to the fir-tree in the valley; and there beneath it was the fountain, and beside the fountain the marble slab with the silver bowl chained to it.

Eagerly Uwaine filled the bowl from the fountain and poured the water over the slab, and instantly he heard thunder greater than any he had heard before. And when the thunder was passed, then came the hailstones, as large as thrushes' eggs, and much ado did Uwaine have to protect his horse and himself. And when the storm was over, the sun shone once more, and, as Sir Cynon had told, from all the valley came the song of birds. But pleasing as he found the singing of the birds, Uwaine mounted his horse and watched eagerly about him for a sight of the black knight; and it was with a great joy and with excitement that he saw him at last, galloping along the valley towards the fountain on his black horse, with the black pennon flying from his lance. 'What harm have I done you, that you should send such a storm to lay waste my lands?' he called.

Uwaine prepared to meet his assault, and they clashed together so that the lances of both were shattered on their shields. Without dismounting from their horses, they fought with their swords, and mighty was the battle they had there, beneath the great fir-tree.

But Sir Uwaine was a more skilled knight, and older,

than Sir Cynon had been when as a youth he had met with the knight in black armour; and Uwaine gained the advantage in the fighting and struck the other a blow upon the head so that his sword cut through helmet and bone. And the knight in black armour, knowing himself defeated, turned his horse's head and galloped away.

Uwaine followed him, all along the valley, until they came in sight of a town with a high wall around it. The knight rode through the gate of the town, and he sat in his saddle as though he were wounded to death.

But as Uwaine made to follow him, the portcullis was lowered upon him, killing his horse, and the inner gate was closed to and barred, so that Uwaine was left a prisoner between the heavy grating and the strong wooden and iron gate, with a great commotion going on inside the town. 'I am caught,' he thought, 'as though in a trap. When the inner gate is opened, I shall be killed, for if the knight in black armour should indeed be lord of this town, then all his men will be seeking my life for the hurt I have done to him.'

After a time the noise died down beyond the inner gate and all was silent. Uwaine found a crack between two of the thick planks of the gate and he peered through. He saw an empty road before him, with two rows of houses and a stone block for the mounting of horses and no gate-keeper in sight. While he watched he saw a damsel come walking down the street. When she neared the gate she called out that it should be opened for her, but there was no one there to open it.

'Fair damsel,' said Uwaine, 'I can no more easily open the gate for you than you can open it for me, and when the townsfolk return I shall be as good as dead.' And he told her who he was and how he came there.

'It would be a pity that one who comes from Arthur's court and speaks so courteously should die,' said the damsel. 'I will save you from death if I can.' She took off from her finger a ring set with a large stone. 'Wear this ring,' she said, 'and when they come to fetch you, turn the stone so that it lies within your hand and close your fingers over it, and so long as the stone is hidden, it will hide you also.' And she rolled the ring to him under the gate. 'When they open the inner gate,' she went on, 'you must slip through and come to me. I shall be standing on the horse-block, and though I shall not be able to see you, I shall know it is you when you place your hand on my shoulder. After that you must follow me.'

'Damsel,' said Uwaine, 'I shall be grateful to you for as long as I live.'

She went away and left him, and after a time a great crowd of men at arms with lances and swords came down to open the gate. Uwaine hid the stone on the ring as the damsel had bidden him, and when the gate was opened and they could not see him there, they shouted to one another angrily; and in the turmoil Uwaine slipped through and made his way to the horse-block. He reached up and touched the damsel on the shoulder, and she whispered, 'Follow me.'

She went to the castle which stood in the midst of the town, and entering by a postern gate, led Uwaine to a small but richly furnished room, and there she locked the door. 'You will be safe in here,' she said.

Uwaine gave back the ring to the damsel, who told him

her name was Luned, and she brought him food to eat. While he was eating he heard a great outcry in the castle as of women wailing. 'What is that?' he asked.

'The lord of the castle was dying; that cry means he is now dead. And it is you who have killed him,' she answered.

A little time later there came the sound of solemn singing from without the castle. 'What is that?' asked Uwaine.

'They are taking the lord of the castle to church for burial,' said Luned.

Uwaine went to the window and looked down, and there he saw the bier and the priest and the chanting choristers, and the mourners following after. And the foremost of the mourners was a golden-haired lady, tall and proud, wearing rich clothes. And the moment Uwaine saw her he knew that he could have no other wife than her.

'Who is that most lovely lady who follows the bier?' he asked.

Luned smiled. 'She is the best of ladies and I serve her. Kind and beautiful and just, she is more like my sister than my mistress. She is called the Lady of the Fountain, and she is widow to the lord of the castle whom you have slain.'

'I have never loved a lady until this moment,' said Uwaine. 'And I will have no other wife.'

'That will be hard for you,' said Luned, 'for she does not love you at all.'

And after that they were both silent, Uwaine thinking of the lady with the golden hair, and Luned wondering how she might help Uwaine, for she liked the strange knight from Arthur's court and would have seen him wedded to her mistress.

After a time Luned made ready a bed for Uwaine. 'Lie down and sleep,' she said, 'while I go a-wooing for you.' And she left him and went from the room to the chamber of the Lady of the Fountain; and there she found her mistress sitting alone, her face sad, with no word to say. 'Why will you not speak to me?' asked Luned.

'Are you not ashamed,' said the lady, 'after I have shown you so much kindness, that in my great grief you have kept far from me, never giving me a word of comfort all the while my lord was dying nor standing beside me when they buried him?' And she began to weep.

'It were better,' said Luned, 'that you dried your tears and considered what will now become of you, since you are left without a lord to protect you and your lands, than that you wept for one whom no tears can bring back.'

'Indeed,' sobbed the lady, 'I have many causes for grief, for as soon as my lord's enemies hear of his death, they will be at the gates of the town, and what shall I do to prevent them?'

'Find another lord,' said Luned.

The Lady of the Fountain grew angry. 'You are a heartless wretch that you would insult my constancy. Had anyone else but you spoken to me as you have done, I should have had her head struck from her shoulders. But to you I will be merciful, and say no more than that I never wish to see you again. Now go and leave me alone.'

'It was for your own good that I spoke,' said Luned, 'but since you send me away, I will go. Yet shame be to the one of us who first seeks out the other in friendship after today. Farewell.' And she turned and went to the door. But as she was opening it, the Lady of the Fountain gave a little cough, and Luned looked back over her shoulder. The Lady of the Fountain beckoned, and Luned went to her.

'Luned,' said the Lady of the Fountain, 'you have spoken wickedly to me, but since it was for my own good that you spoke, tell me what I should do.'

'Lady, you should find a knight who will defend for you the fountain as well as did your dead lord. Then will your lands be safe.'

'But where can I find such a knight?'

Luned pretended to consider, then she said, 'I have heard that there are many brave knights at the court of King Arthur. If you were to send me there, I do not doubt that I should come back with a knight who would keep the fountain well for you.'

'Go,' said the lady, 'to the court of King Arthur, and my blessing go with you.'

So Luned returned to the room where she had hidden Sir Uwaine, and there she remained until time enough had passed for her to have travelled to King Arthur's court and back. Then she went once more to the Lady of the Fountain. 'Have you news?' her mistress asked.

'The best news that I ever brought you,' said Luned. 'The good knight Sir Uwaine, son of King Uriens of Gore, has come with me to guard your fountain for you.'

'Bring him to me,' said the lady. But when Uwaine stood before her, she looked long and closely at him. 'You have not the look of a man who has this day travelled far,' she said. 'And your armour is even as the armour of the knight who slew my lord, as I heard tell of him.'

Uwaine fell on his knees before her and besought her pardon. 'Had I known that I would bring grief on you,

48

lady, I would have stayed my hand. I would have died a hundred times rather than give you distress. But now I only ask that I may serve you and make amends in a little for the harm that I have done.'

And after a time the Lady of the Fountain said, 'You killed my lord in fair fight and you cannot be blamed. I will have you guard my fountain for me.'

So Sir Uwaine kept the fountain, even as the knight in black armour had done, and the lady was glad of his strength and his courage, and took pleasure in his company; and in time she grew to love him, so they were married.

When three years had passed from the day Uwaine had heard Sir Cynon's tale and ridden away from Arthur's court, the king said to Gawaine, 'It is too long since we saw your cousin Uwaine, or heard word of him, whether he lives or has died. It is in my mind that he rode away to seek the knight whom Sir Cynon told us of. Let us go and find him.'

So with Gawaine and Cynon and Kay, and many others of his knights, King Arthur set off, and they searched through all the land until they came by chance to the valley with the castle where dwelt the fair-haired man, and from there they went to the mound where sat the one-eyed, one-legged man, and so at last they came to the fountain beneath the fir-tree.

'My lord king,' said Sir Kay, 'grant me to be the first to challenge the knight who guards the fountain, for I was present on that day when Cynon told his tale.' Arthur gave his leave and Kay poured water over the marble slab. And after the thunder and after the hailstorm and after the song of the birds, they saw a knight come riding all in black armour. And because of the black armour they never knew Sir Uwaine, though he knew them well enough.

Uwaine fought with Sir Kay and unhorsed him and rode away; but the next day another of Arthur's knights poured water over the marble slab, and him too Uwaine overthrew. And so it went on each day, until of all those who had come with Arthur, only Gawaine and Arthur himself remained. 'He is truly valiant, this knight in black armour,' said the king.

Gawaine filled the silver bowl with water and poured it over the marble slab. But when he saw Uwaine riding fast towards him, the day being hot, he threw a cloak of silk over his armour to keep it cool from the heat of the sun, so that Uwaine did not know him for his cousin, and fought with him. All day they fought and neither gained the advantage, while Arthur and his knights looked on and marvelled at them. 'I would that he were one of my knights of the Round Table, this knight in black armour,' said Arthur.

And then, in their fighting, Uwaine struck off Sir Gawaine's helmet, and knew him at once, and knelt down and yielded to him. 'Take my sword,' he said, 'for I am your cousin Uwaine.'

'Yours is the victory,' said Gawaine. 'It is for me to cry you mercy.' And they could not agree, in their courtesy.

'Give me both your swords,' said Arthur, 'and the victory shall be to neither.' And he embraced his nephews and made much of Uwaine whom he had sought so long.

Uwaine told the whole of his adventure, and on the morrow he led Arthur and all the knights to the town, and

there he and the Lady of the Fountain entertained them royally.

'You must return with us to court, good nephew,' said Arthur, 'and bring your lady with you, for it will give Guenever much joy.'

But Uwaine would not, for with him gone there would be no one to keep the fountain or the town.

'That shall be my concern,' said Arthur. And he promised that ever would he and his knights be ready to defend the lands that belonged to the Lady of the Fountain; so that for fear, no enemies troubled her ever again, and she passed much of her time with Sir Uwaine at the court of King Arthur, and a happier lady it would have been hard to find.

VI

Gawaine and the Green Knight

KING ARTHUR and his court had been keeping Christmas at Camelot with joyful feasting and merrymaking, and now was New Year's Day come with gifts and games and much festivity, and a great banquet to crown all. Outside the snow lay white and glittering and a cold wind blew, but in the great hall of the castle all was warm and gay, with huge fires burning on the hearthstones and bright colours everywhere.

Just as the merry company was sitting down to feast, the high doors of the hall blew open and in from the snow there rode a warrior, so tall that he might almost have been called a giant.

Everyone fell silent in astonishment, for the face and the hands of this stranger and all that might be seen of his body were as green as the Maytime grass, and his long green hair and his green beard were cut evenly around him at the level of his elbows, so that they hung like a short cape about him. His jerkin, his hose, and his mantle were green, all embroidered with birds and butterflies in gold. His horse, too, was green and a mighty creature, well fitted to carry such a huge man, with its trappings all of green leather studded with emeralds, and its green mane and tail plaited and entwined with golden ribbons, and little golden bells hanging tinkling from its forelock. In one hand the stranger carried a branch of holly, and in the other a great battle-axe with a green haft and a blade of green steel.

This Green Knight rode up the length of the hall and then called out, 'Where is the master of this house?'

And Arthur stood up and answered him, bidding him welcome. 'Dismount and eat with us, for this is the feast of the New Year, and all guests are gladly received.'

'I have not come to feast with you,' replied the Green Knight.

'This is a season of goodwill,' said Arthur. 'May God grant you come in peace.'

'At home,' answered the Green Knight, 'I have armour and a helmet, a shield and a sharp sword, and many other weapons. Think you that if I had meant to give battle to any man I would have ridden forth unarmed? No, my lord King Arthur, I have come in peace. Because I have heard great talk of the courage and prowess of your knights, I have come to find if there is any here will join with me in a sport I have devised.'

'If you would meet one of my knights in combat,' said Arthur, 'I have no doubt that there will be several here who will give you the sport you ask.'

The Green Knight shook his head. 'It is not fighting that I seek. It is no more than a Christmas game to bring mirth to your feasting.' He held up the green axe which he carried. 'If there is any bold man here who would win this axe for his own, let him come and take it, and with it give me one blow, and pledge me his word that when a year is past from today, he will seek me out and take in return one blow from me.'

At first all were too amazed to answer him; and then from where he sat beside Queen Guenever young Sir

Gawaine, King Arthur's nephew, spoke. 'If you will give me leave, my lord king, I will accept this challenge.'

When Arthur had given his consent, Gawaine rose and went to the Green Knight and took the axe from him. The Green Knight dismounted and looked steadily at Gawaine. 'Tell me your name,' he said, 'and give me your word to seek me out and take a blow from me, a year from today.'

'My name is Gawaine, and you have my word for it, sir green stranger. But where shall I find you, when a year is past?'

The Green Knight laughed. 'That must you discover for yourself. Now give me a blow. Just one, no more.' And he bent his head for the stroke.

Gawaine stood firmly and raised the great axe and swung it downward upon the Green Knight's neck with such strength and skill that the green head was severed from the body and rolled among the rushes on the floor, and a cry of admiration for the blow rose up from all those gathered there.

'He has indeed found the game he asked for, the green stranger,' laughed Sir Kay the Seneschal.

Yet the admiration was turned to amazement when they saw how the Green Knight neither fell nor even staggered, but instead bent down and picked up his green head by the hair. He went to his horse, set his foot firmly in the stirrup, and mounted. Then he held up his head high before them, and the lips parted and the head spoke to Sir Gawaine. 'Forget not to come and seek me, a year from today, to take the blow that I have promised you.' And with that the Green Knight, still carrying his head, rode out from the hall into the snow.

For all the rest of that day the company could talk of nothing else save the Green Knight and his head; and his axe was set up on the wall for all to marvel at. And Gawaine made light of the matter and laughed, and called it a rare Christmas jest.

But as the year grew older and summer followed spring, Sir Gawaine began to consider it less of a jest. And when the red and yellow leaves and the golden moon of Michaelmas were come, he went to Arthur and said, 'It is time for me to ride forth and seek the Green Knight, for I know not where he is to be found nor how long it will be before I find him, and I would not be late at our tryst. Give me your leave to depart.'

So Gawaine rode forth on Gringolet his horse, all shining in gold and scarlet and well armed. He wandered through the whole land, alone, without even a squire to serve him, and in every place he asked if any man had heard of a green knight who rode upon a green horse, but no one could answer him. And the winter came upon him as he travelled, with icy wind and snow, but never a word did he hear of his quest.

At last, on Christmas Eve, he came upon a castle and asked shelter for the night. The lord of the castle and his lady received him gladly, and bade him spend the days of Christmas feasting in their company. The lord was a tall strong man with red hair and beard, and his lady was, so Gawaine thought, the fairest he had ever seen until that moment; and they both gave him such a welcome that he forgot for a while the perils of his quest.

When the three days of the festival were done, the lord of the castle asked Gawaine, 'What brings you so far from

King Arthur's court in the winter-time, when ways are hard?'

And Gawaine told him of the Green Knight and how he must find him, and he sighed and said, 'Tomorrow I must leave you, for there is but little time left to me, if I would be with the Green Knight on New Year's Day.'

The lord of the castle laughed. 'You have no need to seek farther,' he said, 'for the Green Knight dwells but a half-day's ride from here. Be my guest until the morning of New Year's Day, and then I will send you on your way.'

Gawaine was overjoyed, for he had feared above all things that he might not be able to keep faith and be shamed for ever as a coward, and he thanked his host with gladness.

'Before you leave here,' said the lord, 'I would ask a favour of you.'

'I shall do willingly anything you ask,' said Gawaine.

'There are yet three days left to us before you need ride forth. You must still be wearied from your search; it would please me well if you would rest and take your ease for the next three days. Rise late and eat when you will, while I go hunting, and my lady shall stay with you to make you good cheer. And whatever I kill in the forest, it shall be a prize for you; if you will, for your part, give to me on my return any good fortune you have come by during the day.' To this Gawaine gladly agreed.

The next morning the lord of the castle rode out early to hunt the stag, and Gawaine rose late and sat by the blazing fire talking to the lady of one thing and another.

But after a time the lady frowned a little and said, 'Do you not find me fair, Sir Gawaine?'

'Indeed I do, lady,' he replied.

Yet her frown deepened. 'Indeed you do not,' she said. 'For never before have I talked so long with a knight without his asking me to give him a kiss.'

Now Gawaine would have thought shame to ask a lady for a kiss, even in jest, when her lord was not by, yet he did not wish to displease her nor would he have had her believe that he did not find her fair. 'I would not fail in courtesy where other knights have not,' he said.

And he rose and went to her and she kissed him, and straightway her frowns were gone and she smiled again, and they sat and talked further until, at evening, the lord of the castle returned.

In the hall he set out all the deer that he had killed, and a great number they were. 'See what I have brought for you,' he called to Gawaine. 'Have I not done well today? Have you gained any good fortune to be compared with mine?'

'No more than this which I shall give to you,' said Gawaine, and he kissed the lord of the castle.

The lord laughed mightily. 'That is indeed sweet fortune,' he said.

The next morning the lord of the castle rode out early to hunt the boar. As before, Gawaine rose late and sat by the blazing fire and talked with the lady of one thing and another. But as it drew near evening she frowned and said, 'Sir Gawaine, do you no longer consider me fair? You have not asked me for a kiss today.'

And in his courtesy Sir Gawaine rose and went to her, and she kissed him twice and her frowns were smoothed away and she smiled.

After a little while the lord of the castle returned, bring-

Gawaine and the Green Knight

ing with him the boar which he had slain. The boar's head he gave to Gawaine, saying, 'See what I have gained today. Have you had any good fortune to compare with that?'

'No more than this which I give to you,' said Gawaine, and he kissed his host twice.

The lord of the castle laughed loud and long. 'Indeed,' he said, 'that was sweet fortune.'

The next morning the lord of the castle rode out early to hunt the fox, and as before Sir Gawaine rose late and sat with the lady, and they talked of one thing and another. But as dusk was falling she frowned and said to him, 'You are indeed a churlish knight, Sir Gawaine, that you have forgotten that yesterday you thought me fair. Today you have not asked me for a kiss.'

And Gawaine rose and went to her, and she kissed him three times and her frowns vanished and she smiled. 'Since you find me fair,' she said, 'will you not take a gift from me?' And she took off a jewelled ring she wore and held it out to him.

At first he did not know how to refuse her gift with courtesy, and then he said, 'I thank you, lady, but I may not take such a costly gift from you when I have nothing to give you in return. I am here among strangers and all my goods are far away, so it would not be fitting that I should accept a ring from you and offer nothing in exchange.'

'If it is only the value of the ring which troubles you, see, I will give you a gift that is of less worth.' And she unfastened the long green girdle which she wore and held it out to him. 'Let it be for a keepsake,' she said.

But when he tried to refuse it, she smiled, 'Poor gift

though this girdle seems, it is not worthless. For any man who wears it is safe from death, and the blow of no weapon can harm him.'

And Gawaine remembered how in no more than a few hours he would have to ride out to meet the Green Knight and withstand a blow from his mighty strength, and he was tempted and hesitated, looking on the green silken girdle that was embroidered with gold.

'Take it,' pleaded the lady, 'for that is my wish.'

Gawaine took the girdle and thanked her; and at that moment they heard the baying of the hounds in the courtyard and the clatter of hoofs, and they knew that the lord of the castle was home.

Cheerily he called to Gawaine and gave him the skin of the fox with its white-tipped tail. 'What good fortune have you gained today, my friend?' he asked.

'No more than this which I give to you.' And Gawaine kissed him three times. But the girdle he hid and did not give to his host, for he knew that he would have great need of it on the morrow.

The lord of the castle threw back his head and his laughter rang through the hall. 'Indeed, that was sweet fortune,' he said.

That evening they feasted merrily, and though it was Gawaine's last night at the castle there was much mirth and joy between them.

Before they went to rest, Gawaine thanked his host and the lady for all their courtesy. 'I shall ever be grateful to you,' he said.

Very early on New Year's Day Gawaine rode out from the castle, together with a squire whom the lord had bidden show him the way; and over his armour he wore the green girdle. They rode through a wood and up a hill, and then the squire pointed towards a tall rock that lay at a distance before them. 'There, lord, is the cave where dwells the dread Green Knight. May all the saints protect you.'

Gawaine thanked him and bade him farewell and rode on alone towards the rock, and when he came close he dismounted. Then he heard a mighty shout from above, and looking up, he saw the Green Knight, his head firmly on his shoulders, standing upon the rock, sharpening an axe on a whetstone.

The Green Knight leapt down from the rock and stood by him, towering and tall, a sight to bring fear even to the boldest of hearts. 'You are welcome, Sir Gawaine,' he said. 'I am glad to learn that you are one who keeps faith. Now take off your helmet and let me strike my blow.'

So Gawaine took off his helmet and bent his head to the axe, and the Green Knight raised his weapon high and brought it down mightily; but even as it fell, for all his courage, Gawaine shrank aside a little, and the Green Knight swerved his blow so that Gawaine was unharmed. 'Indeed,' said the Green Knight with scorn, 'they told me that Sir Gawaine was among the bravest of all men and that he would quail at nothing. It seems that they were mistaken. Did you see me flinch when you struck your blow at me, last New Year's Day?'

'Strike again, Sir Green Knight, and this time I will not flinch, not even though my head falls in the snow. And unlike you I cannot pick it up and put it on my shoulders again.' And Gawaine bent his head once more, trusting as much as he might in the girdle the lady had given him.

The Green Knight raised the axe again and brought it down in a mighty stroke, and this time Gawaine never stirred. But just as the axe would have touched his neck, the Green Knight stayed his hand and laughed. 'Now that you have found your courage, it is time to strike my blow in earnest.' And he raised the axe once more.

'You threaten too long,' said Gawaine. 'Strike and have done.'

A third time the Green Knight raised his axe and brought it down, but so skilfully did he wield it that it did no greater harm than he had intended, and broke no more than the skin of Gawaine's neck, so that a little blood trickled down upon the snow. And when Gawaine felt the blow and saw the blood, he leapt forward and snatched up his helmet and sword. 'You have had your one blow, Sir Green Knight. If you would have another, you will find it shall not go unreturned.'

But the Green Knight leant upon his axe and laughed. 'I have no quarrel with you, Sir Gawaine. I have given my one blow as promised, in fair exchange, and now is all discharged between us. The first blow which I would have struck you and did not strike was for the kiss you had of my lady and gave freely on to me. And the second time I threatened you was for the two kisses you had of her and restored. But when I struck you in earnest and wounded you, that was not for the three kisses which she gave you and which you rendered to me again, but for the green girdle which is mine and which you kept for yourself. For you must know that I am no other than the lord of the castle whose guest you have been these past seven days and more; and most welcome has your company been. My lady and I, as we decided between us, did but seek to try you with her kisses and my green girdle to see if you were a true knight or no, and well did you acquit yourself.'

But Gawaine was ashamed. 'It was my fear of death that made me keep the girdle. And it was that same cowardice that made me flinch from your stroke.'

'It is but a little stain on so noble a knight, Sir Gawaine. There cannot be your like in all the land, and I am proud to have called you my friend. For I am indeed as you saw me at my castle and not as you see me now. This guise is but an enchantment put upon me by Queen Morgan le Fay, who is King Arthur's sister, for she wished to affright her brother and his knights of the Round Table. She believed that no one of them would dare to take up the challenge of a knight so huge and so fantastical as I when in the shape she gave me. Yet now is she proved wrong, and I am glad.' And the Green Knight bade Gawaine return with him once more to his castle for further feasting and joy.

But Gawaine refused, saying, 'I have been long away from King Arthur's court and I would return to them who perhaps grieve for me.' He took off the green girdle and would have given it back, but the Green Knight prevented him. 'It is no great gift for so rare a knight, for in truth it has no magic powers, but it is of my own lady's making, and I would that you kept it if it pleases you.'

And Gawaine thanked him. 'I will keep it to remind me of the moment when I failed in courage,' he said. 'And may it ever save me from further cowardice.'

Then they embraced and Gawaine bade the Green Knight greet his lady for him, and mounting Gringolet, he rode on his way across the snow.

When he reached King Arthur's court once more, there was great rejoicing, for many had feared that he never would return to them. Much they wondered at the story which he had to tell them, and many there were who blamed the spite of Morgan le Fay. But all praised Sir Gawaine; and ever after the knights of the Round Table wore a girdle of green as a baldric to bear him company, and it was esteemed a great honour amongst them.

VII

Lancelot of the Lake

SOON after Arthur's marriage to the Lady Guenever, there came to Camelot a young man riding on a white horse, and he asked to speak with the king. 'You are welcome to my court,' Arthur greeted him. 'How are you named?'

' I am the son of King Ban of Benwick in France. My name is Lancelot, and I am come to ask knighthood of you.'

Arthur looked at the strange youth and thought how he had never liked any man so well. 'Gladly will I make you a knight,' he said.

He asked more concerning Lancelot, and Lancelot told him of how his father, King Ban, had been slain by an enemy when he himself had been but a babe, and how for grief his mother had gone to a nunnery, and how he had been cared for by a water-damsel very like to that Lady of the Lake who had given the sword Excalibur to Arthur, therefore was he known as Lancelot of the Lake. 'And as soon as I came of an age to consider such things for myself,' he said, 'I determined that one day I should seek out King Arthur, for I had heard him to be the very best of men, that from him I might ask knighthood and a place among those who serve him. And now am I come over the sea from Benwick for that end.'

And Arthur was more glad of this thing than of anything else.

A day was appointed upon which Lancelot should be knighted, and the evening before, he kept vigil in the church at Camelot, and Sir Uwaine, into whose keeping Arthur had given him until such time as he should be a knight himself, remained with him. When dawn was come, Lancelot put on his armour, and there in the church, before high mass, he was knighted by Arthur.

Now, it was the custom that though a knight should be ordained before the service, his sword was not girded on until after he had heard mass. And it happened that, in the agitation of this great hour in his life, Lancelot forgot his sword and left it lying on the flag-stones of the church floor where he had been kneeling; so that when the time came for the king to fasten it about him, he did not have it.

But Queen Guenever had seen it; and as she knelt to pray, that the young knight might not be shamed by lack of it, she dropped the train of her gown over the sword, and when she rose she picked it up and kept it for Lancelot until the moment he had need of it.

And when Lancelot would have given his sword to Arthur and found it was not there, unseen by all the others, Guenever put it into his hands. He could not at that moment speak his thanks, but he looked into her eyes and she gave a little smile, and then Lancelot turned and offered the sword to Arthur who girded it about him. But Lancelot could not even hear the kindly words which Arthur spoke, for in that one moment he had fallen in love with the queen.

Lancelot's love for Guenever grew until it became the most valued thing in all his life; and one day he could no longer keep silent and spoke of it to her. And on that day he learnt that she had grown to love him in return.

'Would God that I had met you before ever I wed with the king,' she said. 'The marriage was none of my choosing, but it was pleasing to my father and to Arthur my lord, and how could I know that this would come to pass?'

'Even though I may never marry you,' said Lancelot, 'I will have no other lady. All my deeds shall be in your honour, my very life shall be yours, and wherever I am you will always be in my thoughts.'

And they kissed and swore faith for evermore and hid their love from the king. And though their love brought them a measure of happiness, it brought them also much pain, for Arthur was very dear to them both and they hated to deceive him.

Sir Lancelot soon showed himself to be a knight without equal, even among the fellowship of the Round Table, and before very long he was considered the best of all knights in the land, and without a match. He was ever first in the jousting, and at the tourneying there was no one like him; in courtesy and gentleness he surpassed even Sir Gawaine, and he rode on many adventures and won the respect of all. And always, secretly, he did all his knightly deeds for the sake of Queen Guenever.

Arthur gave to Lancelot, whom he honoured above all others, a castle named Joyous Gard, close to the city of Carlisle; but Lancelot was not often there, since most of the time he rode on adventures, carrying his red and silver shield; and always his horses were white.

One day he saved Gaheris, the brother of Gawaine, from the hands of an evil knight, and this was how it chanced. He was riding along the highway and there he met with a damsel on a palfrey. 'God keep you, lady,' he said. 'Have you heard of any adventure that I may undertake?'

'Near by there lives a knight named Turquine,' she replied, 'who has long brought grief to many, for he robs and slays where he will. Good knights he takes as his prisoners and holds them in his castle. It would be not only an adventure for him who undertook it, but a great blessing to others, that this knight should be slain. But he is a man of might and I fear that even Sir Lancelot of the Lake would find him hard to overcome. So it were best, sir stranger, that you sought somewhere else for an adventure than near Sir Turquine's lands.'

'Lady, I am Lancelot of the Lake, and I thank you for those kind words you spoke of me. Tell me how I may find this Sir Turquine, and with God's help he may be overcome.'

So the damsel showed him the way to Sir Turquine's castle, and Lancelot knocked at the gate and called to Turquine to come forth, but though he waited for near half an hour, no one came out to him. And then he saw a knight riding towards the castle along the highway, and after him he led a horse with a knight bound and lying across its saddle. 'It is Sir Turquine and one whom he has made his prisoner,' said the damsel.

And when Sir Turquine came nearer, Lancelot saw that the captive was Gaheris, now no longer his brother's squire, but himself a knight of the Round Table.

'Shame on you, Sir Turquine,' called Lancelot, 'to treat a good knight so. Come, leave your prisoner and fight with me, for I have ridden from King Arthur's court to free the land of your evil ways.'

'If you are of the Round Table, and one of King Arthur's knights,' said Turquine, 'then shall I willingly fight with you for the hatred I bear King Arthur and all your fellows.' And he lowered his lance and attacked. They fought long on horseback, and even longer on foot, until at last they were both wearied and breathless and stood to rest, leaning upon their swords.

'Never in all my days,' said Turquine, 'have I met a knight who was my match. For all that you are a knight of King Arthur, I would be accorded with you, for I have never fought with a better knight. Come, let us forget our quarrel, and whoever you are, so long as you are not Lancelot of the Lake, I will deliver my prisoners up to you, to do with as you will, for greatly have you deserved my respect.'

'And if I were Lancelot, Sir Turquine, what then?'

'Of all the knights of the Round Table,' said Turquine, 'of all the knights in the world, it is Sir Lancelot whom I hate the most, and with him could I never be at peace.

One day I shall meet with him, and on that day one of us shall slay the other. But let us not speak of Lancelot. Tell me your name and let us be friends.'

'It would have pleased me well,' said Lancelot, 'if it might have been peace between us. But I see that it cannot be, for I am Lancelot.'

'Then you are well met,' said Turquine, 'and here one of us must die.' And he raised his sword and set upon Sir Lancelot.

For two hours and more they fought while the damsel and Gaheris watched, and first it seemed as though one of them were the stronger, and then the other. But at last Sir Turquine grew weak and he had not the strength to hold up his shield, and Lancelot gave him a great blow on the helmet, and Turquine fell to his knees and Lancelot struck off his head.

The damsel came running to him joyfully. 'Today you will have the thanks of many knights,' she said.

But Lancelot looked down on Turquine. 'He was a worthy enemy,' he said.

Then he and Gaheris entered the castle and released the knights who were prisoned in the dungeons, and in all there were four and sixty of them. Rejoicing greatly, they praised Sir Lancelot, while the damsel hastened away to tell everywhere the glad tidings of Turquine's death.

Because of his fame as the best of knights in Britain, men of evil life, such as Sir Turquine had been, often sought to kill Sir Lancelot, and there was one knight named Phelot who tried to slay him by guile, for he knew that he could never overcome him in fair fight.

Lancelot was one day riding by the castle where dwelt

this knight, Sir Phelot, when he saw a falcon flying as though it had broken free. And while he watched the hawk he saw how the long leash attached to its jesses caught on the branch of a tree, high up from the ground, so that the falcon hung dangling when it would have flown away. Lancelot rode under the tree, full of pity for the fine bird, when suddenly he heard a voice calling to him. 'Sir Lancelot, as you are the best of knights, I pray you help me.' And Lancelot saw a lady coming towards him.

'Willingly shall I help you,' said Lancelot.

'That falcon belongs to my lord, Sir Phelot, and through my own carelessness I have allowed her to fly away. My lord will be angry if I lose her. I pray you, climb into the tree and fetch her down for me.'

Lancelot, though he knew the name of her husband as that of a knight who hated him, would never refuse his courtesy to a lady, enemy or not. He smiled. 'I am but a poor climber, lady, yet I will do my best.' So he dismounted and the lady helped him put off his armour, and with difficulty he climbed the tree to where the falcon hung. Then breaking off a dead branch, he tied the falcon to it by the leash and dropped the branch down to the lady, so that she had the falcon safe.

But when he would have climbed down from the tree himself, he saw Sir Phelot step forth from the bushes, all armed and holding his sword. 'At last I have you, Sir Lancelot,' he said. 'You shall not escape from me.'

Lancelot saw in how great danger he stood, but all he said was, 'You have betrayed me, lady, and I would have done you a service.'

'She did but as I commanded her,' said Phelot. 'Now make haste to the ground, that I may see you die.'

'If ever you held your knighthood in honour, Sir Phelot, if ever you had pride in your skill at arms, then you will think shame to kill a weaponless man, however much you may wish his death.'

'So long as you die,' replied Sir Phelot, 'I care not whether you die armed or unarmed.'

'Then pass up my sword to me,' said Lancelot, 'and I will come down to you. I do not ask for my armour or for my shield, but only for my sword.'

But Phelot laughed. 'I have heard too much of you and your skill to be foolish enough to give you a sword.'

And Lancelot saw how he could expect no gallantry from this enemy and that he would assuredly be murdered. He looked down to where his white horse stood, close by the tree, and then he reached up and broke off a dead bough. 'If you will wait for me, Sir Phelot, I will come down to you.' Then carefully, still holding his broken bough, he came down to a lower branch, and before Phelot guessed what he would do, he had jumped to the ground so that his horse was between them.

Sir Phelot gave a shout of triumph and sprang forward with his sword, but because the horse stood in his way, by the time he had reached Lancelot, Lancelot was ready for him, and caught the sword stroke on his broken bough. Then, before Phelot could gather himself to strike again, Lancelot gave him a great buffet on the head with the bough, so that the dead wood broke in two, then grappling with him before he was recovered from the blow, took his sword and with it struck off his head.

At that the lady screamed as though she were out of her mind. 'You have my pity, lady,' said Lancelot. 'But you and your lord both brought this sorrow on yourselves when you sought to kill me by guile. Above all things I hate treachery.'

Then he saw how her cries were bringing men out from the castle, and he put on his armour hurriedly and, mounting his horse, he rode away.

And these are only two of the many adventures which Sir Lancelot had when he was but a young knight.

VIII

Lancelot and Elaine

BECAUSE Queen Guenever and Sir Lancelot had to hide their love from all the world, it sometimes brought them much grief. Lancelot was handsome and the best knight in the land, so there were many ladies and damsels who would gladly have called him their lord. And though they meant nothing to him, to each of them, that she might not feel herself slighted, he was courteous; so no one of them ever ceased to hope that he might grow to love her. And Guenever watched them and was jealous, because they could smile at Lancelot and speak kindly and flatter him, while she, who loved him above all else in the world, might show him, when in company, no more favour than she might show to any other. And there were times when, in her unhappy jealousy, she could not refrain from becoming angry and upbraiding Lancelot that he was not more cold to these other ladies; though in her heart she knew that she was cruel and unjust. And when it was too late, and the words could not be taken back, she would weep bitterly and ask his forgiveness; and Lancelot would understand and love her all the more.

There was a king named Pelles, of the city of Corbin, whose overlord was Arthur, and this Pelles had a daughter named Elaine. At her birth it had been foretold that a son would be born to her and to the best knight in the land, and that this son would do great deeds and see with his own eyes the Holy Grail, which was said to be the very cup from which Jesus Christ and the Disciples had drunk at the Last Supper. So that the prophecy might be fulfilled, King Pelles determined that Lancelot should wed his daughter, and to this end he sent her to Camelot, to Arthur's court, saying nothing of his reasons to any man. And as soon as Elaine set eyes on Lancelot she wished for no other lord.

The Lady Elaine was fair and young, and Guenever was kind to her; but when she found that Elaine, too, loved Lancelot, she was ill pleased. Elaine had a waiting-woman named Brisen who one day heard her mistress sighing. 'What is amiss, lady?' she asked. And because Elaine was unhappy and needed comforting, she told Brisen how she loved Lancelot and how he cared nothing for her. And Brisen, who pitied her mistress, contrived that Elaine and Lancelot should be alone together, that Elaine might tell her love to him and maybe win him for her lord.

But Guenever learnt of this meeting, and in great anger she went to the room where they were and accused Lancelot of being faithless to the promises that he had made her. She said many harsh and cruel things to him, and at last she commanded him to leave King Arthur's court, and never to see her again. And Lancelot, for grief and despair, went out of his mind, and all unarmed ran from the castle, through the streets of Camelot, and out to the forest.

Elaine wept and reproached the queen for her unkindness. 'If it were not for you,' she said, 'Lancelot might have grown to love me. You have the greatest king in all the world for your lord, why should you have the love of Sir Lancelot as well?'

Guenever bade her leave Camelot and return to her

father. 'But if you value Lancelot's life,' she said, 'you will speak no word of what you have learnt today.'

When Elaine had gone, Guenever sent for three knights who were Lancelot's kinsmen: Sir Lionel and Sir Bors who were his cousins, and Sir Ector de Maris who was his brother. With tears she begged that they would not rest until they had found Sir Lancelot and brought him back to Camelot; and when they understood how well she loved him, they could not hate her, though she had caused so much sorrow and distress to one whom they held so dear. And the three of them went forth to search for him.

Out in the forest Sir Lancelot hid himself from the sight of men, and lived upon roots and berries and drank water from the streams, and knew not what he did. There in the forest one day a good knight named Bliant found him, and because of his wild appearance did not know him for Sir Lancelot. Yet having pity on him, he took him to his castle and gave him food and clothing and a little room to live in; but because he was a madman and might therefore be a danger, he kept him chained.

After Lancelot had been at Bliant's castle for a year or more, one morning he looked out of the window of his little room and saw how Sir Bliant, sorely wounded, rode home alone, pursued by two robber knights. And though he was out of his mind, Lancelot was still too much himself to stand by and watch a good knight slain. With all his strength he broke his chains and ran out through the castle gateway. Unarmed though he was he dragged one of the robbers from his horse, and wresting his sword from him, struck at the other so that the two of them were afraid and rode away as fast as they might.

Sir Bliant made much of Lancelot, and blessed the day when he had found him and brought him home. And after that Lancelot came and went about the castle as he pleased, and sometimes rode out with Sir Bliant, or sometimes alone.

One day while he was hunting alone, Lancelot was wounded by a boar, and a hermit who lived in the forest took him to his woodland cell that he might heal the wound by his knowledge of herbs and medicine. Yet Lancelot would not remain in the hermitage, but railed against the hermit for not leaving him to die; and the moment he was alone, he rose up from the bed where he had been laid and wandered off. But he could not find the way back to Sir Bliant's castle, though he searched long for the path.

A few days later he came by chance to the city of Corbin where King Pelles ruled and where lived the Lady Elaine. When Lancelot limped through the gates of the city, ragged and footsore and out of his mind, the townsfolk jeered and flung stones and gave chase to him up the street as far as the castle gate. And there two young squires came out and drove away the mob. They looked at Lancelot. 'For all he is mad,' they said, 'he is a fine man, and strong.' They took him into the castle and clothed him and gave him a place to sleep in and straw on which to lie. And each day one of the kitchen servants would bring him food.

King Pelles had a nephew, and it happened that he was at about this time ordained knight, and on that day, to celebrate the occasion, he gave clothes to the poor of the city, and gifts to the servants. And to Lancelot he gave a scarlet cloak.

In his scarlet cloak Lancelot wandered into the garden
of the castle, where the ladies of King Pelles' court walked
in the sunshine, and there he sat down beside a well and
slept. And there the Lady Elaine saw him and knew him
at once for Lancelot.

She went immediately to her father and brought him
to where Lancelot lay. 'He is indeed Sir Lancelot,' said the
king. 'How sad a thing is this. We must keep his secret, for
it would be but shame to such a noble knight that all men
should know how he was out of his mind.' He told no
more than his four most trusted knights and Brisen,
Elaine's serving-woman; and they carried Lancelot into
the castle and laid him on a bed and tended him, so that
after a time he grew well again in his mind and wondered
how he came to be in Corbin. 'How did I come here?'
he asked. 'For I was last in Camelot.'

Elaine told him how he had been mad and now was well
again, and how for two years he had not been in Camelot;
and Lancelot remembered everything, his quarrel with
Queen Guenever, and how she had forbidden him ever to
see her again, and he wept. 'There is none but my father
and his four most trusted knights, and Brisen my woman,
who know of your madness,' said Elaine to comfort him.
'So there is no shame to you of it, before all the world.'
But Lancelot thought of Guenever and would not be
comforted.

So Lancelot remained at Corbin because he believed that
he might not return to Arthur's court, and in time Pelles
persuaded him to take as a gift a castle in his lands which
had been built on an island in the midst of a lake. And there
on this island Lancelot lived with Elaine as his lady, and

ever he named himself, no longer Sir Lancelot, but the Knight that had Trespassed. And in fulfilment of the old prophecy, a son was born to Elaine and Lancelot, and Elaine named him Galahad, and King Pelles rejoiced.

Yet neither in the babe nor in his life had Lancelot any joy, for he ever remembered Arthur, and Guenever whom he thought never to see again. But Sir Bors, Sir Lionel, and Sir Ector de Maris still sought him for Guenever's sake; and King Arthur, who understood nothing of why Lancelot had left Camelot without a word to him, had sent forth his nephews to find him.

One day Lancelot, who had for long performed no knightly feats, sent forth a dwarf to cry to all knights that on the island in the lake the Knight that had Trespassed would joust with all who came, and to any who could overcome him, would he give a falcon. But though five hundred knights came to the island, no single falcon was won, for each of the knights Lancelot worsted.

And it happened that Sir Ector de Maris, Lancelot's brother, still searching for Lancelot, passed by the lake at that time and thought to joust with the Knight that had Trespassed. And when he had been rowed to the island and he met with Sir Lancelot, Lancelot knew him for his brother and could not refrain from telling his name. With great joy they embraced, and Lancelot told all his grief.

'Bors and Lionel and I,' said Ector de Maris, 'have sought you these three years by order of the queen. And the king, too, has sent out knights to search for you. You must return with me to Arthur's court.'

But Lancelot would not, and he told Ector de Maris of

the queen's anger and how she had bidden him never to see her again.

'She has regretted her hasty words,' said Ector de Maris, 'and before my eyes she wept for your loss and asked that we, your kinsmen, might seek you and bring you back to her.'

Lancelot was glad beyond measure when he heard this, and at once he prepared to go with Ector de Maris to Camelot, where King Arthur was. But Elaine wept when she knew that she must lose him, as she had ever feared she one day would, and with great sorrow she bade him farewell. 'When Galahad our son is fifteen years old,' she said, 'he shall be ordained knight.'

'That must be as you wish it,' replied Lancelot. 'But God grant he make a good knight.'

And Elaine held her head high, for all her tears. 'I do not doubt, my lord, that he will prove the best of all his kinsmen, save only his father.'

With Sir Ector de Maris Lancelot went back to Camelot, and there Arthur received him with the greatest joy, and bade him tell all his story. And Lancelot told him a little of it. But Guenever wept to see Lancelot again, so that Arthur turned to her and laid his hand on hers, smiling. 'Why do you weep, lady? We have our good friend Lancelot with us once more, so there is cause to rejoice.' Yet Bors and Lionel and Ector de Maris and Lancelot himself knew why she wept.

When they could speak alone together, Guenever besought Lancelot to forgive her for her jealousy, and promised never again to fail to trust in him. And they were more happy than they had ever in all the last three years believed possible, for they might see one another again.

IX

How Tristram Fought against the Knight from Ireland

THERE was in the south of Britain a small kingdom called Lyones where ruled King Meliodas who held his lands from King Arthur as overlord, as did also King Mark of Cornwall whose lands lay close by. King Meliodas had for wife the sister of King Mark, a fair lady whom he loved well; and in time a son was born to them and they named him Tristram. But to the king's great grief, his wife lived not long after the birth of the child.

For seven years King Meliodas mourned for her, and then, on the advice of his counsellors, he took another queen. At first she treated little Tristram kindly, but when sons of her own were born, she grew envious to think that it was Tristram and not they who would one day rule their father's lands. And the more she thought on the matter, the more bitter she grew, so that at last she resolved to kill Tristram.

One day she put poison into the silver ewer from which her stepson was wont to pour his drink; but by mischance, her own eldest son, coming into the room where Tristram was and being thirsty, poured wine from the ewer and drank, and immediately he fell down dead.

The queen's sorrow for the death of her son made her the more eager to kill Tristram, and once again she poisoned his wine and watched carefully that no one else might touch it. But King Meliodas came home from the hunt, tired and thirsting, and after greeting his wife and children, he took up the wine that had been poured for Tristram and made to drink.

The queen ran to him and snatched the cup, spilling the wine upon the floor. 'My lord,' she cried, 'do not drink.'

The king, astonished, looked from the queen's white face to the spilt wine upon the rushes, and from the wine to Tristram's golden cup which his wife still held in her trembling hand, and he remembered how strangely her eldest son had died. 'You would have murdered Tristram,' he said.

Yet she denied it, with indignation and with oaths. But Meliodas drew his sword and swore that he would kill her unless she spoke the truth. So with tears the queen confessed her crime, and the king turned from her in horror. 'You are surely unworthy to live,' he said.

So the queen was, by one accord of the king and his lords, condemned to die by burning. A great fire was built before the castle walls and the king and his lords all gathered there to see justice done. But when the queen was led forth to die, young Tristram knelt at his father's feet and begged for a boon.

'Dear son,' said the king, 'I will give you whatever you ask.'

'Then give me the life of my stepmother, the queen.'

The king was angry, but he could not refuse. 'You are a fool,' he said to Tristram, 'for she would have killed you and set her own sons in your place.'

'I have forgiven her,' said Tristram. 'Can you not do likewise?'

So Meliodas forgave the queen and took her back, and ever after she loved Tristram above all others in the world, for it was to him she owed her life. And indeed, well might she and all others love Tristram, for he was a most fair and courteous youth, skilled in feats of arms and in hunting and hawking, and he played excellently upon the harp and sang most sweetly.

At the time when Tristram was nineteen years old and not yet made knight, King Anguish of Ireland sent to King Mark of Cornwall and demanded that he should pay him much gold, or he would come with an army and take his lands. King Mark sent back word to King Anguish saying, 'Let each of us appoint a champion to fight for him, two good knights and bold. And if your knight has the victory I will pay you all you ask. But if my knight conquers, then shall you remit for ever your demands.'

To this King Anguish agreed, and for the purpose sent to Cornwall his bravest knight and the brother of his queen, Sir Marhaus. But Sir Marhaus was a knight of the Round Table and in all Cornwall there was not a knight to match him, and no one offered to stand against him for the sake of King Mark.

When Tristram saw how his uncle was shamed, he begged that his father might let him fight against Sir Marhaus, and it was granted him. So Tristram rode into Cornwall accompanied by his squire Gouvernail and made himself known to King Mark and asked knighthood of him, and the right to fight Sir Marhaus. And both King Mark granted willingly.

Then Tristram went to meet Sir Marhaus, who was a good and noble knight and much distressed by Tristram's youth. 'Indeed,' he said, 'you would be well advised to turn and seek your home. For you are young and in-experienced in battle, and I would not be the death of one so young and yet so brave.'

But Tristram would not turn back for any man. 'Though I am young,' he said, 'and was but ordained knight today, yet am I the son of a king, and I am proud that my first battle should be with one who has such great fame as yours.'

Then they rode at one another, and with so much force that either unhorsed the other and cast him to the ground; and Tristram was wounded in the side. For long they fought together on foot, until Tristram struck Sir Marhaus such a blow upon the helmet that his sword cut through the metal right into Sir Marhaus's head, so that the Irish knight fell to the ground and could fight no more. And when Tristram looked at his sword, he saw how a small piece of the edge had been broken off, and this piece had remained in Sir Marhaus's wound.

Sir Marhaus was carried back to Ireland, and there he died. And his sister, the wife of King Anguish, kept the broken piece of Tristram's sword to remind her of her brother's death, that one day she might be avenged upon his slayer.

King Mark and his lords made much of Tristram, for he had freed them for ever from the demands of King Anguish; but their sorrow was great when they found how sorely he was wounded. For many days he lay still and like to die, while King Mark sent over all the land for physicians and men and women skilled in healing. Yet could none of them help Sir Tristram. But at last there came to the court a woman who had earned much respect by her gift of prophecy. And when she had seen Tristram and looked to his wound, she said, 'This brave knight will never be healed until he travels to the land where the weapon was forged that wounded him.' So King Mark made ready a ship to carry Tristram to Ireland, and he went, taking with him his harp and Gouvernail his squire.

In Ireland he was given lodging in the manor of a kindly knight whose lands lay close by the castle of the king. For the entertainment of his host, Tristram sat up in his bed and took his harp and played merrily and sweetly each day. And at last the fame of his singing and playing reached the ears of King Anguish, and he sent for Tristram to be brought to his court. There he made him welcome and asked his name.

'Lord king,' said Tristram, 'my name is Tramtrist and I am come from the country of Lyones where I was wounded in a fight for the sake of a lady.' For Tristram dared not tell his true name nor how he had slain Sir Marhaus.

King Anguish pitied the young knight and gave him into the hands of his daughter Isolt, for she was well skilled in herbs and all manner of healing; and under her care, even as the wise woman had foretold, was Tristram cured of his hurts.

The daughter of the king of Ireland was young and very lovely, and for that reason men called her La Belle Isolt, Isolt the Beautiful. And while she tended him so carefully, Tristram grew fond of her, and she became fond of him in return, so that they had much joy in each other's company. For long would they sit together talking, or Tristram would sing to her and make music; and at her request he taught her to play upon the harp, and very pleasingly did she do it.

But one day, when Tristram was from his room, Isolt and her mother went there, and seeing his sword lying upon his bed where he had left it, the queen idly drew it from the scabbard to see how fine a weapon it might be. And she saw that there was a piece broken from the edge of the blade.

'Why have you grown so pale, mother?' asked Isolt, 'What is amiss?'

But the queen gave no answer and only dropped the sword upon the bed and hurried from the room. She went to the coffer where she kept her jewels, and there she kept also the piece of the sword that she had taken from Sir Marhaus's wound, and returning to Tristram's chamber, she fitted the piece to the blade of his sword, and it fitted perfectly.

'This Tramtrist is that same knight who slew my brother your uncle,' she said, 'and he shall die for it.'

Isolt wept; but the queen took hold of Tristram's sword in both her hands, and went in great anger to where he was, and would have thrust him through with his own sword and slain him, but that his squire Gouvernail held her back and took the sword from her. Then, weeping, she ran to the king, and told him what she had discovered.

King Anguish was grieved. 'If it might have been any way but this,' he said, 'I should have been well pleased, for this Tramtrist is a good and noble knight.' And he forbade the queen to meddle in the matter, and went himself to seek out Tristram.

He found him armed and ready to fight, but he said

kindly, 'It would do me small honour, Tramtrist, to kill you under my own roof. Yet if you will tell me truly your name and whence you come, and whether it was indeed you who killed my good champion, then you may go in safety, for I would not slay one who has been my guest.'

So Tristram told him the truth, and King Anguish was very sorrowful. 'You killed him in fair battle,' he said, 'and you could do no other than fight for your uncle King Mark. I bear you no ill will for that. But my queen and her kin will not rest until they are avenged upon you, so it were best that you went from Ireland at once and never returned.'

'Permit me first to bid farewell to your daughter, the Lady Isolt, for she has been good and kind to me, and it was she who healed me of my wound.'

King Anguish was willing, so Tristram went to take his leave of Isolt and found her weeping for his danger. He told her all, even as he had told her father, and thanked her for her care of him. 'I shall never forget your kindness,' he said, 'and I shall ever be your true knight, to serve you faithfully.'

'And I shall always remember you,' said Isolt, 'for I have never had another friend I liked so well.' And she gave him a ring off her finger, and he gave her one of his.

And so, believing that he would never see Isolt again, Tristram departed from Ireland and returned to Cornwall, to the court of his uncle, King Mark.

X

Tristram and Isolt

WHEN Sir Tristram returned from Ireland, King Mark of Cornwall was greatly pleased to see his nephew healed of his wound, and he asked Tristram much concerning La Belle Isolt, whose skill in medicine had saved him. When Tristram told him of how lovely she was and how accomplished, King Mark sighed and said, 'She is even such a damsel as I should wish for my queen. But her father is my enemy since you slew his champion, so Isolt can never be my bride.'

A little time after, in Ireland, a huge dragon came out from a forest close by the castle of King Anguish, and there on the edge of the forest it remained, killing and devouring the cattle and any unhappy folk whom it chanced to catch.

Soon this dragon became the dread of the whole country-side, and King Anguish was in despair to know how it could be destroyed. That it might be an encouragement, he promised the hand of his daughter, La Belle Isolt, to the man who slew the monster; but though the prize was heartening, the task was too hard and the dragon too fearful, and no man won the princess.

At last word of the proclamation of King Anguish came to Cornwall, and Tristram thought how, if he killed the dragon, he might win Isolt for his uncle. 'Surely,' he said to himself, 'if I did such a deed for the king of Ireland, he could no longer consider me an enemy. And when he counts me as his friend, then will my lord uncle also be no enemy.'

So Tristram set sail for Ireland again, with Gouvernail his squire, and once ashore, they rode for the forest where the dragon was. There, leaving Gouvernail with their horses in a place of safety, Tristram went on alone, his drawn sword in his hand, keeping a careful watch on all sides, that he might not be taken unawares. But the dragon saw him coming, and with a roar uncurled itself from about the rock where it had been lying, and came towards him, its poisonous breath like a mist about it.

Tristram stood still and waited for it to reach him, his heart beating fast and his sword held firmly, as it dragged the scaly length of its tail through the brushwood and crushed the grass and woodland flowers beneath its huge clawed feet. The nearer it came the fouler was its poisonous breath, and Tristram gasped for air and wondered how much longer he could retain his senses; and then it was upon him, and he stepped aside, out of reach of the great jaws, and thrust his sword with all his might between the dreadful creature's ribs, and pierced its heart; and then had barely time to leap aside as its tail lashed round in its struggle against death.

But in a while the dragon lay still, and Tristram, thinking to have some proof of his deed to offer to King Anguish, cut out its tongue; though he was so weak from the poisonous fumes that he could hardly hold his sword. He wrapped the tongue in his cloak and walked unsteadily away, but after a few paces he fell senseless.

Now, on that same morning, the steward of the household of King Anguish, having for many days longed to kill the dragon and wed La Belle Isolt, determined, though a coward, to ride out and try his luck. But when he came to the place where the dragon was, he saw it lying dead and still, and close beside it, Tristram, as though he too were dead.

'Here is indeed good fortune for me,' thought the steward. 'The dragon is dead, and the knight who has slain it also. Who is to know that it was not I who did this deed?' And he hacked off the dragon's head with his sword and hung it from his saddle bow, and eagerly rode back to the castle.

King Anguish was overjoyed to hear that the dragon was slain, and though he had no wish to see his daughter wedded to his steward, it did not cross his mind to offer the man any other reward. 'What I have promised shall be yours,' he said, and sent for Isolt. But Isolt knew the steward for a coward, and in spite of the proof of its head she could not believe that he had really slain the dragon; and as soon as she might, she called to her two of her waiting-women and a young squire, and rode out for the edge of the forest. When they came there they found the headless body of the dragon, and beside it, as though dead, a knight in armour.

'Dismount,' said Isolt to the squire, 'and take off that knight's armour and see if he is truly dead, or if there is any help that we could give him.'

But when the squire had taken off Tristram's helmet, Isolt knew him at once, and with a cry she was off her horse and on the ground beside him. Tristram opened his eyes, and seeing Isolt, smiled. 'Tell your father the king that I have slain the dragon,' he said, 'and that it has all but slain me. And take him its tongue which I have wrapped in my cloak.' Then his eyes closed and he said no more.

Once again La Belle Isolt tended Sir Tristram with her great knowledge of healing, and in a little time he was well again. 'Now must you go to my father,' she said, 'and tell him how you killed the dragon and how our steward is lying.'

King Anguish was surprised that Tristram had returned to Ireland; but his lady the queen was angry, remembering how he had slain her brother. The king sent for his steward and told him of Tristram's claim to have slain the dragon, and the steward grew pale, but held to his story. 'It was I who killed the monster, my lord king, and I have its head to prove my words.'

'But I,' said Tristram, 'have its tongue, which I cut out before you took off its head.'

King Anguish did not know which of them to believe. 'Let the two of you meet in the lists and decide this matter with the sword,' he said. 'And to the victor shall go the claim of having slain the dragon and the hand of my daughter Isolt.'

But though Tristram was willing, the steward was afraid and he dared not fight with Tristram; so he confessed how he had lied, falling on his knees before the king. And King Anguish arose and embraced Tristram, calling him the saviour of the land; and even the queen said, 'He has done so brave a deed for us and for all Ireland, that it far outweighs the slaying of my brother. Let him now be our good friend.'

The king sent for Isolt, and said, 'Sir Tristram, I promised the hand of my daughter to the man who slew the dragon. If you will take her, she is yours.'

But Tristram replied, 'It is for my uncle, good King Mark, that I would woo her, and not for myself, if that is pleasing to you.' And he told them of how King Mark had loved Isolt since first he had heard of her, and how he sighed for just such a queen; and though King Anguish was surprised, he did not refuse her hand to King Mark, since it was Tristram who asked for it. 'I would rather,' he said, 'that you had asked to wed with her yourself, for you are a man whom I know and respect. Yet since King Mark is your uncle, and since you seem to me to love him well, he must be a worthy man. I give you my daughter Isolt to take to him. May she be happy and make him a good queen.'

But Isolt went apart and wept, and her mother came and found her. 'Why do you weep, my child?' she asked. 'Is it because you must go to Cornwall?'

'If I had to leave my home and go to a strange land,' said

Isolt, 'why could it not have been to marry a husband whom I knew? Why could good Sir Tristram not have asked for my hand for himself, for I know him to be brave and kind? King Mark is a stranger to me and an older man, and he is besides, no knight, or else he would have come a-wooing for himself and not sent his nephew.'

The queen gave her daughter all the comfort that she could; but saying nothing to her, she prepared a potion which would cause those who shared it to love each other evermore. This potion she poured into a little flask and gave it to Isolt's favourite waiting-woman, Bragwaine, swearing her to secrecy. 'On their wedding day,' she said, 'give half of the potion to the Lady Isolt and half to King Mark. He may be an older man and no knight, and he may be a stranger to her, but when they have both drunk of this potion, it will not matter, for their love will be undying, and so they will be happy.'

When the day came for Isolt to set sail from Ireland escorted by Sir Tristram, they went aboard a ship, and in a chest in the cabin of her mistress, Bragwaine hid the little flask. The sea was calm and they had a fair voyage; and in the company of her old friend Tristram, Isolt forgot much of her sorrow at parting from her parents, and she and Tristram sat and talked long together, or Tristram played upon his harp and sang to her.

One day when the voyage was almost done, after he had been singing, he asked for wine to drink, for he was thirsty; and Bragwaine not being by, Isolt herself went to fetch it. She opened the chests which stood in her cabin to find in which of them Bragwaine kept the wine, and in one she found the little flask. She unstoppered it. 'It must be the best wine of all, there is so little of it, and Bragwaine is keeping it all to herself. She deserves to lose it for her greediness.' And she laughed and poured the potion into a silver cup. She carried it to Tristram. 'I will pledge you,' she said. 'May you ever be happy, my friend, and may you ever sing as sweetly as you have this moment done for me.' And as was the custom, she drank from the cup before she handed it to him. He took it from her and drank what remained of the potion, and immediately their hearts were filled with undying love for one another.

At first there was no joy to compare with theirs, in those moments when they thought only of their love; but as the coast of Cornwall came in sight, they remembered how Isolt was to wed with King Mark and might never be Tristram's own lady, and they were overcome by despair. And it was thus, weeping, with Tristram's harp lying forgotten on the floor and the empty flask beside them, that Bragwaine found them a little later, and went almost out of her mind when she knew what had happened.

King Mark welcomed his bride and embraced his nephew with gratitude for all his services. 'Do not return yet to Lyones,' he said, 'for it gives me much happiness to have you at my court. I think of you more as my own son than as the child of my sister.' And that he might be near Isolt, Tristram remained with his uncle.

But in time it grew more than Tristram could bear, to be so close to Isolt and see her the wife of another; and for her too there was no joy in her marriage, loving as she did her lord's nephew; and at last, from fear that they might betray their love and let it be seen by King Mark, they parted, and Tristram went from Cornwall with his faithful

Gouvernail. 'If I travel all about Britain,' thought Tristram, 'maybe I shall forget Isolt.'

He travelled from one end of Britain to another, having adventures in many places, but always he remembered Isolt; and because of the love-potion, never was he able to forget her. After a while he came to the court of King Arthur, and there he was well received, both for his prowess and for his lovely singing, and Sir Lancelot and King Arthur himself held him in great honour. In time he was made a knight of the Round Table, and his skill at arms was reckoned second only to that of Lancelot and Sir Gawaine.

But in spite of the noble companionship of the other knights and the kindness of Arthur, and in spite of the friendship of Sir Lancelot, Tristram was for ever sad. 'I can stay in no one place for long, my lord king,' he said at last. 'I must ever be wandering, so give me your leave to go.'

And though he grieved to see Tristram depart, Arthur would not hold him against his will, and bidding him return one day, he sent him on his way.

So that he might be as far as possible from Cornwall where Isolt dwelt, Sir Tristram crossed the sea to France, to the land of Brittany, where he was welcomed by King Ganhardin who ruled there. Tristram and Ganhardin, both being young, rode on many adventures together, and Ganhardin grew to count as his dearest friend the quiet handsome knight who sang so well and always seemed so sad.

Ganhardin had a sister, and she too was named Isolt: Isolt Blanchemains, Isolt of the White Hands, and she loved Tristram from the moment that she saw him. But because he never looked at her nor showed by any sign

96

that he regarded her more than any other damsel, she hid her love and spoke of it to no one, not even to her brother.

But one day when he thought himself alone, Tristram took up his harp, and as he often did, he sang a song in praise of La Belle Isolt. And while he did so, Isolt of the White Hands passed by the room and stopped to listen. Hearing her own name spoken of with love in Tristram's song, and believing it to be herself he praised, she was over-joyed and went immediately to her brother, telling him what she had heard. 'I have loved him ever since he came to Brittany,' she said. 'And if now, as it seems, he loves me in return, I beg you, brother, offer him my hand.'

Happy at the thought of a marriage between his sister and his friend, Ganhardin kissed Isolt of the White Hands and hurried off to Tristram and found him sitting un-happily, his harp silent at his side. 'You are sad, my friend,' said Ganhardin. 'Is it for love of the lady of whom you were singing?'

Surprised, Tristram answered him, 'It is, but how should you know?'

Ganhardin laughed. 'Then your sadness is over, my friend, for she loves you in return, and has sent me to offer you her hand. It has brought me much joy, Tristram, to have you for my friend, but even greater joy will it be to call you my brother.'

And when he understood how they were mistaken, though he could never love her, out of friendship for Gan-hardin and from courtesy to his sister, Tristram married Isolt of the White Hands. But always his heart was in Cornwall.

There came a day when Tristram fell sick of a strange

malady, and in all Brittany there was found no cure for it; and even though men and women skilled in healing came at the command of Ganhardin from all the land of France, still Tristram lay pale and sick upon his bed, and it was feared that he was dying.

Then Gouvernail his squire, with tears for his beloved master, knelt beside the bed and said, 'Do you remember, lord, how once before you lay sick and in all Britain there was no cure for you? And how we sailed together to Ireland where the Lady Isolt healed your wound?'

'Why do you remind me of those days?' sighed Tristram. 'This time there is no cure for me, and I shall die.'

'Give me your leave, good lord, to sail for Cornwall and speak with Queen Isolt and beg that she will come to you and save you by her skill, for there is no one so versed in healing in all the world.'

'She could not come,' said Tristram. 'She is my uncle's queen and must remain at his side.'

'If she still loves you, lord, she will come to you.'

'I am dying, Gouvernail, and I shall be dead before you return from Cornwall, whether you come with Isolt or alone.'

Gouvernail wept. 'Lord, stay alive until I am with you once again. Wait until I have brought Queen Isolt here to help you.'

'It is too long to wait,' said Tristram.

'Wait only until the ship which carries me is in sight of land. Then you will gain strength to wait a few hours longer, until Queen Isolt stands at your side.'

'But what if Isolt will not come, Gouvernail?'

'If she is with me, the sails of the ship shall be white, my lord; and if she has not come, then they shall be black. That way you will know the truth before even you see me. Give me your leave to go.'

And after a time Tristram sighed and said, 'Go to Cornwall, Gouvernail.'

With all the speed he might, Gouvernail set sail, and went at once to the court of King Mark and asked to speak with the queen. When she heard of Tristram's sickness, Isolt rose up immediately and asked no man's permission, but rode from the castle with Gouvernail and went aboard the ship; and with white sails flying in the wind, they set out for Brittany.

By the bedside of her lord, sat Isolt of the White Hands. 'What is this other Isolt,' she asked, 'who is to come from Cornwall to cure your sickness? Is she one skilled in healing, or a witch?'

And because he was feverish and did not guard his words, Tristram answered her the truth. 'She is no witch. She is the lady whom I love.'

Isolt of the White Hands forced back her tears and calmed her voice. 'Tell me of her, lord,' she said.

And Tristram told her of how he had first seen La Belle Isolt in Ireland, and of how they had drunk the love-potion together, and of how Gouvernail was to hoist white sails if Isolt were on board the ship. And Isolt of the White Hands wept, for she saw how her lord had never loved her.

The next day Tristram said, 'If the wind has been favourable, Gouvernail should return today. Go to the window, Isolt, and watch for the ship.' And Isolt of the White Hands stood in the window place and watched. At midday it came in sight, white sails against the blue green sea. 'I can see the ship,' she said.

Tristram raised himself a little in his bed. 'What colour are the sails?' he asked eagerly.

Isolt of the White Hands noted how his voice was stronger than it had been for many a day. She stared out at the ship and saw it through a mist of tears, and her hands clenched until the nails pierced through the skin. 'The sails are black, my lord,' she said. And she held to the window frame to prevent herself from falling, and waited for his next words. But Tristram spoke no more.

After a while Isolt of the White Hands went to the bed and sat beside it, her arms about Sir Tristram. But he would not be comforted, and turned his head from her; and because he had no will to live, he died. And Isolt of the White Hands did not move her arms away, but sat there weeping.

When La Belle Isolt came into the room with Gouvernail close after her, Isolt of the White Hands looked up. 'You are too late,' she whispered. 'He is dead.'

Gouvernail knelt at the foot of the bed and wept; but La Belle Isolt came forward slowly until she stood beside Tristram, looking down on him, and at the grief in her quiet face, Isolt of the White Hands rose and backed away.

La Belle Isolt took down Tristram's harp from where it hung on the wall at the head of the bed and she laid it by his hands. Then she bent her head and kissed him; and in that moment her heart broke, so that she died.

XI

Gareth and Linette

ONCE King Arthur went to keep the feast of Whit-suntide in a castle close by the border of Wales. Now, he had a custom that on Whitsunday he would never sit down to meat until he had seen some wonder or heard of some marvellous adventure.

On this day as he waited to begin the feasting, a youth followed by a dwarf rode into the courtyard, dismounted, and came into the hall. He was a very tall and broad young man, with a happy face and hands that were large and strong; and as he strode up the hall all eyes watched him with approval.

'You are welcome, stranger,' said Arthur. 'Sit down and eat with us.'

But the youth replied, 'Greetings to you, my lord king, and to your fellowship. I have come here this day to ask three favours. The first I shall ask now, if you will permit me, and the other two a year from today.'

Arthur smiled. 'Ask what you will. I do not think that I shall refuse you.'

'I ask only,' said the youth, 'that you will give me meat and drink and a place in your household until a year is passed and I may ask for the last two boons.'

'It is a poor request,' said Arthur. 'I should be glad to give you more than that.'

'It is all I ask,' said the youth.

'Then you shall have your fill of meat and drink for

twelve months,' said Arthur. 'God forbid that I should refuse his keep to any man. But tell me now your name.'

'Forgive me, my lord king,' replied the youth, 'but that I cannot tell you yet.'

Arthur smiled again. 'Let it be as you wish.' Then turning to Sir Kay the Seneschal he said, 'Let this young man have of our best for a year, and though we do not know his name, let him be treated as if he were the son of a nobleman, and see that he lacks nothing.'

But Kay was indignant that Arthur was prepared to spare good food and drink for one who might not merit it. 'The son of a nobleman!' he exclaimed. 'He is more likely the son of a peasant. The son of a nobleman would have asked you for a horse and armour, not for a twelvemonths' food. And as for his having no name, I can find him a name easily enough.' He glanced with scorn at the youth's hands, which were so large that they seemed almost clumsy. 'I shall call him Beaumains, Fair-hands, and unless he is as lazy as he is large, I shall find him work enough in the kitchen, where he may earn his keep.'

'Do not be over hard in my interests, Kay,' said Arthur, who knew well his foster-brother's cross-grained loyalty and loved him for it.

But the stranger smiled. 'I will do whatever work you demand of me, Sir Kay.'

Yet Sir Lancelot, hearing Kay's words, did not smile. 'Shame on you, Kay,' he called from where he sat, 'to mock at a lad who has done you no harm, and who, I dare say, will one day prove himself worthy of our fellowship.'

And though he said nothing, Sir Gawaine, King Arthur's nephew, stared closely at the youth, wondering why, though he had seen the tall stranger for the first time not above a few moments before, he should instantly have felt that he knew him.

'What he has asked for, I have offered him,' said Kay. 'Now let him find himself a place and sit and eat, for we have seen a wonder sufficient to satisfy our lord the king this Whitsunday: a youth, tall and strong enough, with his wits and his health, who has no wish for anything in life but food and drink.'

So Beaumains, as they called him from that day, went and sat below the salt, among the serving-lads, without another word. And the dwarf who had accompanied him mounted his master's horse and left the castle, answering the questions of none.

But when the feasting was over, Gawaine went to the youth, wondering why he did so, and offered to take him as his squire. Beaumains turned his head away and would not look him in the face. 'I thank you for your kindness, Sir Gawaine,' he said, 'but I will do as Sir Kay has bidden me, for in all things he must be my master.'

'It shall be as you wish it,' said Gawaine.

Then Sir Lancelot, with his usual courtesy and gentleness, came and spoke to Beaumains, offering him food and wine and lodging and good company; and this time Beaumains did not turn away, but looked Lancelot in the face and smiled and said, 'I thank you for your kindness, Sir Lancelot, but I will do as Sir Kay has bidden me, for in all things he must be my master.'

'It shall be as you wish it,' said Lancelot. 'But if ever at any time you would ask a service of me, it shall willingly be rendered.'

'One day,' replied Beaumains, 'I hope to ask a service of you, Sir Lancelot.'

So for twelve months Beaumains worked in the kitchen, turning the meat on the spits, baking the bread, and fetching pails of water from the well, and never a word did he say as to his name or whence he had come, and never once did he grumble at his lot, but was always cheerful and well mannered. And in the summer evenings, when the kitchen-lads would gather in the courtyard after their day's work was over, to try themselves with feats of strength and wrestling, Beaumains was always proved the strongest of them. And always when there were jousting and tournaments, so long as his work did not forbid it, Beaumains would be there, among the servants, looking on eagerly, a great light of longing shining in his eyes.

When a year had passed and Whitsunday came round once more, again King Arthur would not sit down to the feasting until some wonder or adventure came to him; and while he waited a richly dressed damsel rode up to the castle and asked to speak with him.

'I would have the help of one of your boldest knights, lord king,' she said, 'for the sake of my lady who is besieged in her castle by the evil Red Knight of the Red Plain, whose name is Sir Ironside.'

'I have heard of this Red Knight,' said Gawaine. 'He is indeed an evil knight, and with the strength of seven men.'

'Willingly shall I and my knights give you our help, damsel,' said Arthur, 'if you will tell us the name of your lady and where she dwells.'

'That I may not do,' replied the damsel.

'It is asking too much of one of my knights,' said Arthur gently, 'that he should ride with you to serve an unknown lady in lands you will not name.'

'I did not think that King Arthur would refuse me my request,' said the damsel. 'But now I see that I must ask elsewhere.' And she gathered up the train of her gown and made to leave the hall.

But Beaumains stepped forward from among the servants and knelt before Arthur. 'My lord king,' he said, 'I have been in your service for a year, may I now ask of you the last two favours?'

'Ask what you will,' said Arthur.

'Then, my lord king, let me undertake this adventure for the unknown lady who is assailed by the Red Knight, and also grant that when I shall ask it, I may receive knighthood at the hands of that one of your knights whom I most respect.'

Arthur was glad that the unknown youth showed a desire for adventure and for knighthood, and he answered, 'It shall be as you wish.'

But the damsel was indignant and cried out, 'Is this the far-famed courtesy of King Arthur, that he offers me no more than a kitchen-lad to serve my lady?' And with her head held high she swept from the hall, mounted her horse, and rode away.

Beaumains went out into the courtyard, and even as he stood there, the same dwarf who had accompanied him to the court twelve months before came through the gates, leading a fine horse and bearing armour and a sword. 'I have returned as you bade me, master,' he said, and helped Beaumains arm himself. Then Beaumains, having neither shield nor lance, mounted the horse and rode after the damsel, with the dwarf running at the horse's side.

'This is a fine thing,' grumbled Sir Kay, 'that my kitchen-lad arms himself like a knight and the son of a lord and rides off on an adventure. Let us see how he acquits himself when a true knight opposes him.' And with that he called for his own horse and his armour and rode off after Beaumains, in spite of the protests of Lancelot and Gawaine, who wished no ill to come to the youth.

Just as Beaumains overtook the damsel, Sir Kay caught up with him and called out to him to wait. 'I am going to fight the Red Knight for the sake of this damsel's lady, and I may not wait,' said Beaumains quietly.

'You are impertinent,' said Kay. 'Do you not know who I am?'

Beaumains smiled a little. 'I know you well. You are the most ungentle knight in all King Arthur's court.'

Kay was angry and rode straight at Beaumains, for all that the youth had neither lance nor shield; but Beaumains thrust Kay's lance aside with his sword and struck him such a blow that Sir Kay fell from his horse and lay stunned upon the ground. Then Beaumains bade his dwarf give him Kay's shield and lance, and ordered him to ride upon Kay's horse since he had none of his own.

But as Beaumains was about to ride on again after the damsel, he caught sight of Lancelot who had ridden after Kay and seen all that had happened. 'Sir Lancelot,' he called, 'will you joust with me?'

'Willingly,' said Lancelot. They rode at each other and at the first blow Lancelot unhorsed Beaumains, and dismounting drew his sword and fought with him on foot.

And Lancelot was glad to find how strong and quick young Beaumains was, that even he, who was the best of knights in Britain, was well matched by him, and he laughed and cried out, 'Come, Beaumains, we have no quarrel so great that we should fight all day for it.'

'I did but wish to prove my worth to you,' said Beaumains, lowering his sword.

'And you have proved it well,' said Lancelot.

Beaumains took off his helmet. 'Shall I soon be worthy of knighthood?' he asked eagerly.

'You are worthy of knighthood at this moment,' replied Lancelot.

Beaumains's face was alight with joy. 'Then before I go on my first adventure, will you make me a knight? For of all in Arthur's court there is no one by whom I would rather be knighted than by you, who have shown me so much kindness and are the best knight in all the land.'

'It is a thing which I shall do most willingly,' said Lancelot, 'but first you must tell me your name.'

'I am Gareth of Orkney, brother to Gawaine and nephew of the king. But I beg that you will tell no one of it until I am returned from this adventure.'

'I had no doubt that you were of noble birth,' said Lancelot, 'for all that you asked so little of the king.'

So Gareth, who had been called Beaumains, knelt down on the grass and Lancelot took up his sword and knighted him. Then he said, 'Now ride on your adventure, and may you be successful, and I will see Kay safely home.'

So Gareth rode on quickly, followed by his dwarf, and after a time he caught up with the damsel who had ridden on as soon as she had seen Sir Kay unhorsed. She greeted

Gareth with scorn. 'I hoped that I would see no more of you, you kitchen-lad. Must you still plague me with your company? Why do you follow me? For you will never dare to face the Red Knight.'

'I can but try,' said Gareth quietly. And for a time they rode on in silence, the damsel with her head held high and Gareth a little way behind.

Then suddenly, towards evening, as they journeyed through a wood, a man came running towards them and clutched hold of the bridle of Gareth's horse. 'I beg you, help my master,' he cried. 'For he has been attacked by robbers and I fear that they will kill him.'

'Take me to him,' said Gareth. The man led him a little way off the path to where his master lay bound, with six robbers dividing his arms and his gold between them. When they saw Gareth approaching, they leapt to their feet and made to run away, but with three strokes Gareth killed three of them and then pursued the others until all six were slain.

The knight whom he had rescued made much of Gareth, and since it was close on nightfall, offered him the hospitality of his near by castle until the morning.

'I follow this damsel on an adventure,' said Gareth. 'If it is pleasing to her to ride on all through the night, then so must I. But if she will accept your offer, then I will follow her to your castle.'

And because it was growing dark and she was weary, the damsel rode with the knight to his castle, talking most courteously to him, but ever bearing herself as though Gareth were not there.

In his castle the knight called for meat and wine and

set the damsel at his high table and bade her eat. But when he would have called Gareth to the place beside her, she cried out, 'Shame on you for a discourteous host, who would expect a noblewoman to eat in the company of a kitchen-lad.'

And the knight was ashamed that she should speak thus of one who had done him so great a service, and he ordered his servants to set a small table for Gareth at the other side of the hall, and went himself and ate apart with him, while the damsel supped alone in angry silence.

In the morning Gareth and the damsel took leave of their host and rode on. After a time they reached a wide river, and there was in sight only one place where it was shallow enough to be forded, but on the farther side the ford was guarded by two knights who called out that none might cross the river unless he fought with them.

'You had best ride home, scullion,' taunted the damsel.

'Indeed I shall not,' said Gareth, and he rode on into the river.

One of the knights rode forward, and in the very midst of the river they met and fought, and the strange knight was thrown from his horse into the water, and so drowned. On the farther bank Gareth fought with the second knight and slew him with a mighty stroke. Then he bade the damsel cross in safety.

All the way across she railed at him, 'That I should ever have lived to see the day when two fine knights should perish at the hands of a greasy kitchen-lad! Yet you need not flatter yourself that you have fought manfully today, for I saw the horse of the first knight slip and throw him, and so was he drowned by misadventure. And as for the second, you struck him from behind, false and cowardly as you are.'

But to all her unjust words Gareth gave no answer save, 'I have come to serve and win your lady, and I shall do it or die.'

'You will not die, never fear,' scoffed the damsel, 'for at the first sight of the Red Knight you will turn and fly.'

A little way beyond the river, beneath a gnarled old hawthorn tree, stood a great black horse with a knight in black armour upon its back, bearing a black shield.

'It is the Black Knight,' said the damsel. 'He is famed for his strength. Turn and make for home, scullion, while there is yet time.'

'I thank you for your care of me, lady,' said Gareth, 'but I will allow not even you to make me a coward.'

The Black Knight recognized the damsel and called out to her, 'Greetings, Lady Linette. Is this the champion from King Arthur's court whom you went to fetch?'

'Indeed it is not,' replied the damsel indignantly. 'It is no more than a kitchen-lad who has followed me against my will. I shall be much in your debt if you will rid me of his company.'

'It would be a lasting shame to me that I should fight with a kitchen-lad,' said the Black Knight. 'But his horse and his armour I will take from him, and he may return to his kitchen on foot.'

'My horse and my armour are mine,' said Gareth, 'and I can well defend them.'

And they rode against each other, while Linette and the dwarf looked on. The Black Knight's lance broke, so that he and Gareth drew their swords and fought on foot, and at last Gareth killed him. And because Kay's shield which he carried had been battered in the fight, he took with him the black shield that had belonged to the Black Knight, and rode upon the Black Knight's horse, for it was fresher than his own.

And ever Linette upbraided him for a cowardly kitchen-lad who slew good knights by mischance, and bade him begone from her.

'Lady,' said Gareth, 'you might as well leave your railing, for I will follow you as long as I may. And as for your counselling me to flee whenever danger shows, it seems to me that it would have been better had you saved your counsel for those I fought against.' But his words only made her more angry.

Then suddenly they saw approaching them a knight in green armour, with a green shield, and green harness on his horse; and seeing the shield which Gareth carried, this knight called out, 'Are you my brother, the Black Knight?'

But before Gareth could reply, Linette cried, 'It is not the Black Knight. It is no more than a common scullion who has killed your brother and carries his shield.'

Then the Green Knight was angry and bade Gareth defend himself, calling him a murderer. 'I slew your brother in fair fight,' said Gareth. And he fought with the Green Knight while Linette stood by and rallied his opponent, reminding him of the shame it would be to a knight to be worsted by a kitchen-lad. But at last Gareth overcame the Green Knight, who yielded to him and begged his mercy.

'Your life is lost,' said Gareth, 'unless this damsel asks for it.'

'Do you think that I would ask a favour of a scullion?' cried Linette.

'Then must this brave knight die,' said Gareth, 'and all for want of a word from you.'

'Lady, have pity on me and speak for me,' pleaded the Green Knight.

Yet Linette would not hear him and only said, 'I will ask no favours of a greasy kitchen-lad.'

Gareth took off the Green Knight's helmet and made as though he would cut off his head, and Linette pitied the Green Knight and cried out, though reluctantly, 'Release him, scullion, or you will repent it!'

Gareth smiled. 'It is a pleasure to do you a favour, lady.' And Linette stamped her little foot and turned away.

That night they lodged at the Green Knight's manor which was close by. And once again Linette would not sit to eat with Gareth, though the Green Knight rebuked her for it; so Gareth ate alone at a little table.

The next day Gareth and Linette set out again, and after a short ride they reached a tall white tower. As they passed by this tower a knight in crimson armour, carrying a crimson shield, rode forth to them, calling out to Gareth, 'Is it you, my brother the Black Knight?'

And Linette replied immediately, 'It is not your brother. It is no more than a kitchen-lad who has slain the Black Knight and carries his shield.'

When the Crimson Knight heard that his brother was dead, he rode in anger at Gareth and a great combat they had there, while Linette watched them. And at last the Crimson Knight yielded to Gareth and pleaded for his life; and Gareth answered, 'I will spare you only if this damsel will speak for you.' And he flourished his sword as though he would have cut off the Crimson Knight's head.

Linette was angry, but she could not see a brave knight die for want of a word from her, so grudgingly she said, 'Release him, wretched kitchen-lad, or it will be the worse for you.'

Gareth smiled. 'It is a pleasure, lady, to do you a favour.'

Gareth and Linette rode on together, followed by the dwarf, and all the way she never ceased to taunt him and upbraid him, though he answered her no word in reply. At last they came to a field before a castle where there were many pavilions set up as for a jousting, and they were all blue with blue pennons flying in the breeze. And the moment that she saw them Linette grew silent and thoughtful.

As they rode by, a knight spied them from his pavilion, armed himself, and rode forth to meet them; and he was all in blue armour, carrying a blue shield, and the harness of his charger was blue.

Linette reined in her horse and said to Gareth, 'That is the Blue Knight coming towards us, and he is stronger by far than his brothers. Fly while there is yet time.'

'I have fought with the others, I shall fight with him,' replied Gareth.

But Linette spoke again, and this time her voice was no longer scornful and cold, and she turned away as though she were ashamed. 'Even though you are a serving-lad, you have proved yourself brave. Well have you fought and gently have you received my harsh words. I would not see you shamed or slain through engaging with one too strong for you.'

'Now that you have spoken kindly of me, I have all the more reason for courage. Fear not for me, lady.' And Gareth rode forward to meet the Blue Knight and fought long with him, until at last the Blue Knight was overcome and pleaded for his life. And this time Linette spoke at once. 'Give him his life, Beaumains, for he is a noble knight.'

Gareth and Linette were welcomed at the Blue Knight's pavilion, and there they ate together in good company and fellowship, and there they passed the night. And in the morning, when they would have set out again, Linette begged Gareth that he would agree to be knighted by the Blue Knight. 'For,' she said, 'today we shall reach the castle of my lady, who is my sister, the Lady Lionesse, and there you will meet with the Red Knight of the Red Plain, and it is only right that one who has proved himself worthy should be made a knight before undertaking a fearful task.'

But Gareth told her how he had been knighted by Sir Lancelot after he had fought with Sir Kay, and he told her that he was Gareth of Orkney and nephew to King Arthur, and she rejoiced that he was after all of noble birth and not a serving-lad, and asked his forgiveness for her scorn. 'Lady,' he replied, 'I have forgotten all you said to me.'

So they went on towards her sister's castle, and before it they saw the pavilions of the Red Knight and his men, and near by a tree with a horn hanging from a branch. 'Whoever would challenge the Red Knight must blow on that horn,' said Linette.

Gareth set the horn to his lips and blew a mighty blast, and the evil Red Knight, Sir Ironside, came forth from his pavilion and armed himself all in red; and mounted upon a flame-coloured horse, he awaited Gareth on a level stretch of ground right below the castle walls.

'See,' said Linette, 'where my sister looks down upon you from that window. Now at last may she be delivered from her enemy.'

And Gareth looked up and beheld the most beautiful lady he had ever seen, and swore to himself to save her and win her or die, and he galloped forward to meet the Red Knight. They came together with such force that either unhorsed the other, but as quickly as they might they rose to their feet and drew their swords. And so they fought for more than half a day. The Red Knight was a hardy fighter, and much experienced in battle, so that Gareth was all but overcome. Then he looked up at the window where the Lady Lionesse watched, and he took courage and made one final effort and struck the Red Knight upon the helm so that he was stunned and dropped his sword. Gareth unlaced his helm to cut off his head, and the Red Knight yielded and asked mercy.

'I will spare you only if you will promise to leave off your evil ways,' said Gareth. And the Red Knight gave his word to live peaceably from that day, and with all his men he departed to his own lands, and the Lady Lionesse was free.

Later, when Gareth was healed of his wounds, he entered the castle and met the Lady Lionesse, and she seemed to him even more beautiful than when he had first seen her at the window. And he seemed to her the finest and the bravest knight in all the world. He took her back to King Arthur's court with him, and there they were married. And a little time later, his brother Gaheris married the Lady Linette.

Arthur had made much of Gareth when he knew that he was his nephew, and Gawaine and Gaheris had greeted him joyfully as their younger brother whom they had not seen since he was a child. But of all knights Gareth loved best Sir Lancelot, who was ever a good friend to him.

And in time the Red Knight of the Red Plain, whose name was Sir Ironside, having thought long on the courtesy and courage of Gareth, came to Arthur's court and offered his services to the king. He proved himself as good as he had once been wicked, and was at last admitted to the fellowship of the Round Table.

XII

The Marriage of Gawaine

ONE year King Arthur kept Christmas at Carlisle, and right merry was the feasting that he and his knights had there, with games and minstrelsy and all manner of good cheer. Soon after Christmas Day Arthur was riding alone one morning in the forest of Inglewood, and as he rode by the frozen waters of Tarn Wadling he met with a huge man armed with a mighty club.

With one hand this huge man took hold of Arthur's lance and dragged it from his grasp, and with the other he snatched Arthur's sword, Excalibur; then he laughed loud and long. 'Now are you my prisoner, my lord King Arthur,' he said, 'and in my castle shall you abide for so long as it pleases me, save if you give me the ransom that I require.'

'What ransom is that?' asked Arthur.

'That you will return to me here on New Year's Day and bring me the answer to this question: What is it that every woman most desires?'

'I will bring you the answer to your question,' promised Arthur.

The huge man laughed again. 'If you bring me the wrong answer, sir king, you will never see your knights or fair Guenever your queen again.'

'Nevertheless,' said Arthur, 'I will be here on New Year's Day, whether I bring you the right answer or no.'

With a last chuckle that rumbled like thunder and shook all his great body, the huge man handed Arthur his lance and his sword and strode away swinging his club.

Arthur rode slowly back to Carlisle, wondering what it might be that every woman most desired, and the more he pondered on it, the harder the question seemed. Back in his castle he sat alone, still wondering, all the joy gone out of Christmastide for him.

Sir Gawaine, King Arthur's nephew, saw how he kept himself apart and would not speak, and going to his uncle he asked, 'What is amiss, my lord king?'

And though at first he would not, at last, after Gawaine had long entreated him, Arthur told of his encounter with the huge man and of the question to which he had to find the answer.

'It is a hard question,' said Gawaine, 'but do not despair, my lord uncle. We will each one of us here, your knights of the Round Table, think of an answer, and perchance among all our answers the true one will be found.'

So for all the time that remained to them between that day and New Year's Day, each knight puzzled out an answer to the question and told it to King Arthur. And when New Year's Day was come, Arthur set forth alone and rode through the forest of Inglewood.

But before he came to Tarn Wadling he passed by a place where he saw an oldish lady sitting on a fallen tree-trunk which lay between two trees, a holly with its dark green leaves and scarlet berries and a leafless oak. This lady was clad all in red no less bright than the holly berries, and as Arthur came by her, she called out a greeting to him. But so amazed was Arthur at the sight of her that he forgot all his courtesy, staring at her and giving her no greeting in reply.

And well indeed might he have stared, for surely nowhere in all Britain could there have been another lady so ugly as she. Her eyes were set, one high up and the other low down in her face, her mouth was twisted to the left side, her great hooked nose was crooked, and all her brave red silken finery could not make her one whit less ugly. Yet her voice was low and sweet. 'Why do you stare at me so, King Arthur, and never speak a word? Even an ugly lady likes a courteous reply to her greeting. And maybe you would do well to offer me fair words, for I can tell you the true answer to that question which troubles you so.'

'If you will tell me the answer to that question, lady, I shall be grateful to you for all my life.'

She laughed. 'That is not enough, that you should be grateful. I should want more than that for my help.'

'Ask whatever you will, lady, and it shall be yours, so long as you tell me the true answer to the huge man's question.'

'You have a nephew, King Arthur, a brave and noble knight, and one known as much for his beauty as for his courtesy. Give me Sir Gawaine for my husband, and you shall have the answer.'

But Arthur would not hear her. 'Gawaine is young, yet he is held in great honour: his choice of a wife must be his own. He is handsome, as you have said: shall he wed with such as you?'

'You have promised,' she said, 'to give me whatever I asked. Shall Arthur break his word?'

'A promise given by one man, lady, cannot bind another.'

'He loves you, King Arthur, your nephew Gawaine, and he is dutiful. He will do as you bid him, even in this.'

'I would not ask it of him, not though it is the price of my freedom.'

'Then break your word which you have given to a woman,' she said, 'and go your way without help, and bitterly will you rue it when you have no true answer to give by the shores of Tarn Wadling. And cruel will be the shame of the memory of your broken promise through the long days of captivity that lie ahead of you.'

The more that Arthur thought on the fate that would be his, the more he dreaded it, and at last he said, 'I will bring you Gawaine, and if he is willing, you shall have him for your husband. But his consent must be freely given; I shall not force him in this. If that will content you, tell me the answer and let it be true.'

'Gawaine is a noble knight and a man of honour. It will content me,' she said. And she told Arthur the answer to the huge man's question.

Arthur rode on to Tarn Wadling, and there on the frozen shore where the ice glistened blue in the sunlight, the huge man waited for him. 'What answer have you brought to my question, Arthur the king?' he called.

'Here is the answer, sir giant.' And Arthur gave him the words of the most ugly lady.

The huge man was angry and roared until the bare branches of the trees shook and trembled, and he flung his club upon the ground and stamped his great feet in his rage. 'You had that answer from my sister,' he said, 'from a crook-nosed, wry-mouthed hag. There was no one else who could have told you. When I find her she shall die for it.'

But he could do Arthur no harm, for all his wrath, and Arthur turned his horse and rode back to Carlisle, sick at heart for the price he had paid for his freedom.

When Arthur reached the castle he was met with great rejoicing, and each of his knights asked him, 'Whose answer was the true one? Was it mine?' But Arthur would speak to none of them, and went alone to his chamber and sat with his head bent in his hands. And there Gawaine followed him. 'What is amiss, my lord king?' he asked.

Slowly Arthur raised his eyes and looked at him, so young, so noble and so fair, and he shuddered. 'There was a most hideous lady in a scarlet gown, sitting on a fallen tree. She is sister to the huge man, and it was she who gave me the true answer.'

'What price did she ask, my lord uncle? Tell me, and I shall see that she is paid.'

But looking at him, Arthur could not bring himself to tell Gawaine all the truth. 'She asked for one of my knights for a husband,' he said.

'Then must she have her husband,' said Gawaine. 'Good uncle, do not grieve so. We have you safely back with us, and what matters the rest?'

In the morning, King Arthur and his knights rode forth into the forest of Inglewood; but only Gawaine and Arthur himself knew that they did not go to hunt. And there in the forest, on the fallen tree, between the holly and the oak, sat the most ugly lady in her scarlet gown.

'Greetings to you, King Arthur, and greetings to you, lord knights,' she called.

They all reined in their horses and stared at her, for never had one of them seen a lady so ugly as she.

'By my faith,' laughed Sir Kay, 'I would not care to kiss that crooked mouth. Nor can I tell which I like the less, the eye that is up or the eye that is down.' And many of the knights laughed with him.

'Peace, Sir Kay, do not jest,' said Gawaine quietly, 'for one of us must marry her, so our lord the king has promised.'

And at that all the knights fell silent; and then one by one they moved away, some calling to their hounds, some saying that the hour grew late and they must be gone, and others whistling a gay tune as though they had not heard his words; and even Lancelot, though he pitied the lady with all his heart for her ugliness, thought of lovely Guenever and did not stay; until at last there were only Arthur left, and Gawaine. And Arthur turned his head away and would not look.

'It shall never be said that King Arthur broke a promise,' said Gawaine. He dismounted and went to the most ugly lady where she sat between the holly and the oak, and knelt down before her and kissed her hand. 'Lady,' he said, 'will you marry me?' And her twisted mouth smiled a little as she answered him.

Sir Gawaine set her before him upon his horse and rode with her to Carlisle; and there in the castle Gawaine was wedded to the most ugly lady. There was a great feasting in celebration, and since it was a wedding, there was a show of rejoicing; but in his heart, there was no one there who did not pity Sir Gawaine.

When the feasting was done, Gawaine and his bride were

led to the bridal chamber, and the door was closed upon them and they were alone.

'This is our wedding day, my lord,' said the most ugly lady, 'yet you have not kissed me once, and you have kept your eyes from me. Am I so very hateful in your sight?'

Gawaine looked straight at her and all her ugliness, and then he looked away again. 'God forbid that you should think that,' he said.

'Then kiss me, dear lord,' she said.

And Gawaine, of his courtesy, took her in his arms and closed his eyes and kissed her twisted mouth, and it seemed to him that it was not so crooked after all. And when he opened his eyes he saw that he held in his arms the fairest young damsel he had ever seen.

She smiled at his surprise. 'You have broken half of the spell that my stepmother laid on me,' she said, 'and now I may keep my own shape, which is such as you see it at this moment, for either the day or the night, and it is for you to choose whether it shall be by moonlight or sunlight that I am a hideous hag.'

'It is a hard choice,' said Gawaine, 'but I think that I would rather that you were beautiful for me alone, than for all the world. Dear lady, be fair as you are now each night, and a hideous hag each day.'

She turned a little away from him. 'Would you wish me to have to hide myself during the hours of light? Would you wish me never to hold my head high when other ladies are by? Would you wish me ever to endure the shame of my hideousness as I read it in the shudders of others?'

And after a while Gawaine answered, 'Forgive me,

dearest, for I was selfish. Let it be as you wish: you shall have your own way in this thing.'

And she flung her arms about his neck and kissed him, saying, 'Now is the whole of the spell broken, and I shall ever be as you see me at this moment, both by day and by night, for you have given me that which a woman most desires: Her own way. And that was the answer to the question which King Arthur was asked by my brother, who will now also be freed from the spell which made of him a huge man to frighten all who passed by Tarn Wadling.' And she told him the whole story of her stepmother's evil enchantments, and how they could only be broken if a good knight took her as his lady and gave her her own way.

Great was their joy together; and in the morning, when Gawaine led his lovely lady into the hall, and everyone saw how fair and sweet she was, then the rejoicing for the marriage began all over again; and this time there was true joy in every heart for Gawaine's happiness.

XIII

Geraint and the Knight of the Sparrow-hawk

ONE summer's evening, as King Arthur and his knights sat at meat in his castle at Caerleon, there came a young lad to the king and told him of a white stag which he had seen in the forest.

'We shall hunt that stag tomorrow,' said Arthur, 'for it sounds a rare beast.'

'My lord king,' said Guenever, 'I would ride with you tomorrow to see the hunting of this stag; have I your leave?'

Arthur smiled. 'You have indeed.'

Arthur rose early in the morning and all his knights with him, for no one of them wished to miss the hunting. But when they were gathered together, mounted and waiting, with the hounds leashed and eager to go, Arthur saw that Guenever was not with them. 'Perchance the queen has changed her mind and would lie abed instead,' he said. 'Let us not wait for her.' And he led the company out to the forest.

A half-hour later Guenever awoke, and her ladies told her that all in the castle save a few servants had already ridden forth. Guenever frowned a little. 'It is indeed a mishap that I should oversleep today of all days. But let us make haste and maybe we shall catch up with the king.' And she sent a damsel to the stables to see the number of horses left. But in all the stables no more than two horses remained, so many knights had ridden forth to see the hunting of the white stag. 'Then can only two of us ride after

126

my lord the king,' said Guenever. And she chose out one of the damsels to accompany her.

They set off into the forest, following the tracks of the horses of Arthur and his company, and after a while the queen saw a young knight riding towards them on a grey horse. He was auburn-haired and handsome, his clothes were gay, and a gold-hilted sword hung from his baldric. 'It is Sir Geraint,' said Guenever, and she called to him.

He greeted her with courtesy. 'God keep you, Queen Guenever.'

'You are well met, Sir Geraint,' said she, 'for you can ride with us and give us your company until we reach my lord the king.' And she told Geraint how all at the castle had ridden forth to hunt a white stag.

'That will surely be a fine sight,' said Geraint.

The three of them rode on together, and in a little while they saw approaching them a tall knight in armour, accompanied by a lady on a white horse, and in front of them rode a dwarf. 'That tall knight is a stranger to me,' said Guenever. 'Is he known to you, Sir Geraint?'

'He is no one I have ever seen before,' answered Geraint.

Upon that Guenever sent her damsel to ask who the stranger might be, in case he was bound for Caerleon and wished for hospitality. The damsel rode towards the dwarf and gave him a greeting and asked him the name of his lord.

'That is no concern of yours, lady,' he replied.

'Since you are so churlish,' said the damsel, 'I must ask the knight himself.'

But when she would have done so, the dwarf prevented her, saying, 'You are not worthy to speak with my lord.'

And he struck her across the face with the whip he carried, and laughed when she rode back to Guenever in tears.

Guenever was angry. 'Do you go, Sir Geraint, and ask who is this knight whose servants deal so discourteously with the lady of a queen. Perchance the dwarf will be less bold with a man.'

But when Geraint had asked the question, he too was met with the same answer. 'That is no concern of yours.'

'Then shall I ask your master himself,' said Geraint.

But the dwarf placed his horse across the path in his way, saying, 'You are not worthy to speak with my lord.' And he struck Geraint across the face with his whip.

Geraint laid his hand on the hilt of his sword, and he would have drawn it but that he thought, 'If I slay this wretched dwarf then shall I have his master to contend with, and the tall knight is well armed while I have no more than my sword. Small good will I get of a battle with him if I have no armour.' So he rode back to Guenever, angry and ashamed.

But she praised him for his prudence. 'If the knight is as unmannerly as his dwarf, little would he have cared whether you wore armour or no.'

'If you will give me leave, good queen, I will follow this knight and his lady until they reach a town, and there I shall borrow armour and fight with him. And may it be given me to avenge the slight his dwarf put on your damsel.'

Guenever gave him leave to go, only warning him against meeting with the knight before he was fully armed, and Geraint set off after the strangers.

They rode through the forest and across the open land,

with Geraint following them, and at last they came to a town where there was a castle. The knight and his lady rode into the castle, and when Geraint was certain that they would remain there, he looked around the streets of the town for any man he knew from whom he might beg the loan of armour and a shield. But it was a town where he had never been before and all those about him were strangers to him.

Just beyond the town stood an old manor that must once have been fair and rich, yet now was all but a ruin. Geraint rode into the courtyard, thinking that if the house were indeed as deserted as it seemed, he might rest there awhile. But an old man in tattered clothes came out to him. 'If you are seeking shelter, sir knight, you are welcome,' he said. And for all his rags his voice and his bearing were courtly as he bade Geraint dismount and follow him.

They entered the great hall where all was dust and emptiness, and the old man led Geraint up a stairway to an upper room, where, on a stool before a little fire, sat a lady in a gown of faded silk, with a young ragged damsel standing beside her. And in spite of their poverty it was apparent to Sir Geraint that they were all three of noble birth.

'This is my lady, and this is my daughter Enid,' said the old man. And they both greeted Geraint kindly.

'My child,' said the old man to the damsel, 'go you and carry corn and water to our guest's good horse, and then make haste and buy food for us,' and he gave her a coin.

Geraint would have prevented her when she went to stable his horse in the empty hall, but she only shook her head and gave a little smile and slipped quietly from the room. 'It is not fitting that a noble damsel should act as groom to my horse,' said Geraint.

But the lady said gently, 'We have no servants, yet that is no reason why we should not show all honour to a guest.'

So Geraint sat and talked with the two of them of one thing and another until the damsel returned with a loaf and meat and a leather bottle of wine, and then they sat to eat upon stools at a trestle table, while the damsel waited on them.

When the meal was over, Geraint asked to whom the castle belonged that stood in the town. For a moment there was silence and a tear trickled down the lady's cheek.

'It was once mine, sir knight,' said the old man quietly. 'All the land that lies about here was once mine in the days when I was an earl.' He sighed. 'I will tell you how it was. I had a brother who died and left me guardian of his heir, my young nephew, and of all the lands that were to be his when I considered him old enough to rule over them. But my nephew and I could not agree when that time had come. I was all for his giving me guardianship for a year or two longer, and he was all for being master of his own lands right away. So he left me and gathered together friends to support him and men at arms to fight for him, and he fell upon me in my castle. I and my followers were defeated, and thus did my nephew gain not only his own lands but also mine, and so I have lived in this poverty in which you see me, ever since that day.'

'That is indeed a sad tale,' said Geraint, 'and much do I pity you, good lord.'

'Let us not talk of it, sir knight,' said the old earl. 'But tell me instead why you have come to this town.'

So Geraint told him of the tall knight. 'And how think you, lord,' he asked, 'that I may enter the castle and do battle with him?'

'Each year,' said the old earl, 'there is held at the castle a great jousting. Every knight who comes to fight must bring with him the lady whom he loves best, and the prize for the knight who proves himself worthiest is a sparrow-hawk. This knight of whom you tell me, for two years he has won the sparrow-hawk, and in honour of the same lady, so that now he is always known as the Knight of the Sparrow-hawk. No doubt he thinks to win for a third time this year. The jousting is to be held tomorrow, so if you would match yourself against this knight, it were well that you went in the morning and challenged him.'

'I have no armour with me,' said Geraint.

'My armour is old and rusty, I have not worn it for many a day, but you are welcome to wear it, if you do not scorn the offer.'

'Indeed,' said Geraint, 'how should I scorn a kindly offer? I am grateful to you, good lord. But I fear that I have no lady of my own to take with me to the jousting.'

'A lady you must have,' said the old earl, 'or you will not be allowed to fight.'

Geraint looked at the young ragged damsel where she sat at her mother's feet. 'If you would permit it, and she were willing, might not your daughter go to the jousting with me, as my own lady?'

'Any service that I or mine can render you, we shall render willingly,' said the old earl. And when Geraint looked again at the damsel Enid to ask her leave, she smiled at him and blushed a little and seemed glad.

The next morning Geraint armed himself in the old earl's armour, and it was indeed battered and rusty, the poorest he had ever seen. Then he mounted his grey horse and set Enid before him, in her ragged gown; and with the old earl walking on one side of him, carrying the lances that he would need, and the countess walking on the other and holding to the horse's bridle, they set off for the meadow before the castle where the jousting was being held.

When they came there, they found that the Knight of the Sparrow-hawk had been victorious over all those few who had dared to fight with him; and having stood up before all the remaining knights and found no one else to challenge him, he had been adjudged the winner, and was even then bidding his lady fetch the sparrow-hawk that was his prize.

But Geraint called out, 'A moment, sir knight, for there is a damsel here who is more beautiful than your lady, and it should be for her to fetch the sparrow-hawk.'

'If you maintain that, còme and fight with me,' said the Knight of the Sparrow-hawk. And when Geraint rode forward in the rusty armour there were many there who laughed. But when they saw his damsel, in her faded and ragged gown, there was even more mockery.

'Indeed,' said the Knight of the Sparrow-hawk, 'the lady and the armour are well matched. I would not care for either to be mine.'

Geraint and the Knight of the Sparrow-hawk fought together, and three times they broke their lances on each other. Then the old earl handed Geraint the last of his lances and said, 'This is the best of all the lances that I ever had.'

'I will try to be worthy of it,' said Geraint. He rode at the Knight of the Sparrow-hawk and struck him with all his might, so that he fell to the ground. Geraint dismounted and the Knight of the Sparrow-hawk rose to his feet and they fought long with their swords. And after a time the Knight of the Sparrow-hawk gave Geraint such a blow that he thought he could fight no longer. But the old earl came to him and whispered, 'Good friend, have you forgotten the insolence of this knight's dwarf to you in the forest, and his insult to Queen Guenever's lady?'

Geraint made a last effort and with all the strength that remained to him he struck the Knight of the Sparrow-hawk upon the helm, so that he fell to his knees and could fight no more, and asked quarter of Geraint.

'I will spare you,' said Geraint, 'if you will take your lady and your dwarf and go to King Arthur's court at Caerleon, and there ask pardon of Queen Guenever for the injury you did her damsel.' And this the knight promised to do; while the Lady Enid fetched the sparrow-hawk and gave it to Geraint.

Then the young earl who was the old earl's nephew came to Geraint and made much of him, for he had overthrown the knight who had been accounted the finest among them, and he bade Geraint come to the castle with him.

'I thank you, lord,' said Geraint, 'but the house where I lodged last night shall be good enough for me. For there I found the best of company.'

Then the young earl was aware how his uncle stood near by with his lady, and when he saw how poor they were and how tattered, he was ashamed and hung his head.

'Lord,' said Geraint, 'I would that you were accorded

with your uncle.' And he went with the old earl back to the tumbledown house.

But the young earl came after them and spoke with Geraint. 'I would repair the wrong I did my uncle,' he said. 'Tell me what I should do.'

'Give him back those lands that are his and keep to yourself only those which you had from your father.' To this the young earl agreed, and they all feasted together that night and swore goodwill for ever. And in the morning, as he had said, Geraint rode for King Arthur's court, with Enid in her ragged gown, holding the sparrow-hawk.

Meanwhile, at Caerleon two days before, after a long morning's hunting, Arthur and his knights had at last killed the white stag, and in triumph they carried it back to the castle. 'To whom shall the head with the antlers be given?' asked Arthur. And one knight after another claimed it as his own.

'My lord king,' said Guenever, 'let the head be kept until Sir Geraint returns to us, for while you hunted this morning he rode to avenge an injury done to one of my damsels.' And she told them of what had passed in the forest.

'The stag's head shall surely be his,' said Arthur, 'if he comes to Caerleon safely.' And all agreed with him.

The following day was the day of the jousting for the sparrow-hawk, and no word of Geraint came to Caerleon, so that Guenever grew anxious. But the next morning the Knight of the Sparrow-hawk, full weary from his battling, together with his lady and his dwarf, rode into the castle and knelt before the queen, saying that Sir Geraint had bidden him do thus.

Great was the rejoicing when it was known that Geraint

was safe, and even greater was the joy when he came himself with the Lady Enid. Guenever herself chose out a gown and jewels for Enid, that she might be clad fittingly for a marriage feast; and Geraint and Enid were wedded with the well-wishes of everyone. And at the festivities the white stag's head was given to Enid. 'For,' said Guenever, 'it was through her courtesy that Sir Geraint avenged the insults of the tall knight's dwarf, since without a true and lovely lady of his own he could not have won the sparrow-hawk.'

XIV

Geraint and Enid

FOR a time after their marriage Sir Geraint and his lady Enid remained at King Arthur's court, and very welcome they were, for Enid was of a sweet and modest disposition and much loved by Queen Guenever and her damsels, while Geraint ever proved himself in the jousting and in the tournaments to be one of the best of the younger knights.

But there came a day when Geraint's father sent to him, saying, 'My son, I am growing old and I am no longer able to rule our lands as they should be ruled. Come and manage these matters for me.' So Geraint and Enid set out for their home.

There Geraint took care to govern all things well, and since, his father being old, knightly feats among his followers had fallen into disuse, he held on all the feast days tourneys such as he had grown used to in King Arthur's court. To these gatherings came not only knights from all over his father's lands, but many stranger knights as well; but to them all was Sir Geraint superior in the jousting and in all knightly exercise. And so at last, for want of worthy rivalry, Geraint became slack and careless, no longer giving of his best in the tournaments, and in time no longer taking part in them, but watching them only from the side of Enid his lady.

And soon there came a day when even this gave him so little pleasure that he kept from the tourney-field and the tilting-yard even as a watcher; while his very horses forgot his voice and the touch of his hand, he rode so seldom. His days were passed in idleness, in eating and drinking and sleeping, and in the companionship of Enid, and he thought himself well content.

But the Lady Enid grieved for the loss of his knightly prowess, though she dared speak no word of it to him, and she longed again for the old days when there had not been many knights his equal, even in Arthur's court.

One morning she awoke early in the great bed where she slept with her lord, and looking down on Geraint where he lay with his eyes fast closed, and thinking he was yet sleeping, she sighed and whispered, 'Would God that you were still as you were before, when there were few to rival you in all the land, and you were my brave and beloved knight.'

But Geraint was not asleep and he heard her words, and thinking them to mean that she no longer loved him, he was angered. He said nothing to her, but rose and called for his armour and ordered two horses to be saddled. Then he bade Enid rise and dress herself in her oldest gown and come to him in the courtyard. And he left her, thinking bitterly, 'She shall see that I am still skilled in knightly feats, and much pleasure may it give her.'

Wondering, Enid put on the old faded and ragged gown in which Geraint had first seen her, for she had kept it for its memories of that happy meeting. Then she fastened up her hair and ran down to the courtyard where Geraint waited.

'We ride out together,' he said, 'and we come not home again until you are satisfied that I have lost neither strength nor courage. Mount your horse and ride on ahead, and whatever you may hear concerning me, take no heed of it and turn not back.'

Poor Enid mounted her horse and rode slowly in the way he had directed her, and, some hundred paces or so behind, came Geraint. In this fashion they rode along the highway until they reached a forest, and there Enid saw four armed knights ride out from among the trees, and she heard them say among themselves, 'Here is a knight alone, save for a woman. Let us take his armour and his horse.'

'Even if he is angry with me for speaking,' thought Enid, 'I cannot see these men fall upon my lord and hurt or slay him. I would rather his anger than that.' And she reined in her horse and waited until Geraint caught up with her. 'Lord,' she said, 'yonder are four armed men who wait to fall upon you. I beg you take care.'

But Geraint turned on her in anger. 'I bade you not speak to me, whatever you saw or heard. No doubt it would please you were they to slay me and leave you a widow and well rid of me. But you shall see that I am not afraid of four robber knights.'

The first of the robbers rode at Geraint and Geraint met his charge and flung him from his horse, so that he lay dead upon the ground. In the same way he served the second, the third and the fourth. Then he dismounted and stripped the armour from the dead men and fastened it upon the saddles of their horses. He tied the reins of the four horses and bade Enid lead them and ride on ahead. 'And this time,' he said, 'obey me and speak no word, whatever you may hear concerning me.'

Enid rode on ahead, with difficulty leading the four horses, and there were tears in her eyes and great sorrow in her heart, for never before that day had she known other than kindness from her lord.

They passed through the forest and came out on to open country, and there, from the shelter of some bushes, Enid saw three knights ride. When they drew closer to her, she heard them say, 'Here is indeed a prize for us, six horses and much armour, and only one knight to defend them.'

'My lord is wearied from his fighting,' thought Enid, 'and may well be slain. No matter how wrathful he is with me, I must speak to him.' So she reined in her horse and waited for Geraint. 'Lord,' she said, 'yonder are three robbers. I heard them tell how they will fall upon you and slay you and take the horses and the armour.'

'That would doubtless please you well, that they should slay me and you could find yourself a new lord who was no sluggard knight as I am,' said Geraint bitterly.

'Truly, lord, it was for your good I spoke.'

'I need none of your care for me,' said Geraint. And even as he was speaking, one of the robber knights rode at him, but Geraint met his attack with great strength and toppled him from his horse. And likewise he did with the two other robbers; while Enid watched, full of terror at the sight. Then Geraint dismounted and took the fallen knights' armour and placed it on their horses, and fastening together the reins, he bade Enid lead the seven horses and ride on as before. 'And this time,' he said, 'take care that you obey me, and say not a single word to me until I bid you.'

Sadly Enid rode on before, and great trouble she had with the seven horses; while Geraint followed her. After a time Enid saw five knights all in armour halted across the path. 'See here,' they laughed to one another, 'nine horses and much armour and a fair damsel as well, and no more than one knight to defend them. Great booty shall we gain today.'

And though she tried to obey him, Enid could not see her husband slain, so she turned and rode back to him. 'Lord, I have heard the five knights there laughing to each other, and they say they will easily slay you and take what they will. I beg you have care for yourself.'

But Geraint upbraided her angrily for a prattling disobedient wife; yet as he spoke the five knights rode on him at once. But Geraint fought fiercely and well, and in a little while the five knights lay on the ground and made no move. Geraint dismounted and took off their armour and laid it across their saddles. Then he fastened the reins of their horses together and bade Enid lead them.

If seven horses were hard for her to control, twelve were far worse, and a great task did she find them as she rode on ahead, sick at heart; with Geraint following after her. And if Geraint had not been so angry, and had he not believed that she loved him no longer, he would have pitied her, so dejected she was.

They rode through another forest, and when the sun had set, Geraint called out to Enid and bade her halt. 'Here shall we pass the night,' he said.

'As you will, lord,' she answered.

He dismounted and lifted her from her horse. 'I am tired,' he said, 'and I shall sleep. Watch the horses that they do not stray.'

And while Geraint slept fitfully in his armour underneath a tree, Enid remained unsleeping, watching the horses, though her head ached with weariness and her heart with misery.

At dawn Geraint awoke. 'Let us be on our way,' he said. 'Ride on before as you have done, and let me hear no word from you.'

So once again Enid rode on ahead with the twelve horses, and in time they left the forest and found themselves in meadow land beside a river, where in the distance rose up the walls of a town. In the fields there were men mowing the grass, and Geraint called to a lad and asked him to direct him to an inn. 'If you will do this for me,' he said, 'I will give you your pick of these horses.'

The youth, surprised and pleased, led Geraint to the best inn of the town and Geraint bade him choose for himself one of the horses and the armour it carried, and the youth rode off happily, telling his good fortune to all he met. At last the story came to the ears of the lord who ruled in that town, and he determined to see for himself the strange knight who gave a good horse and fine armour away for no more than a slight courtesy.

At the inn the horses were stabled and Geraint and Enid were shown to a comfortable room. 'This chamber is large enough,' said Geraint to Enid, 'therefore keep to one end of it. I have no wish to have you near me.'

'It shall be as you command, lord,' replied Enid, weeping. And she went to the far end of the room and lay down upon a straw pallet. And Geraint lay down on the bed and slept, for he had rested but little in the forest.

But soon came the innkeeper with word that the lord of the town was come to speak with Geraint, and Geraint rose and bade the lord welcome, and they greeted each other courteously. The lord asked Geraint whither he travelled. 'I travel for adventure, to no especial place,' he replied.

The lord looked across at Enid and thought how fair she was. 'The damsel who travels with you,' he said, 'have I your leave to speak with her?'

Geraint shrugged his shoulders. 'As you will.' And he turned away as though he cared nothing for Enid.

The lord of the town went over to her and greeted her. 'It cannot be pleasant for you to travel without a servant to wait on you, lady,' he said.

'I travel well enough,' she answered.

'Indeed, it is a shame that a knight should treat a fair lady so, neither to speak with her nor to comfort her, but only to turn his back.' And the lord smiled much on her.

'It must be as he wills,' said Enid. 'And I should rather his indifference than any other man's love.'

But for all her words the lord was not to be discouraged. With a glance to see if Geraint were watching, he whispered, 'I will give you great riches and much honour if you will leave this knight and come to my castle with me.'

'How should I leave this knight,' asked Enid, 'since I am pledged to him for ever?'

'I have never seen a fairer damsel than you,' said the lord of the town, 'and you shall be my lady, though I have to kill your knight to win you.'

And Enid remembered how all her warnings to Geraint had met with hard words and scorn, so she thought it best to dissemble lest Geraint refused to listen if she spoke to him. She leant near to the lord of the town and whispered, 'I dare not leave my knight of my own accord, for fear that he is angered and seeks to do me injury. But if you come here early in the morning, with all your men, then can you take me to your castle as if by force, and I shall have no blame of it.'

The lord smiled. 'You are crafty as well as beautiful, lady. I shall be here again tomorrow.'

All that day Enid said nothing to Geraint of the matter, and for his part he said no word at all to her. That night they lay down to sleep, still as far away from each other as might be, but at midnight Enid arose and laid out Geraint's armour and his weapons, and then she went to the bed where he lay and woke him. 'You are in danger, dear husband,' she said. And she told him of what the lord of the town had planned.

Geraint was angry with her. 'I did not bid you speak to me,' he grumbled. But in spite of his anger he arose and armed himself and sent Enid to call the innkeeper. And to the innkeeper he said, 'My eleven horses in your stable and the armour they carry I will give to you in payment of my reckoning, if you will receive them.'

The innkeeper was astonished. 'Good sir knight,' he said, 'no more than one of the suits of armour would suffice to pay your reckoning.'

'Then that is all the better for you,' said Geraint. 'Now tell me how I shall leave this town most quickly.'

With many thanks for his bounty, the innkeeper showed Geraint the way he should go, and saddled his horse and Enid's; and once again the two of them rode off, out through the town gates and on to the highway.

After an hour or two the dawn came, and with it the lord of the town and his men, all mounted and armed and clattering into the innyard. When the lord found that Geraint and Enid were gone, he was angry, and with his whole company he rode out of the town and along the highway, following the tracks of Geraint's horse.

As the sun rose, Enid looked back along the roadway often, watching to see if they were pursued. And at last she saw what she feared, a great cloud of dust from the galloping horsemen, and she called out to Geraint, warning him. 'I bade you hold your tongue,' he said. 'Will you never learn to obey?'

But he turned to face the lord and his men, and he fought against them, every one, and overthrew them all.

While he had been fighting, Enid had stood by the roadside wringing her hands and weeping; yet when the battle was over, Geraint had never a good word for her, but only bade her mount her horse and ride on again.

The road that they were following led towards a bridge over a river, and as Enid came near this bridge, a man met them and called out to Geraint that he might not pass that way unless he fought with the lord who owned all the land that lay thereabouts. 'He is named the Little King,' said the man, 'and though little in stature he may be, he is mighty in the fight.'

'I care not,' said Geraint. 'I shall cross the river in spite of your Little King.' And he ordered Enid to go forward over the bridge.

Yet they had not gone very far before they saw a horseman come galloping, and a voice called out to Geraint to halt and fight. And on a huge black horse they saw a small man, the smallest man Geraint had ever seen, but well armed and fierce. 'It was ill done, stranger,' said the Little King, 'to ride over my bridge unbidden.'

Geraint laughed, thinking that such a small man would be easily overthrown, but the Little King's blows were powerful and his lance as tall as any knight's; and they had not been fighting together for very long before Geraint had learnt how hard it is to strike at an adversary so small. For though each one of the Little King's mighty thrusts told home, so that Geraint's armour and his shield were all battered, no more than one in ten of Geraint's strokes reached their small mark. But at last they were both down off their horses, and on foot Geraint had the advantage from his greater height. He swung his sword in a mighty blow upon the Little King's helmet, so that the metal was cracked, and the Little King's sword flew out of his hand.

Then the Little King asked for quarter, and Geraint answered him, 'I will give you your life on condition that if ever I require your service, you will come to my aid. For you are indeed a mighty fighter, and would be a good friend in need.'

'That do I promise you, by my honour,' said the Little King. And he would have had Geraint come with him to his castle near by to be healed of his wounds; but when Geraint saw how Enid would have urged him in this course, he refused, that she might have the more sorrow of it. So, weary and wounded though he was, he mounted his horse and bade Enid ride on, and with many a backward glance to see that he still had the strength to follow her, she did as she was bidden.

But Geraint's wounds gave him great pain, and the heat of the midday sun increased his weakness, so that on the edge of a forest he bade Enid dismount, and dropped wearily from his saddle and stood beneath a tree, leaning on his lance. Yet when Enid would have come to him, he harshly ordered her away, and she stood at a distance, weeping for his hurts.

Then there came to them both the sound of hunting horns and the ring of merry voices, and after a moment a single knight came riding by. Geraint and Enid saw at once that it was Sir Kay the Seneschal, and Enid thought with hope, 'It will be King Arthur and his knights hunting in the forest. Perchance my lord will give them leave to tend his wounds.' But though Geraint knew Kay at once, Sir Kay did not know him, for he still wore his armour and the painted device had been all worn off his shield in his battle with the Little King.

Sir Kay looked at Geraint. 'What do you here, sir knight?' he asked.

'I do no more than rest beneath a tree,' replied Geraint.

'I am the seneschal of my lord King Arthur,' said Kay. 'Come you with me to where he waits.'

But Geraint would not, for he knew that it would be hard for him to see all his friends again and to have them know how Enid no longer loved him, but instead despised him for his idleness. 'I will not go with you, sir seneschal,' he said.

But such an answer ever made Kay offended, and in anger he said, 'Then will you be forced to come, you churlish knight.' And he rode towards Geraint and made as though to seize him. But Geraint lifted up the lance he leant on and with it gave Sir Kay a buffet under the chin so that he was thrown from his horse. Kay picked himself up, grumbling mightily, mounted his horse, and rode to where Sir Gawaine was. 'I have heard but now,' he said, 'that there is a wounded knight yonder in the forest. Would it not be good to fetch him to King Arthur?'

'It would indeed,' said Gawaine, and made to ride off in the direction Kay had pointed out.

'It were best you took armour and a strong lance with you,' warned Kay, 'for I have heard that he is churlish and attacks all well-wishers.'

Gawaine laughed. 'If he is wounded, I doubt not I can manage him without armour or a lance.'

But by the time Gawaine reached the tree where Geraint stood, Geraint, for the pain in his head, had taken off his helmet, and Gawaine knew him at once and greeted him gladly.

'Go your way, good Sir Gawaine, and let me be, for I wish no company today,' said Geraint.

'Shall one of our lord King Arthur's best knights be so near without the king's gaining a sight of him? I will take no refusal, Sir Geraint.'

And though he was unwilling, Geraint suffered himself to be led to where Arthur was, and Enid followed.

The king was glad indeed to see Geraint again, and he made much of him, as did Guenever of Enid, though she marvelled greatly that Enid should be travelling alone with her lord, shabby and ragged, with not a single squire, yet she asked no questions. At Arthur's command Geraint remained with him until his wounds were healed, but as soon as he was whole he sought leave to go again, and though Arthur had no wish to lose him, he did not deny him what he asked.

So once again Geraint and Enid rode off together, Enid ahead and Geraint following after her. As they rode along a track that ran beside a wood, they heard a woman's scream, and a little way among the trees they found a lady kneeling on the grass, wailing over a dead knight. 'How came this to happen?' asked Geraint.

'But even now,' said the lady, 'three giants passed this way, and for no cause they slew my lord.'

'I will avenge him for you, lady,' promised Geraint. And bidding Enid comfort her, he rode after the giants. When he overtook them, he saw how each was taller than three men, and carrying a mighty club; but giving them no time to prepare themselves, he rode at the first of them and pierced him right through the body with his lance, so that the giant fell dead. The second he served likewise; but before he could strike one blow at the third, a mighty club crashed down upon him so that he all but lost his senses. Yet he still fought on, and because the giant was slow to strike again, him also Geraint ran through with his lance and left him dead beside his brothers. He rode back to where Enid waited, trembling, with the strange lady; but as he would have dismounted from his horse he fell from the saddle to the ground, as though he were dead.

Enid cried out and went to him, taking off his helmet. His face was pale and still and there seemed but little life in him. While she sought to tend him, a band of knights with the earl who was their lord came by and paused to see what was amiss. When he heard what had passed, the earl praised the courage of Geraint who had slain single-handed the three giants, then he ordered his men to bury with all honour the body of the strange knight and escort his widow to her home, but he bade them carry Geraint to his castle. 'For,' he said, 'there is a little life in him yet, and perchance he may mend, though there is but faint hope.'

In the great hall of the castle Geraint was laid upon a bench with his sword beside him. He lay unmoving and seemed scarcely to breathe, so that no one doubted that he was already dead. Enid sat beside him and would not speak a word. After a time the earl came to her and said, 'See, my servants have brought in food for us that we may eat. Leave your grief for the dead knight and sup with me.' But she would not, for all his persuasion, so that at last he took her roughly by the hand and led her to the table. 'It is folly,' he said, 'to fast because a knight is dead.'

In that moment Geraint's senses came back to him, and he lay there on the bench and heard their voices speaking, but still he made no movement, for he was very weak.

Enid sat at the table beside the earl, but she would neither eat nor drink. When he would have urged her to taste the meat that was set before her, she only said, 'It would be shame to me to eat food while my lord is lying there.'

The earl poured wine for her and put the cup into her hand. 'Drink, fair lady,' he said, 'and when you have drunk my good wine the world will seem a better place.'

'It would be shame to me,' said Enid, 'to drink while my lord is unable to drink.'

And so long as he tried to persuade her, all she would answer was, 'It would be shame to me to do thus when my lord is lying dead.'

At last the earl grew angry. 'If courtesy does not prevail with you, let us see what discourtesy can do.' And he struck her. 'Eat when you are bidden,' he said.

Enid cried out with the pain of the blow. 'Ungentle knight,' she said, 'you would not use me so if my lord were still alive.' And she wept.

And at the sound of her cry and her tears Geraint sat up on the bench and took hold of his sword and rose and went unsteadily to where the earl sat, and with one blow he killed him. In great terror all those in the hall fled, thinking that the dead man had risen up to slay them, so that Geraint and Enid were left alone. Geraint looked at Enid and he knew at last that she still loved him and was true to him, and that he had misjudged her, and he was ashamed and could think of no word to speak, save only, 'We must not tarry here, or they will grow bold enough to come back again to see whether I am truly dead or no.'

They went out to the courtyard together and Enid fetched and saddled his horse, and Geraint, who could hardly stand for weakness, mounted, and Enid set herself before him, and together they rode through the castle gates in the darkness, and no one saw them go.

As they went along the road, Enid heard the sound of hoofs following and she grew sick with fear. She reined in the horse and waited, and when the horseman came near in the gloom she called out, 'Whoever you are, small glory will it be to you to slay a dead man.'

'Alas,' said a voice, 'is that Sir Geraint and his lady?'

'It is indeed,' said Enid. 'And who may you be, stranger?'

'I am the Little King, come to the aid of Geraint, when I heard that he was hard beset, even as I promised.'

'You are well met,' said Geraint, and his voice was no more than a murmur.

'Better would it have been had you come with me to my castle when I so counselled you. Yet it is never too late to take good advice.' And the Little King led them to his castle and there Geraint was healed of his hurt, though he recovered but slowly. And Enid tended him with loving care all the days that he lay sick; until at last he was strong and well again and they could ride for their own home.

And this time they rode side by side and talked gaily all the way; and never again did Geraint doubt that Enid loved him, but always after he considered himself the most fortunate knight in his lady that ever there was.

XV

How Percival Came to Arthur's Court

IN King Arthur's days there was an earl in the north of Britain who had seven sons. This earl cared for nothing but war and combats, and when he could not be fighting his enemies, he was ever at tourneying, he and his sons. And it happened that in this way he and his six eldest sons were all slain, and it was only because the seventh was too young to know anything of fighting and had to remain at home with his mother that he was not also slain.

When the earl's widowed lady heard how she had lost both lord and six sons, she wept bitterly and set her heart for ever against all manner of warfare and knightly deeds. 'I have still one son left to me,' she thought, 'and never shall he take part in any battle or jousting. So may he stay long in this world.'

She left her lord's estates and went to live in a forest clearing, far away from other folk, and there she had to serve her only women and boys and simple souls such as had never handled weapons, nor indeed knew aught of such things. There, in this unfrequented place, her youngest son, who was named Percival, was reared, and he grew to be a tall lad, strong and brave, with a merry smile and a merry heart, and knowing nothing of the ways of the knightly world. Every day he played in the forest alone, fashioning little darts of holly wood and throwing them at a mark, until he was very skilled in this game.

One day, near a forest track, he saw a man go by and gave him a greeting. The man answered him, but did not pause, and Percival marvelled much at the strange fashion in which the man was clad, and at the great horse that he rode.

A while later, when his mother had joined him with her spinning and they were sitting together in the sunshine, he saw, along that same forest track, two more men riding. 'Look up, mother, and tell me what those men are,' he said.

His mother looked and saw that they were two knights, riding in full armour on their great war horses, and the spindle fell from her hand and her face grew pale. Then she picked up her spindle, smiled at Percival, and said, 'Those are two angels, my child.'

'Then I will go and speak with them,' said Percival. And before she could prevent him, he had run after them.

Now, the knights were none other than Sir Gawaine

and Sir Uwaine who travelled on a quest, and when they saw Percival running after them they reined in their horses and called to him, 'Have you seen a knight ride by here today?'

Percival stopped beside them and considered. 'What is a knight?' he asked.

Sir Uwaine laughed. 'Why, lad, it is even such a man as I.'

At once Percival remembered the man who had ridden by that morning. But he was curious about these strangers, the shining clothes they wore and their great horses, their iron-tipped staffs, and the painted metal things they carried; and so he said, 'I will answer your question, strangers, if you will first answer mine.'

'That is fair enough,' said Gawaine.

Percival pointed to the fine saddle that was on Uwaine's horse. 'What is that?'

'A saddle.'

He pointed to Gawaine's lance. 'And this?'

'A lance.'

'And this?'

'Why that is my shield.'

'And this?'

'My sword in its scabbard.'

And so it went on, until Percival had heard the names of all those things which he had never seen before that day. Then he thanked the knights for their courtesy and told them what they wished to know. And Sir Gawaine and Sir Uwaine bade Percival farewell and rode on their way after the other knight.

Percival returned to his mother and his eyes were bright.

'You were mistaken, my mother,' he said, 'for they were not angels, but knights. And I am going to be a knight, even as they are.' And nothing his mother could say might alter his resolve.

He went to the sheds where they kept the few horses that carried the wood from the forest for their fires, and chose out the largest of them all, a skinny old piebald nag with the bones almost through its hide. He put a ragged cloth on its back to serve as a saddle, and with plaited withies he made bridle and reins and all a horse's trappings as well as he could remember them. Then he went to his mother to ask her blessing before he rode forth.

She sighed and said, 'Since you are determined to leave me, my son, let me give you three words of advice. First, go to the court of King Arthur, for there the best knights are to be found. Second, wherever you are, if you come to a church or a chapel, say a prayer. And third, if ever you meet with a lady in trouble or distress, never fail to give her all the help you can.'

'I will remember and do as you say, good mother. And now farewell to you.' He took a handful of his holly darts, mounted the old piebald nag, and rode off.

After two days he saw before him, in a little forest glade, a gay pavilion. Thinking it to be a chapel, he remembered his mother's words, and dismounting, he knelt down and said a prayer. Then he rose and went closer and looked inside. The knight who owned the pavilion had ridden forth, but his lady was within, and a fine meal prepared against her lord's return.

'God save you, lady,' said Percival. 'I am hungry.'
'There is food,' she said. 'You are welcome.'

So Percival ate and drank and thanked her, and remembering his mother's advice, asked her in which direction King Arthur's court might lie.

Several days later he came to the castle where Arthur was then holding his court, and as he neared the gateway, he saw how a tall, grim-faced knight rode up to the gates a little way ahead of him and on into the great hall. So Percival went after him, on his old piebald nag.

Now, this tall knight bore no love to Arthur nor to any of his knights and he had long desired to do them dishonour, and for this purpose was he come. On that day King Arthur and most of his knights were hunting in the forest, and besides Queen Guenever and her damsels, only Sir Kay the Seneschal and Sir Uwaine, now back from his quest, were with her.

As the strange knight entered the hall, a page was pouring wine for Guenever, and seeing this, the knight dismounted, snatched the silver goblet from her hands, and flung the wine in her face. Then taking the goblet, he mounted his horse and shouted, 'If there is any knight so bold as to attempt to take back this goblet and to avenge the insult to his queen, let him follow me to the meadow beyond the castle, and he shall find me waiting.' And with that he rode out of the castle and away through the gates.

While the damsels made a great outcry around Guenever, Sir Uwaine looked at Sir Kay. 'The knight who would dare to treat our queen thus must be very sure of his skill in arms,' he said.

'I do not doubt,' said Kay, 'that he is skilled in more than arms who would be so daring. He has enchanter's powers,

I warrant.' And this, indeed, is what the knight had hoped that they would think.

And both Kay and Uwaine hesitated, since neither of them wished to leave the queen unprotected and go alone to battle against an enchanter in the meadow.

Then Kay looked up and saw Percival there on his bony horse, with neither saddle nor leather trappings, and a sight less fitted to a king's court he thought he had never seen. He instantly came forward and made as though he would have ordered Percival away. But Percival faced him calmly. 'Tell me,' he said, 'where is King Arthur?'

'What do you want with King Arthur?' asked Sir Kay.

'My mother bade me come to him that he might make me a knight.'

'A fine knight indeed would you make with that horse and those weapons,' exclaimed Kay. And in the hall they began to laugh at Percival, glad of a chance to forget the shame that the strange knight had put on them.

But at that moment, two dwarfs, a man and a woman, came bearing sweetmeats on a dish for the queen, and when they saw Percival they stopped and stared at him. And then going to him, they cried out, 'Welcome to you, Percival, one of the greatest among great knights.'

Sir Kay became angry. 'You wretched dwarfs, you have been serving the king for a twelvemonth and yet in all that time you have not uttered a word, though the best of company has been yours. And now today you choose to salute this ragged beggar-lad who would make a jest of knighthood and a mockery of Arthur's court. Begone with you.' And he gave them each a box on the ears.

'That was ill done,' said Percival. 'You are a most un-kindly knight. Now tell me where I shall find King Arthur.'

'Go first,' shouted Kay, 'to the meadow beyond the castle and there encounter with the strange knight who laid an insult on Queen Guenever. Take his horse and his arms and then come back and you shall be ordained knight.'

Percival thought of his mother's advice that he should always give aid to any lady in distress. 'I will do it,' he said. He rode out from the hall and through the gates and on to where the tall knight waited in the meadow, cantering his horse from one end of the field to the other, twirling the goblet on the end of his lance. When he saw Percival he called out haughtily, 'Tell me, lad, is there anyone from the castle who will come out and fight with me?'

'There was a knight there,' replied Percival, 'and he bade me take your horse and your arms for myself.'

'Enough of your impudence. Go back and bid Arthur come out and fight with me.'

'This fight is mine,' said Percival.

The tall knight was angry and he struck Percival a great blow on the shoulder with the butt of his lance. 'Now begone,' he said.

Percival took one of his holly darts, and flung it at the knight, and it pierced the joints of his armour and passed right through his body, so that he fell dead.

A little while later Sir Uwaine came out to the field and there he found Percival dragging the dead knight over the grass. 'Tell me,' Percival asked him, 'how I can get these iron garments off him.'

And Uwaine recognized him for the youth who had questioned him in the forest, and he marvelled that one so simple should have slain the tall grim-faced knight. He stripped off the dead knight's armour and smiled at Percival. 'Now you have armour and a horse worthy of your courage, my friend. Come back with me to the castle and you shall be made knight.'

But Percival shook his head. He picked up the goblet and held it out to Uwaine. 'Take this cup back to Queen Guenever and tell her I send it to her. And tell the king that I shall ever be loyal to him. And tell also to that most ungracious knight who spoke to me, that I shall never return to Arthur's court until I have met him in combat.'

Percival put on the armour and mounted the horse that he had won, and set off to seek adventures; while, full of wonder, Uwaine returned to the castle and told the others there of all that had passed. And Kay was none too pleased by what he heard.

Percival rode from one adventure to another, ever learning more of knighthood and feats of arms, until many months had been spent in that way. And during all that time King Arthur had not ceased to look for him, hoping that in one place or another where he held his court the young stranger who had avenged the insult to Queen Guenever might be found.

Once in winter Percival passed the night in the cell of a kindly hermit, and when morning came he found that in the darkness there had been a fall of snow, and the earth lay white and silent all around. 'How beautiful indeed is the world which God has made,' said the old hermit as he bade Percival farewell.

Percival rode on his way up a little hill, and as he reached the top and looked out over the valley which lay below him, the sun rose in a pink and golden sky and all the snow-covered valley glittered. 'It is indeed beautiful,' thought Percival, and he remained motionless, contemplating the scene, quite forgetful of the time that was passing by.

In the valley King Arthur and a party of knights were hunting. 'What manner of man is that,' asked Arthur, 'who sits his horse at the top of the hill as though he were a statue?'

'I will inquire for you, my lord king,' said one of the squires. He rode to the top of the hill and called out to Percival, 'Who are you, sir stranger, and what are you doing?' But Percival was so wrapped in his thoughts that he neither saw the squire nor heard his question. Upon this the squire insolently gave Percival a blow with the shaft of his hunting-spear. Percival left his thoughts for long enough to strike at the squire with his lance and fling him from his horse.

The squire picked himself up, shook the snow from his clothes, and rode back to Arthur. 'He is some savage man who answers courteous questions with blows, my lord king,' he said.

Sir Kay, who was beside Arthur, was indignant. 'I shall teach this stranger a lesson.' And he rode off at once for the top of the hill. 'For what reason, foolish stranger, do you remain looking out over the valley as though you had lost your wits—if indeed you ever had any to lose?'

And without a word Percival left his thinking and struck at him with his lance and flung him from his horse to the ground, so that his arm was broken and he lay there in the snow, while Percival returned to his thoughts. Sir Kay's horse, finding itself riderless, turned and trotted back to where the others waited, and Arthur was concerned. 'Perhaps good Sir Kay is slain,' he said.

Several knights immediately went up the hill, found Kay, and carried him back to Arthur. 'It is a most churlish and unmannerly stranger who sits his horse on the top of the hill,' groaned Kay.

'Let me go to speak with him, my lord uncle,' asked Gawaine. 'Perchance I can win a word from him.'

'No doubt you will succeed where the rest of us would fail,' sneered Kay. 'You and your glib tongue, Gawaine. If all knights were as you, little fighting and feats of arms would there be, but always pretty speeches and fine words.'

But Gawaine only smiled at the taunt and rode up the hill. 'Greetings, stranger,' he said. 'If it would be as pleasing to you as it would be to me, I would stay and speak with you awhile, but I am sent from King Arthur to bid you come to him and tell him of yourself.'

Percival turned his head and looked at Gawaine. 'Those others who came to me,' he asked, 'did they come on the same errand?'

'The very same,' replied Gawaine.

'I was meditating on the beauty of the morning,' said Percival, 'and most roughly did they drag me from my thoughts.'

Gawaine smiled. 'It is ill to disturb a knight when he would be left in peace to think. But when your thinking is finished, will you not come with me to the king, for he wishes greatly to speak with you?'

Percival considered a moment, and then he asked, 'That knight who is King Arthur's seneschal, is he still with the king?'

'Sir Kay? That was he whom you threw last from his horse. His arm is broken.'

'Then have I avenged the wrong done to the two dwarfs,' said Percival, 'and now may I go to Arthur's court.'

And Gawaine knew at once that this was no other than the lad whom Arthur had been seeking for many months. He took Percival's hand in his. 'You are indeed well met, my friend, after so long a search. Tell me your name and come with me at once to my uncle the king.'

So Percival told his name, and together he and Gawaine rode down the hill to Arthur, who was glad out of measure when he knew who the stranger was.

And Percival was ordained knight by King Arthur, and was admitted to the fellowhip of the Round Table, with a great welcome from all, even from Sir Kay, who, whatever his own disliking, wished Arthur ever to have the best of knights about him.

XVI

How Galahad Came to Arthur's Court

IT was at a time when King Arthur was keeping the
Whitsun feasting at Camelot that, on the day before
Whitsunday, a strange damsel rode into the great hall
and asked for Sir Lancelot. He rose. 'What would you of
me, lady?'

'I am sent,' she said, 'in the name of King Pelles of
Corbin, to bid you go with me to a place which shall be
made known to you when you are come there.'

'I will do as you ask, since you ask in King Pelles' name,'
said Lancelot. And he bade a squire make ready his horse
and bring his armour.

But Guenever frowned a little. 'Sir Lancelot,' she said,
'will you leave us to go on an unknown quest just at the
Whitsun feasting?'

Before Lancelot could answer her the damsel had
spoken. 'He will be back here tomorrow by the time of
the midday meal, I promise you, good queen.' And with
that Guenever had to be content, since Arthur was willing
for Lancelot to go.

Lancelot rode beside the damsel out of Camelot and into
the forest which lay near by, and in a clearing in the forest
they came upon a nunnery. 'It is here that we are awaited,'
said the damsel.

The abbess of the nunnery greeted Sir Lancelot kindly.
'There are here already two of your kinsmen,' she said.
'Sir Bors and Sir Lionel rested here last night. They are

on their way to Camelot for Whitsunday.' And she took Lancelot to where his two cousins sat at meat, and they were indeed glad to see him.

'What brings you here?' asked Bors. 'We had thought you already at Camelot.'

Lancelot told them of the strange damsel and her request made in the name of King Pelles. 'It is more than fifteen years ago that he showed me much kindness, in that sad time of my madness. I could refuse nothing that he might ask of me,' he said.

While they were speaking twelve nuns came into the room, and with them a youth of great beauty. 'Sir Lancelot,' they said, 'we bring you this youth at King Pelles' request, that you may make him a knight.'

Now, the youth was no other than Galahad, son of the Lady Elaine and of Lancelot himself, and now that he was fifteen years old, his mother, as she had promised, was sending him forth to be a knight. Lancelot looked long at him and thought that he had never seen so comely a youth, nor so open and so frank a face; but he did not know him for his son. 'Is it your own wish that you should be ordained knight by me?' he asked.

'By you and by no other, if it pleases you,' replied Galahad.

So Lancelot knighted Galahad. 'May God grant you make a knight as good as you are beautiful,' he said.

In the morning Lancelot rode back to Camelot, and Bors and Lionel went with him; and Arthur and Guenever and all the knights of the Round Table were glad at their coming. Arthur led the way that they might sit down to eat, and called for the meat to be brought.

'My lord king,' said Sir Kay, 'today is the feast of Whitsunday; if you eat before you have seen a marvel or heard of an adventure, you will break your old custom.'

Arthur laughed. 'I had forgotten the custom in the joy of having our good Lancelot here with us when I had not thought to see him again so soon. Let us wait, by all means, for a marvel.'

But at that very moment a young squire came hurrying in and knelt before the king, breathless and excited. 'Down on the river there is a strange thing, my lord king. A great block of marble floating on the water, and in the marble a sword.'

'A wonder for us already,' said Arthur eagerly. 'Let us go and see this thing.'

Led by Arthur and Guenever, all the knights and their ladies hurried to the river's edge, and there, as the squire had said, floating on the water within reach of the bank, as though it were no heavier than a feather, was a great block of marble, and in the marble a sword with a jewelled hilt. On the marble was written in letters of gold, 'This sword can never be taken from hence save by him who is the best knight in the land. And those who try and fail to draw it forth shall in time receive a wound from it.'

At once Arthur turned to Lancelot. 'This sword must be for you, for you are without a doubt the best knight in the land.'

But Lancelot looked long at the sword and knew in his heart that it was not for him, and he shook his head. 'That sword will never be mine,' he said. And for all Arthur's protests and Guenever's entreaties, he would not lay his hand on the hilt.

Then Arthur turned to Gawaine. 'Since Lancelot will not, good nephew, do you try to draw out the sword.'

'If it is your command, my lord king,' said Gawaine, 'I will attempt it.' And he took hold of the hilt of the sword and tried with all his strength to draw it forth, but it would not move.

And someone said to Gawaine, 'It would have been best had you not set your hand to the sword. Do you not see what is written on the marble concerning those who try to draw it forth and fail?'

Young Sir Percival stepped forward. 'I am in no way the best knight in the land,' he said, 'but if ill fortune is to come to Sir Gawaine through this thing, then I would share in it.' And he took hold of the sword. Yet by him also it could not be drawn forth.

While Arthur stood dismayed at the failure of his knights, Sir Kay spoke to him. 'We have indeed seen a marvel enough to satisfy us all today. Give the word for us to return to the castle, and let our meal begin.'

So Arthur and the knights and their ladies returned to the great hall of the castle, and each knight seated himself in his place at the Round Table. And since by this time, from the best knights in his land Arthur had found the full number, of the hundred and forty places only one was empty, and that was the Perilous Chair of which Merlin had said many years before, 'No knight shall sit here save only one, and the time for him to be of your company is not yet come.'

But no sooner was each knight in his place than there came into the hall an old man leading a youth. This youth wore armour, but he carried no shield, and an empty scabbard hung by his side. 'I bring you here, my lord king, a new-made knight,' said the old man. 'Welcome him, for one day he shall do a marvellous thing.'

And when Lancelot looked up, he saw that the youth was Galahad, whom he had knighted in the nunnery.

The old man led Galahad to the Perilous Chair, beside which Lancelot sat. 'This,' he said, 'is your place.' And before the eyes of all gathered there, there appeared on the Perilous Chair the name of Sir Galahad. Galahad sat down, while all wondered at it, and without another word the old man went away. And Lancelot, watching him closely, knew suddenly who Galahad was, and he was filled with a great pride in his son.

'After we have eaten,' said Arthur, 'Sir Galahad shall see the marvel of the sword in the block of marble that floats on the river. But for now let us be merry.'

Later, all the knights and their ladies stood once more on the bank of the river, and Arthur showed Galahad the block of marble with the sword held fast in it. 'Two of my best knights have tried to draw it forth and failed,' he said. 'Is that not strange?'

But Galahad shook his head. 'It is not strange, my lord king,' he answered quietly, 'for this adventure is not theirs but mine. And to this end I brought no sword with me, but only an empty scabbard.' Then he took hold of the hilt of the sword, and with no effort drew it forth, while all there marvelled at it.

And a damsel called out to Sir Lancelot, 'It is not now as it was yesterday, Sir Lancelot. Now you are no longer the best knight in the land, for you have been surpassed by another. And should you still make claim to be the first

168

of all the fellowship of the Round Table, then would you be no better than a liar, for see how young Sir Galahad has drawn out the sword which you dared not touch.'

But Lancelot answered her gently. 'Lady, I have never considered myself the best knight in the land. It was but a name which others gave to me.'

Wondering at the adventure they had seen, they all returned to the castle, and Queen Guenever asked to speak with Galahad. When he stood before her she looked long at him and at last she said, 'Is your mother the Lady Elaine, King Pelles' daughter?'

'She is, good queen.'

'Then your father must be Lancelot, for you are much like him.' And when Galahad did not answer her, she said, with pride and a challenge in her voice, 'You need have no shame that Sir Lancelot is your father, for he is the most courteous knight of all, and the bravest, and there is no man so handsome in all the land.'

'Indeed, good queen,' said Galahad, 'you speak truly and I do not deny it.'

She was pleased by his answer, 'May you too be a great knight,' she said. And she smiled, no longer jealous.

That evening when they had sat down to feast, with Galahad among them, there came a sound as of thunder and a bright light filled the hall, and each knight saw a shining vessel covered with a silken cloth, that went the length of the hall, carried by unseen hands, and there came from it a scent as of the loveliest incense. Then it vanished as suddenly as it had come.

'It was the Holy Grail,' said Arthur. 'The Holy Grail from which Our Lord and His Disciples drank. My friends, we have been granted a sight of the Holy Grail.'

And everyone was silent in awe and wonder, until Sir Gawaine said, 'But we did not see the Grail in all its glory, for it was covered by a cloth. What blessed joy it would be to see it as it is, in all its brightness. I for one, shall not rest until I have looked upon the Grail uncovered. For a year and a day I shall search for it, if it is to be found.'

And immediately all the knights cried out with one accord that they too would seek the Holy Grail and look upon it unhidden.

But Arthur wept and said, 'Good nephew Gawaine, you have taken all my knights from me and scattered the fellowship of the Round Table. For this is a hard quest upon which you will all go, and many of you will surely never return.'

'Be comforted, my lord king,' said Lancelot, 'for this quest will be a great honour to you and to us alike. And since a knight must die sometime, how better can he die than in quest of the Holy Grail?'

Arthur sighed. 'You above all others, Lancelot, I would not lose.'

In the morning the knights armed themselves and made ready to go on the quest, and when they were prepared it was seen that there were one hundred and forty of them, even the whole fellowship of the Round Table. After they had heard mass they took leave of Arthur and his queen. But for weeping Guenever turned away and went alone to her room, and she thought that her heart was breaking.

Lancelot went after her. 'You have betrayed us, Lancelot,' she said. 'Is this your love for Arthur, that you will not stay with him?' She wept as though she could never cease. 'Is this your love for me, Lancelot, that you will leave me now?'

'Would you have me hold back from a quest such as this?' he asked gently. 'Would you wish me alone of all the fellowship of the Round Table to remain safely at your side?' He took her hands in his. 'Guenever, I will return to you. I promise that whatever befalls, I will return to you.' But she did not answer him, and after a time he said, 'Do not let me leave you like this. Let me go with a blessing from you.'

She tried to smile at him. 'May God keep you, Lancelot, and send you back to me.'

From the courtyard of the castle of Camelot, and along the streets of the town, rode the knights of the Round Table on the start of their quest. At the town gates they parted, some riding alone and others in company, in one direction or another, and all high in the hope of seeing with their own eyes the Grail uncovered.

But of all those who set out, there were to be no more than three knights who were to achieve the quest of the Holy Grail.

XVII

The Death of Uwaine

OF all King Arthur's knights who rode forth from Camelot to seek the Holy Grail, few were more eager than Sir Gawaine who had been the first to call the other knights to the quest. As he had bidden her farewell, his lady, who had once been so ugly but now was so beautiful, had wept, and he had found it hard to leave her. Yet once out of the town of Camelot, his spirits rose, and he rode on alone, refusing all company, ever watching for an adventure in which he might show his skill. But he met with no adventure of any kind.

One night he rested at an abbey, and asked of the monks if any other knights of the Round Table had passed that way. 'But a few days since, young Sir Galahad was here,' replied the abbot.

'Had he met with any adventures on his way?' asked Gawaine.

'He told me of one.'

'I would that I had ridden in his company,' laughed Gawaine, 'for neither adventure nor jousting has come my way since I left Camelot.'

The abbot smiled. 'If you set your mind to it, you may yet catch up with him.'

Gawaine considered. 'He will be hard to find,' he said, 'for he bears no shield and may be known by no device.'

'He bears a shield now,' said the abbot, 'so you may know him by it. It is a white shield with a red cross upon it.'

While Gawaine and the abbot were speaking together, Sir Gareth rode up to the abbey and asked shelter.
Gawaine greeted him with joy. 'You, brother, are the
first of our fellowship whom I have met with since
I left Camelot. Have you found any adventures on the
way?'

'Little enough,' replied Gareth, 'yet I will tell you of
them.'

'You are more fortunate than I,' sighed Gawaine, 'for I
have found none.'

The knights and the abbot talked together until supper
time, and the next morning, after they had heard mass in
the abbey, the two brothers rode away. On the highway
they fell in with Sir Uwaine, their cousin, and the three of
them kept together for company.

'What adventures have you met with since you left
Camelot?' asked Gawaine.

'Why, none at all,' laughed Uwaine. 'Perhaps your
fellowship will bring me better fortune, good cousin.'

'Not mine,' said Gawaine, 'for all adventures keep from
me these days.'

But the very same day they saw, riding towards them,
seven knights who seemed as though they fled from an
enemy. The seven knights reined in their horses. 'Who are
you?' their leader asked.

'We are Uwaine, Gawaine, and Gareth of the Round
Table,' answered Gawaine.

'We have been driven forth from the Castle of the
Maidens which we held by force of arms for seven years,'
said the strange knights, 'and that by one Sir Galahad of
King Arthur's court. Therefore for his sake we hate all

those of the Round Table and will destroy any we meet.'
And with that all the seven knights fell upon Arthur's
nephews.

'An adventure at last,' cried Gawaine, and lowered his
lance and charged.

The battle was short but hard, and at the end of it all the
seven strange knights lay dead. 'Now let us ride to this
Castle of the Maidens,' said Gawaine, 'and perchance we
shall catch up with Sir Galahad and have some adventures
in his company.' But when they came to the castle, Galahad was already gone.

'Truly,' said Gawaine, 'we are ill starred on this quest.
For if any knight should achieve the quest of the Holy
Grail, I believe it to be Sir Galahad.'

'He is young,' said Gareth, 'and untried. If any achieve
the Grail it will be Lancelot.' For of all knights Gareth
loved best Sir Lancelot.

'Galahad is young,' said Uwaine thoughtfully, 'and for
that reason his mind will be set upon one thing only: the
sight of the Holy Grail. He has as yet no wordly ambitions
as have we other knights with our past glories to exceed.
He has no damsel whom he loves; but older knights have,
as have we three, their own ladies.'

There, outside the Castle of the Maidens, the three
cousins parted company and went in different ways. 'I
think,' said Gawaine, as he bade the others farewell, 'that
as soon as I may, I shall find for myself a shield without a
device. Perhaps if men believe me to be a knight of no
account I may meet with some adventures.'

Uwaine looked at the black shield which he had carried
since he first had sworn to serve the Lady of the Fountain.

'Perhaps I shall do likewise,' he said. 'You and I, Gawaine, bear shields which are too well known.'

After they had parted, Gawaine did as he had said, putting aside his crimson shield with the golden pentangle and taking a white one without a device. But still he met with no adventures, nor with any of his friends, until the summer was passed and Michaelmas was come. And then one day he saw Sir Ector de Maris, Lancelot's brother, riding on ahead. He spurred on his horse and caught up with him, and at first Sir Ector de Maris did not know him, because of the white shield which he carried. 'I am Gawaine,' he laughed, 'and never was I so glad to see anyone. For I have lacked both company and adventures for many days.'

'I have met with a score of knights of our fellowship and they all complain the same,' said Ector de Maris. 'Truly, it seems, this quest of the Holy Grail has brought little adventure to any of us.'

'I am weary of it,' sighed Gawaine, 'and I would I were back in Camelot with my lady.'

They rode on together a little way, and Gawaine asked, 'What of Lancelot, how has he fared?'

'I am seeking him now, but have so far no word of him.'

'Then let us seek him together,' suggested Gawaine. And the two of them promised that they would not leave each other's company until either they had met with Lancelot or achieved the quest and were come home to Arthur's court.

For many days they travelled together, and one night darkness found them far from any dwelling save only a ruined chapel, and there they decided to spend the night.

Being tired, they both fell asleep in spite of the discomfort of their resting-place, and while he slept Gawaine had a strange dream. In this dream he saw a wide meadow in which grazed a herd of bulls, one hundred and forty in all. And of these bulls, three were white and the others black. And while Gawaine watched them in his dream, it seemed to him that they said amongst themselves, 'Let us find better pasture,' and one after another the whole herd wandered away until the meadow was empty. And then, after some time had passed, a number of the bulls returned, but they were thin and weary and it seemed as though they had not found that which they had sought. And though in his dream Gawaine watched for a long time, there were never again the full one hundred and forty in the meadow. And of the white bulls, no more than one returned.

When he awoke, he told his dream to Ector de Maris. 'What think you that such a dream signifies?' he asked.

But Ector de Maris shook his head and answered, 'I cannot tell. Let us seek out one skilled in reading such things, that he may explain it to us.'

So they went to an old hermit and Gawaine told him all his dream and asked, 'Tell me, good father, do you know what that dream should mean?'

After the hermit had thought for a while, he said, 'Those bulls which you saw in your dream were the knights of the Round Table who number one hundred and forty. And when they left their meadow to seek new pasture, it was when the knights rode on the quest of the Holy Grail. Some of them will return to King Arthur's court, and some will come home no more. But only three out of all the great number will achieve their quest and see uncovered the Holy Grail, and those are the three knights whom in your dream you saw as the three white bulls. Yet of them, two shall perish and only one return. That, my son, is the meaning of your dream.'

For a time Gawaine was silent, then he asked, 'Who are the three who shall achieve the quest?'

The hermit smiled and answered gently, 'You are not one of them, my son, for you think too much of the things of this world.'

'Since I shall not achieve the quest,' said Gawaine to Ector de Maris as they rode away from the hermit's house, 'I could as well abandon it, but that I swore to seek the Holy Grail for a full year and a day.' And he sighed, thinking of Camelot and his lady, both still half a year away.

Gawaine and Ector de Maris rode through a valley and there they met with a knight who bore a plain white shield and who offered to joust with them. Gawaine was overjoyed. 'This is but the second time that I shall have matched myself with a knight since I left Camelot, so this battle is mine, Sir Ector de Maris, and the next we meet shall be yours.' And he rode hard upon the strange knight and so eagerly did he smite him in his pleasure to be fighting once again, that his lance passed right through the stranger's armour and into his body so that he was thrown from his horse with the broken head of the lance in his wound. Gawaine dismounted and drew his sword, but the other knight had no strength to rise. 'Will you yield to me, or be slain?' asked Gawaine.

'I am slain already, sir stranger. Of your charity, carry me to the abbey which stands near by, that I may die in peace.'

But when Gawaine and Ector de Maris would have raised him up, he was too weak to bear it; so they laid him back upon the grass, and Gawaine unfastened his helmet and put it off and saw that he was Uwaine. 'What have I done?' he cried. 'I have slain my own cousin.'

'Who are you then?' asked Uwaine.

'It is I, Gawaine. I did not know you from the white shield which you bore.'

'And I did not know you, cousin, because you carried not your golden pentangle.' Uwaine smiled, but his voice was weak. 'Do you remember, Gawaine, that time before when we fought and did not know each other, beside the fountain in the valley?'

But Gawaine could not answer for weeping.

'Do not grieve,' said Uwaine, 'for all men must die sometime, and I could not have died by a nobler hand than yours. When you come again to Camelot, tell our uncle the king of me, and my father King Uriens, and all our friends, and give my last greeting to my Lady of the Fountain.'

'I will do that,' said Gawaine.

And after a little time, Uwaine died.

From then Gawaine and Ector de Maris had no inclination for any further adventures, and they rode whither they cared not and met with no one who knew them, until a certain day when they came by a castle in which was being held a tournament. And that it might in a little comfort his companion, Sir Ector de Maris said, 'Let us join with those gathered here, and fight.' Gawaine cared nothing either way, so they rode into the lists. And there they saw a knight who performed great feats, and he carried a white shield with a red cross upon it. 'It is Sir Galahad,' said Ector de Maris.

'I have no heart to tourney with him or any man,' said Gawaine; yet to please Ector de Maris he took part in the fighting, and by chance he came up against Sir Galahad and received from him a mighty blow of his sword, which cut through his helmet even to the bone. Ector de Maris carried Gawaine from the fight and sent for one skilled in medicine to bind up his wound.

'Do you remember,' asked Gawaine, 'what was written on the block of marble that was floating on the river near by to Camelot on Whitsunday? How any man who tried to draw forth the sword and failed would receive a wound from it? I tried to draw it forth and failed, where Galahad succeeded, and it was Galahad's sword that cut me down today.'

'The quest is over for you,' said Ector de Maris, 'though the year is not yet up.'

'But it is not over for you, my friend. Leave me here to be healed of my wound and ride on alone. For the hermit never told me that it would not be you who saw the Grail.'

Yet Ector de Maris would not leave Gawaine, and he remained with him until he was so much recovered that he might return to Camelot. And there they were both welcomed by Arthur and Guenever, even though they had failed in their quest; and as for Gawaine's lady, she cared nothing for quests so long as her lord was safely home.

XVIII

Lancelot and Galahad

WHEN Sir Lancelot rode forth from Camelot on the quest of the Holy Grail, he journeyed without adventure for the first few days. Then in a forest he fell in with young Sir Percival. They greeted each other gladly and rode on together.

'In this forest,' said Percival, 'there dwells a holy woman. She is my mother's sister and would give her blessing on my quest. I was even now seeking her out. Will you not come with me?'

So together Lancelot and Percival rode to the holy woman's hermitage. But when they came there, before they could dismount, a knight came riding towards them, carrying a white shield with a red cross, and the device was one which they did not recognize. This knight cried out to them to joust with him. Lancelot rode against the stranger and such was the force of their meeting that the lances of both were broken. Then, without dismounting from his horse, the unknown knight drew his sword and rode at Sir Percival, giving him a mighty blow on the head, so that his helmet was broken and the sword cut through to the bone.

At the sound of their fighting the holy woman came forth from her house and stood watching them. 'Truly,' she called to the strange knight, 'you must be the first knight of all the land, that you can strike such blows as that. There is only one name you can bear.'

But when the knight heard her he rode quickly away, as though he did not wish to be known. And as he went, Lancelot knew him. 'It was Galahad,' he said.

'If it was Galahad,' said Percival, 'then was the writing true which was on the block of marble that was floating on the river, for it is a sad stroke he has given me with the sword that he won.'

'You shall stay here and be healed of it, nephew,' said the holy woman.

'Remain with me, Sir Lancelot,' said Percival, 'and when I am whole again we can ride forth once more.'

But Lancelot shook his head. 'I would speak with Galahad. If I ride fast enough, perhaps I shall catch up with him.' And with a farewell to the holy woman and to Percival, he mounted his horse and galloped away. But though his horse was one of the best in the land, and though he pressed on eagerly, he gained no further sight of his son.

Twilight found him, sad at heart, in the very midst of the forest with no human habitation near, but seeing a wayside cross that had been set up for the comfort of those who passed by, he put off his armour and tethered his horse to a tree, and lying down at the foot of the cross, he laid his head on his shield and slept.

But while he was sleeping a knight came by who had through misadventure lost his horse, and seeing Lancelot's fine white charger, he quietly untethered it and rode away, taking with him Lancelot's armour and sword as well, for they were better than his.

When Lancelot awoke in the morning and found his horse and his armour gone, his heart grew even heavier than it had been the evening before. 'Truly,' he thought, 'I am having but ill fortune on this quest.' And sadly he set himself to walk on through the forest, carrying his shield.

At midday he came upon the cell of a hermit who welcomed him kindly and shared his simple meal with him. Lancelot told the hermit his name, and how he was on a quest for the Holy Grail, and how his horse and his armour and his sword had been stolen from him.

'A horse and armour and a sword shall I find for you, said the hermit, 'and you may continue on your adventure. But do not think that you will ever achieve your quest. It is only those who have no thought for the things of this world who may see the Grail uncovered. Those whose love is for holy things alone are worthy of such a privilege. Give up all earthly love and pride and do all your deeds for the glory of God alone, and you may yet see the Holy Grail.'

And Lancelot wept, for though he longed to achieve the quest, he could not leave his love for Queen Guenever, and all his knightly deeds had ever been done in her honour, though only he and she knew that.

Sir Lancelot remained with the hermit for three days, and then, early on the fourth day, while Lancelot still slept, the hermit left his cell and went forth. When he returned he was leading an old horse. 'I could find you no better mount than this,' he said. But Lancelot thanked him gratefully. Then the hermit went to a chest which stood by the wall, and from it he took old armour and a rusty sword and a lance. 'I fear they are not worthy of Sir Lancelot of the Lake,' he said.

'Good hermit,' said Lancelot, 'all kindly gifts are worthy of him to whom they are given, no matter who he may be.' And he armed himself and mounted the horse, and with thanks to the hermit rode on through the forest, thus journeying for several days.

But before he left the forest for the open land, he saw riding towards him a knight on a white horse which he knew for his own. Immediately he challenged the stranger, demanding his horse and his armour, and the knight prepared to defend himself. Lancelot attacked so mightily that at his first blow the other knight was thrown to the ground and lay there stunned. Lancelot dismounted and took off his armour from the fallen knight and put it on, and girded his own sword about him once again. Then thinking, 'It is an ill thing for a knight to be without horse and armour, as I well know,' he tethered the old horse to a tree and laid beside it the armour and the sword which the hermit had given him, so that the knight might find them when he came to his senses again. Then he mounted his own horse and rode on.

But before many days had passed, Lancelot had lost his good horse again, and this time for ever. For he came to a wide and rushing river, and when he had crossed over and his horse was barely out of the torrent it had so bravely swum across, a huge knight in black armour, on a great black steed, came by with a mighty shout, and with one sweep of his sword he slew Lancelot's horse and was gone. Lancelot was grieved for the death of his horse, for it had been a good friend to him, and he feared that the giant in black armour could have been no human knight, so swiftly had he come and gone.

That night Lancelot lay down to sleep on the bank of the river, and to the sound of its waters he fell asleep. As he slept he had a dream. In this dream a voice told him to go to the seashore and there enter the first ship that he saw.

When he awoke the voice still seemed so real to him that he took up his shield and his sword and followed the course of the river down to the sea. The shore was deserted and the sea stretched wide before him with never a ship in sight, but believing in his dream, Lancelot waited patiently, and after a time he saw a ship approaching the land. When she was close in to the shore, Lancelot did not hesitate but leapt aboard, and at once the ship moved out to sea again. And Lancelot saw that he was alone on a ship which moved of herself, needing neither rowers nor wind, yet a great peace came over him and he was in no way afraid.

On this strange ship all things were done of themselves. When Lancelot was hungry, dishes of meat and bread and fruits appeared before him; and when he was thirsty, there beside him was a cup of wine. And so it went for several days, until in the distance land appeared, growing ever nearer until the ship touched the shore. And then Lancelot saw a knight riding towards the sea, who, when he was close to the ship, dismounted and turned away his horse and leapt aboard.

'You are welcome, stranger,' said Lancelot. He could not see the shield which the other knight bore, for it was covered by his cloak. 'What is your name?' he asked. 'For I am Lancelot of the Lake.'

The knight stepped forward, 'I am Galahad, your son.' He put off his helmet and knelt for his father's blessing, and Lancelot raised him up and kissed him. And there was great joy in the hearts of both at this meeting, with either asking the other how he had come to that place.

'I followed a voice I heard in a dream,' said Lancelot.

'And I,' said Galahad, 'was likewise sent by heaven.'

And when they had eaten and drunk together, they sat and talked, and much had they to tell each other. Galahad related to his father all his adventures since he had started on the quest for the Holy Grail, and while he spoke the ship moved gently out to sea once more.

'First,' said Galahad, 'must I tell you how I came by my shield, for it is a strange story. Some days after King Arthur had sent us all forth from Camelot, I came at evening to an abbey where the monks received me kindly, and there I found another of the knights of the Round Table, and he told me his name was Bagdemagus.'

'I know him,' said Lancelot. 'He is a bold and hardy knight, and father to Sir Meliagrance.'

'While we supped together,' Galahad went on, 'Sir

Bagdemagus told me of a wondrous shield that the monks had, hidden in their chapel, of which it was said that no man might carry it save one, unless he came to misfortune thereby. "Tomorrow," Bagdemagus told me, "I shall try the adventure of this shield, come what may." And he asked that if he failed, I should also try. And since he was so bold himself, and urged me to it, what could I do, my father, but promise to do likewise? So all I said was, "Since I have no shield of my own, I should be glad to gain one." In the morning a monk showed us where the shield was hidden, behind the altar, and it was white with a red cross, even that shield which you see there. The monk told us how it might not be carried save by one knight alone, but the name of that knight the monk did not know. So Sir Bagdemagus took the shield and I wished him good fortune and he rode off with his squire. Within three hours his squire was back at the abbey, bearing the shield, and he told how Sir Bagdemagus had been challenged by a knight in white armour riding upon a white horse, with a light about his helmet that made him seem unearthly. And when Sir Bagdemagus would have held the shield before him, it gave him no protection and he was so sorely wounded that he might no longer fight. "Then," said the squire, "did the knight in white armour take up the shield and bid me bring it to you, for he said it should belong to Galahad and to no man else." And that, father, was how I came by my shield. It is strange that it should have been waiting for me in that abbey for so many years.'

'It will have been after that when Sir Percival and I met with you in the forest, for when we saw you, you had your shield,' said Lancelot. He smiled and asked, 'Why did you ride away, Galahad? I followed, but I could not catch up with you.'

'Did it seem very discourteous? I longed to stay, but I wanted to have a real adventure to tell you of before we spoke together. Can you understand how I felt?'

And Lancelot, who had once been fifteen himself, laughed and said, 'I understand. Now tell me what happened next.'

'Why, I had that real adventure,' said Galahad. 'I rode westward and in time I came to a great castle on the bank of a wide river. Here I was halted by an old man with a long white beard. He told me that the castle was known as the Castle of the Maidens and warned me to beware of the seven evil knights who dwelt there. But I was in search of an adventure, and so I rode on towards the castle. A band of damsels whom I met with called out to me and also warned me from going there, telling me that no strangers were ever welcomed at the Castle of the Maidens. When I asked them why this was, one of them said, "When the old lord of the castle died, seven years ago, he left no son but only two daughters, and seven knights who were his enemies took the castle by force from the damsels, and ever since they have held it, and ill have they treated all those who are in their power." At that I thought how good a deed it would be to drive out the seven knights and free the castle with God's help, and so I rode on, even to the castle gates, and there a squire came out to me and told me how the seven knights had seen me from the castle keep and were arming to come out and fight. And close upon him they came, riding forth and calling to me to defend myself. I cried to them that I would give battle to them one by one, but they only laughed and said that they ever held together to fight, the seven of them, against a single enemy or against twenty. And then, father, I was a little afraid, for never even in a tourneying had I fought with seven knights at once, but I put my faith in my shield with the red cross and in my good sword that I had drawn out from the block of marble on the river at Camelot, and I met their charge as boldly as I might. It was a great battle that we had there, father, and I could not now tell you how it went, for I was too hard pressed, and it seems to me that when a man is fighting he has no time to watch how the battle goes. But I know that I struck down two of them, and I know that my lance broke on the shield of another, and I know too that suddenly they were flying from me, right across the plain before the castle, away from the river. Then I entered the castle and everyone greeted me joyfully. And the next day word was brought to us of how the seven knights had in their flight met with Sir Gawaine and Sir Uwaine and Sir Gareth and been slain by them. So at last, after seven years, the Castle of the Maidens is free, and the old lord's daughters rule there now.'

'It was a good deed you did that day, my son,' said Lancelot. 'God grant you many years to bring such happiness to others.'

'After I had left the Castle of the Maidens,' said Galahad, 'I went on alone, and in one place and another I took part in tournaments, and always I was looking for you, my father, for we had spoken so little at Camelot, and now I had an adventure to tell you of, and I hoped that you might have a little pride in me.'

'I have more than a little pride in you,' said Lancelot, smiling.

'But tell me, father,' asked Galahad, 'what of Sir Percival whom I met with in the forest outside the house of the holy woman? I saw him once again, many days later, but we had no chance to speak.'

'I left him with the holy woman, for you had wounded him sorely when you fought with him.'

Galahad was distressed. 'That grieves me, for it was through no will of mine. I did but wish to joust with him.'

So Lancelot told Galahad of how Percival had tried to draw forth the sword from the block of marble that was floating on the river, risking a wound from it that he might keep Gawaine company. 'Therefore,' he said, 'the wound you gave him was no more than the fulfilment of the writing on the marble, and could not have been avoided.'

Lancelot and Galahad were on the ship together for half a year, and great joy they had in each other's company; and a deep affection grew between them, so that neither felt the lack of all those fifteen years when they had not been together nor known each other in the way of other fathers and sons.

But there came a day when the ship touched land, and while they stood watching from the deck, a knight all in white armour with a strange brightness about his helmet and leading a white horse came riding across the shore to the very water's edge and called out to Galahad, 'It is time you were gone from your father's side, for there is a great deed for you yet to do. Come from the ship and continue on the quest of the Holy Grail.' And with that he was gone, leaving the white horse.

Lancelot and Galahad came from the ship on to the shore. 'God keep you, father,' said Galahad, 'and may we meet again soon.'

But when they looked into each other's eyes, they both knew that they would never meet again. 'You are destined to do great things, Galahad. I will always pray for you,' said Lancelot.

And Galahad smiled as well as he might for his sorrow. 'There is no one else whose prayers I would rather have.'

They embraced and Galahad mounted the white horse and rode away swiftly along the coast, while Lancelot watched him out of sight; then slowly and sadly he returned to the ship, and at once she moved out to sea.

After a time she touched land again, as evening was coming on, and Lancelot went ashore; and immediately the ship vanished, leaving him, as though he were meant to be gone from her. Since he had no horse, he walked inland, and at midnight he reached a castle and looked up at it by moonlight. It was a strange and hallowed place, like to no other Lancelot had seen before, and as he stood there he was filled with awe, and he thought, 'If the Holy Grail is anywhere, it is in this castle.' He walked about the castle walls until he came to a little door, but when he would have entered it, he saw how it was guarded by two lions who growled and lashed their tails at his approach. At first he hesitated and half drew his sword, and then, after reflection, thrust his sword back into its scabbard and walked forward unarmed. And when he was right by the angry lions, they ceased their growling and lay down and suffered him to pass through the door.

Once within the castle there was no one to prevent him

from going where he would, and he wandered here and there in the darkness until he stood before a closed door and saw coming from it a brightness that filled the corridor, and he knew that behind that door was the Holy Grail. He tried to open the door, but it could not be opened, yet a sweet scent as of incense came from the room and the sound of a voice singing that was more lovely than any earthly voice.

Despairing, Lancelot knelt down to pray, asking that though unworthy to see the Grail unhidden, he might be allowed just once again to see something of what he sought. He rose and the door opened slowly, and within the chamber he saw a table of silver and upon it the Holy Grail, brightly shining and covered with crimson silk, and he knelt again and worshipped it. And with the glory of the sight Lancelot swooned and fell senseless.

When he came to himself and opened his eyes once more, he found he was in that same castle, lying in a bed and tended by strangers. 'Where am I?' he asked.

'You are in the Castle of Carbonek,' they told him.

'Here in this castle,' said Lancelot, 'God has shown me much mercy, for unworthy though I am, he has given me a partial sight of that which I have come so far to seek.'

He rose and put on his armour and the people of Carbonek gave him a horse, and he rode back once more to the sea, where he found a ship to carry him to the land of Britain. And so he came to Camelot where he had not been for a twelvemonth.

He found that Sir Gawaine and Sir Ector de Maris were already there, and together with King Arthur they gave him a great welcome and asked him all his adventures, marvelling at what he told them of Galahad.

And Guenever was filled with a deep joy and pride, that though Lancelot had not seen the Grail uncovered, he had at least gained sight of it again. But above all, she was happy that he was safely returned.

XIX

The Quest of the Holy Grail

AFTER Lancelot had left Sir Percival at the house of the holy woman, Percival fretted much that he had not defended himself against Galahad. 'If only this wound of mine were healed, I would ride after him,' he complained.

The holy woman smiled. 'Would you fight with him, good nephew?' she asked. 'Truly, you are like your father and your brothers, always at jousting and tourneying. Would you end as they did and give yet more sorrow to your mother?'

And Percival was ashamed at her words and only said, 'But he is a fine knight, and I would one day be matched against him.'

'It would avail you little if you were,' said the holy woman, 'for I know that he is blessed by heaven and may be overcome by no mortal man.'

Percival thought over her words in silence, and then he asked, 'Good aunt, is it Galahad who will achieve the quest of the Holy Grail?'

'That is as God wills, nephew,' she replied.

'When I am healed of this wound,' said Percival, 'I would seek Galahad in friendship.' And he waited impatiently until the time when he could ride forth again.

Then one morning he bade his aunt farewell, and she gave him her blessing as he rode from the little house in the forest to look for Galahad. Yet it was many days before he met with him, and even then he had no chance to speak to him, and this was how it came to pass.

As Percival rode through a valley he came upon a score of men-at-arms who walked about the bier of a knight who had been slain. When they saw Percival they called out and asked him whence he came, and he replied, 'I am from the court of King Arthur.'

Immediately the men-at-arms cried out, 'Let us slay him, for our dead lord was ever against King Arthur's knights while he lived.' And forthwith seven of them rushed upon him at once, while others struck down and killed his horse, so that Percival fell to the ground surrounded by a number of armed men all intent on slaying him.

'This,' thought Percival, 'is the end of my questing for ever,' and from the ground he hacked with his sword at arms and legs; but such was the press about him that his blows had but little effect.

Yet even as he gave up hope, he heard a young voice which cried out, 'For shame, that one knight should be set upon by so many men.' And he was aware of a knight on horseback who attacked his assailants, so that they were forced to defend themselves, leaving Percival to struggle to his feet and join in the attack. And as they fought, Percival saw that the knight who had come to his rescue carried a white shield with a red cross upon it, and he knew that it was Galahad.

At every stroke Galahad felled a man, so that at last, from fear of his blows, those of the men-at-arms who remained on their feet fled to the safety of some near by trees and Galahad rode after them. Percival called to him, but Galahad did not hear, and though Percival followed, he could not catch up with him. Then weary and horse-less and dispirited, he sat down and wondered what he should do.

'To find a horse must be my first task,' he thought. But it was growing dark and he had no idea how far from human company he might be. 'It would be better to sleep here for tonight,' he thought, 'and walk on tomorrow when it is light.' And he lay down, and after a time he slept.

At midnight he awoke suddenly and saw standing before him a tall damsel in a dark cloak. 'What do you here, Sir Percival?' she demanded.

'No more than try to sleep, lady,' he answered.

'You lack a horse,' she said. 'If you will give me your word to come to me when at any time I send for you, then shall I lend to you my own horse to travel where you will.'

Percival was grateful for her offer. 'I will serve you whenever you bid me, lady.'

In an instant she had gone, and soon she was back again, leading by the bridle a huge black horse with eyes which glowed in the moonlight like embers. 'I shall ever be grateful to you, lady,' he said. And even as he mounted, the horse galloped away with him.

It seemed to Percival that never had he travelled so fast. Over hills and valleys, over rough ground and smooth, the black horse carried him, until in the space of one hour they had done a four days' journeying; and Percival saw how the horse had brought him to the brink of a wide and rushing river.

He had no more than time to hear the roaring of the

waters and shudder at their darkness before the horse had leapt into the torrent, and all he could do to hold the creature back was of no avail. 'Now heaven protect me, for I shall surely be drowned,' thought Percival, and he signed himself with the cross. And immediately the horse disappeared from under him and was gone with a great scream of rage; and Percival, struggling in the water, saw how the horse had been a fiend that would have destroyed him. With difficulty he dragged himself to the river's bank, and knelt and gave thanks for his deliverance.

In the morning, when the sun rose, he found himself in a wild and barren land with no habitation or tree in sight. 'I will follow the course of the river down to the sea,' he thought, 'and maybe there I shall find a ship, or men to tell me where I am.' And taking up his shield and his sword, he set off.

It was many days later, after a weary walk, that he came at last to the sea, and there, close in to the shore, he saw a ship, and no one in her. He went aboard, and, as Lancelot had done upon another ship, he found all manner of food and drink as though prepared against his coming. 'I will wait in this ship and see what befalls,' thought Percival. 'For this is no ordinary ship, and it may well be an adventure.'

When Sir Bors, who was the cousin of Sir Lancelot, rode out from Camelot on the quest of the Holy Grail, he rode alone and not with his brother Lionel. Along the roadway he saw a priest riding on a palfrey, and because the quest meant much to him, he determined to ask this priest's advice as to how best the quest of the Grail might be achieved. He reined in his horse and greeted the priest. 'Good day, sir priest. I would ask counsel of you.'

The priest smiled kindly. 'My house is near,' he said. 'Come there with me and pass the night beneath my roof, and we will talk together.'

So Bors told him how he longed to see the Holy Grail uncovered. 'Only a knight whose mind is free from the ambitions of this world may see the Holy Grail, my son.'

'I believe that I have no worldly ambitions, father,' said Bors earnestly.

'I have a little knowledge of what things shall be,' said the priest, 'and I know that though but few of the knights of the Round Table shall achieve this quest, you will be one of them.'

And Bors gave thanks to heaven for the priest's words.

In the morning Bors rode again on his way, and at nightfall found himself before a castle where he asked shelter. The lady of the castle welcomed him and bade him sup with her.

As they ate, a squire came, saying, 'Mistress, your sister sends word to you that tomorrow her champion Sir Pridam the Black will be here and ready to fight for her cause.'

'That,' said the lady of the castle, 'is the worst news of any that you could have brought to me.'

'Is there a way in which I could serve you?' asked Sir Bors.

The lady wept. 'For long has my sister tried to take my lands from me, and now has she found a champion to fight for her, while I have no knight to defend my rights.'

'Lady,' said Bors, 'you have been a kindly hostess, it

would be but courtesy in a guest to offer you his aid. Give me leave to fight in your name tomorrow and perhaps save your lands for you.'

Gratefully the lady dried her tears and thanked him and sent word to her sister that she too had a champion to fight for her. 'But,' she said, turning to Bors, 'I beg of you to take care, for this Pridam is a doughty knight and it goes ill with most who joust with him.'

'With God's help, lady, I will do my best for you,' said Bors.

In the morning, came the lady's sister, and with her Sir Pridam the Black and all her followers; and a herald called out the names of the two knights who were to fight and the quarrel they fought in, and the sisters swore to respect the outcome of the battle.

Then Bors and Pridam met in the lists and Bors found that it was even as the lady had said, and Pridam was a strong and well-experienced knight, and much strength of his own did he need to oppose him. But he remembered how the lands and the castle belonged by right to his hostess, and he thought shame that so good and kind a lady should lose what was hers by right, and he fought as strongly as he could, riding at Sir Pridam until they had both unhorsed each other; and then they fought on foot with swords. And at last Sir Pridam began to tire, and when Bors saw this he pressed upon him harder than ever before, and finally he gave Sir Pridam such a mighty blow that he fell to the ground. And Bors smote off his helmet and bade him yield or be slain.

Sir Pridam the Black asked quarter of Bors, promising never more to take arms against the rightful lady of the castle, but instead ever to be ready to fight for her. And the lady's sister rode away with her followers, heavy at heart.

The lady would have given Bors great gifts for the service he had done her, but he refused, saying, 'I travel in quest of the Holy Grail; it is not fitting that I should travel richly.' And within a few days he was on his way again.

One morning as he rode through a forest clearing, he saw coming towards him two armed knights, and riding between them on a sorry nag, stripped of his armour and bound, was a man. And as they rode, the two knights would ever turn and strike him with rods which they carried. 'Here,' thought Bors, 'is some poor knight fallen into the hands of enemies. Shame it is that two knights should misuse another so.' And he made ready to challenge them when they came nearer.

But at that moment, from somewhere behind him in the forest, he heard a cry. Turning, he saw among the trees a damsel struggling in the arms of a knight who would have carried her off upon his horse. 'Here are two at once who need my help,' thought Bors. 'What shall I do?'

But while he hesitated he heard a familiar voice call out his name, and realized that the man whom the knights ill treated was his own brother Lionel. 'Bors,' cried Lionel again, 'make haste or I shall be slain.'

Bors held his lance in readiness to ride upon the knights, but even at the same moment the damsel caught sight of him, and breaking free from the knight who would have carried her off, she ran towards him. 'Good sir stranger, have pity on me,' she called. But in a moment her captor had caught up with her and was lifting her again upon his horse.

And to Bors it was the hardest decision that he had ever had to make. He thought, 'Lionel is a knight and brave, he will not fear death. And if he should be killed, then I can avenge him. But the damsel is weak and alone, and I cannot refuse her my help.'

So he rode against the knight who would have carried off the damsel and called to him to release her; and the knight set her down and prepared to meet Bors' charge. With his first blow Bors cut through the strange knight's shield and his armour and into his shoulder, so that he fell senseless. Then Bors turned to the damsel. 'How is it with you, lady?' he asked.

'It would have gone ill with me had you not come to my aid. Good knight, I beg of you to see me safely home.'

So Bors set her upon the fallen knight's horse and went with her through the forest, and soon they came upon twelve men-at-arms riding fast. The damsel said, 'They are my father's men and they will be seeking me.' And she called to them and told them how Bors had saved her. 'You will be welcome at my father's castle,' she said to Bors. 'I beg you, come and receive his thanks.'

'Forgive me, lady, if I seem discourteous, but there is a deed which I must do, a knight to whom I must give aid, before it is too late.' And hastily taking his leave, Bors rode swiftly back the way that they had come until he reached the place where he had seen his brother Lionel. Then following as well as he might the path which he thought his brother's captors would have taken, he hastened on. But though he searched for several days, he found no trace of Lionel or of those who held him, so that he was in despair.

And then, on a day when he had all but given up hope, beside a forest hermitage where lived a holy man, he saw Lionel armed and safe. With great joy Bors dismounted and ran to him. 'God be thanked that you are safe,' he said. 'How came you here?'

But Lionel answered him angrily. 'What concern is that of yours? If all the help I had found had been that which you offered me, then would I be dead by now. A fine thing is it when a knight must look to strangers for rescue when he has a brother knows his plight.'

Bors knelt before Sir Lionel and begged his forgiveness. 'It was not through my fault,' he said, 'that others had to save you. My heart was with you in your distress, yet I knew that my duty as a true knight lay elsewhere.'

'You need not ask my forgiveness,' said Lionel, 'for you shall never have it. Indeed, it is to my shame that one so base as you should live longer on this earth.' And in his great wrath he snatched up his sword and mounted his horse and shouted to Bors to do likewise. But Bors rose and went to him and knelt again beside his horse and once more pleaded with him to forgive his unwilling fault.

'You have shamed our noble name and our father's blood,' said Lionel, 'and you have disgraced our kinsman Sir Lancelot. Now mount your horse and draw your sword or I shall kill you where you are.'

'Remember, Lionel, how we two have always loved each other, how we have been true brothers in all things. Listen to me and do not in this madness of yours do something which you will afterwards wish undone.'

But Lionel would wait no longer, and even while Bors knelt to him he rode him down beneath his horse's hoofs, so that he lay senseless on the ground; then, dismounting, he struck off Bors' helmet and made to cut off his head. But the good hermit, hearing the quarrel, came running out from his house, crying to Lionel to hold his hand. 'Have mercy on your brother, good knight,' he said, and would have come between them. But Lionel did not have time to pause in his stroke, and his sword fell upon the hermit and the old man was slain. Yet such was Lionel's anger and his madness, that even this thing did not prevent him from his design, and with never a glance at the hermit he moved once more to cut off Bors' head.

Sir Colgrevance, who was a knight of the Round Table, chanced at that moment to be riding by. He leapt from his horse, and taking Lionel by the shoulders, dragged him away from his brother. 'You cannot do this thing,' he said.

'Let me be,' cried Lionel, 'for he deserves to die.' And he broke free from Sir Colgrevance and raised his sword once more.

'Slay him if you will,' said Colgrevance, 'but first shall you fight with me, and only after, when I can no longer prevent you, shall you do such a terrible deed.'

So Lionel and Colgrevance fought together, while Bors lay there upon the grass; and after a time he came to his senses and sat up and looked about him, and saw how his brother fought with Sir Colgrevance and guessed it to be for his sake. 'Great shame will it be to Lionel and myself if Colgrevance is slain. And great sorrow will it be to me, and great shame, if Lionel is killed.' And he rose and tried to part them, but he was too weak.

In his mad anger Lionel gained the advantage in the fighting, so that Colgrevance was sorely pressed and called to Bors, 'It is for your life that I am fighting. Come you now and fight for mine.'

Yet Lionel laughed. 'I will kill you both if I am given time.' And with a mighty stroke he cut down Colgrevance so that the good knight was dead.

'What have you done, brother?' cried Bors. 'He was of the Round Table, and our friend.'

But Lionel said, 'Now is it your turn to die.'

'It would be a sin, Lionel, if one of us slew the other.'

'It would be a sin,' said Lionel, 'if I left such a one as you to live.' And he fell upon Bors, so that Bors could see no help for it but was forced to draw his sword. 'May God have mercy on me that I draw my sword against my brother,' he said.

And in that instant a mist came about both of them so that they could no longer see each other, and a great flame parted them, so that for fear they dropped their swords and fell upon the ground. Then it seemed to Bors as though he heard a voice which said to him, 'Leave your brother and go now towards the sea where Sir Percival awaits you.' And then the mist was gone, and Bors saw how Lionel was unhurt.

'I must go,' said Bors, 'for I have been commanded by heaven. We may never meet again. Tell me before I go that you forgive me, Lionel.'

'It is you must forgive me,' said Lionel, 'for I think that I was out of my mind from anger.' And he wept.

Together they buried the hermit and brave Sir Colgrevance; then the brothers embraced, and Bors mounted his horse and rode, as he had been ordered, towards the sea, while Lionel rode sadly back to Camelot with the tidings of the death of Colgrevance.

When he reached the shore, Bors saw a ship close in to the land, and in the ship a knight who called to him. At once he leapt aboard and found that the knight was Percival, and they greeted each other with joy and told all their adventures. And Bors said, 'Truly, it seems that heaven has saved us for this intended meeting, and I believe that we are nearing the end of our quest for the Holy Grail. It is a wondrous thing how we two should have been chosen to succeed where so many good knights will have failed.'

'My mother's sister, who is a holy woman,' said Percival, 'has told me how Galahad too is blessed by heaven and how he may be overcome by no mortal man. It cannot be that he should not also see the Grail. We but lack Galahad for this adventure, and I do not doubt that he will join us soon.'

And together they waited on the ship, ever watching the land for a sight of Sir Galahad. After they had waited a certain time, there came a day when they saw him riding along the shore to them; and they greeted him as he came aboard.

He told them how, some days before, in another place along the coast, he had left his father, Sir Lancelot, and ridden away to find them at the bidding of a knight in white armour. 'I have no doubt,' he said, 'that he was no earthly knight, as this is no earthly ship.' And even as he was speaking, the ship was moving out to sea.

The three knights recounted all their adventures, and by

the time their tales were done they saw in the distance a strange land appear. Of herself the ship came close in to the shore. 'It is here that we are meant to disembark,' said Galahad. The knights armed themselves and went ashore, and immediately the ship put out to sea again.

Galahad, Percival, and Bors walked inland, and after a time they came to a castle, like no other castle they had ever seen, and in the wall of this castle there was a low door guarded by two lions. It was the Castle of Carbonek where Lancelot had been a little time before. The lions fawned upon them as they passed through the door, and in the castle all was bright and clear, though no torches burned.

'This,' said Bors, 'is the end of our quest.' And he felt a great happiness such as he had never known. He looked at his companions and saw how they, too, were filled with a strange and blessed joy.

When they came to the door of the room where was the Holy Grail, it opened wide for them and they went in; and there upon the table of silver stood the Grail, in all its brightness, uncovered and plain to see. Their quest over, the three knights knelt down and worshipped it and prayed.

Galahad prayed that, since he could imagine no greater joy than was his at that moment, he might die; and Percival prayed that he, too, might die before the joy of that moment grew faint in his memory; but Bors asked that he might return once more to his king and his kinsmen and his friends, to tell them of his happiness, that they might in some measure share in it. And to all three of them their prayers were granted.

When he knew that death was near, Galahad bade

farewell to his companions and embraced them. 'God keep you both,' he said. And of Bors he asked, 'Greet my father, Sir Lancelot, for me when you see him once again, and bid him not forget me.' Then he knelt down to say a last prayer, and so died. And in that same moment Bors and Percival saw how the Holy Grail vanished, never to be seen again on earth.

Percival put off his armour and his knightly clothing, and leaving the Castle of Carbonek, dwelt as a hermit, ever living over in his mind his joy at the sight of the Holy Grail; and in all this time Bors never left him. But when a year and two months were passed, Percival embraced his companion and said, 'The day has come for us to part.' And so he died.

And Bors went down to the sea and found a ship, and returned to the land of Britain to Arthur's court, where all had believed him dead, he had been so long away. He told them of the Holy Grail and of the deaths of Galahad and Percival, and to Lancelot he gave Galahad's message.

'Well shall I ever remember,' said Lancelot, 'that happy half-year we were together. May his soul find peace in heaven for, though young, he was a good knight, and my son.'

And so was achieved, by three knights only, out of all the fellowship of the Round Table, the quest of the Holy Grail.

XX

The Poisoned Apple

HAPPY though she was that Sir Lancelot had returned safely from the quest of the Holy Grail,
Queen Guenever still could not overcome her
jealousy of the other ladies and damsels who made much of
him, and though she said nothing of it to him for a time,
there came a day when she could keep silence no longer,
and she quarrelled with him once again, and in her anger
ordered him to go from Arthur's court.

Sadly Lancelot went to his brother Sir Ector de Maris,
and to his cousins Bors and Lionel, and told them of the
queen's command. 'It would perhaps be best if I went for
ever from Britain,' he said.

'No,' said Sir Bors, 'for remember how once before the
queen bade you never to see her again, and afterwards she
regretted it, and a great search did we have to find you. Go
rather to old Sir Brasias who has ever been a good friend
to us. He has left off all knightly living and now dwells
as a hermit near Windsor. He will welcome you, and with
him you may live unknown to the queen, until such time
as she would see you again, and there may we easily find
you, should she send us to seek you out.'

Lancelot took his cousin's counsel and went to Sir
Brasias, and there he waited sadly for word from his
kinsmen of Guenever's forgiveness.

But though she longed for him to return to her, Guenever
was a queen and proud, and she hid her grief and said no

word to Lionel or Bors or Ector de Maris, but acted as though Lancelot's absence were nothing to her.

And that others might think her to be happy, she wore her gayest garments and went much to the jousting and rode a-hunting often; and one day it came to her mind to give a merry feasting to certain of the knights of the Round Table. Four and twenty knights she bade to her banquet, and among them were Sir Gawaine and his four brothers, Gaheris, Gareth, Agravine, and Mordred; as well as Sir Ector de Maris, Sir Bors, Sir Lionel, and Sir Kay the Seneschal. There also was one Sir Mador, who brought with him a knight who was a stranger to the others, his cousin Sir Patrice, lately come from Ireland.

The queen herself chose the foods that were to be served at the feasting; and since Sir Gawaine was to be one of the guests, she sent for a bowl of apples, because of all the knights whom she had bidden to the feast Gawaine alone liked apples, and she knew that he ever ate an apple at supper, for they were his favourite fruit.

'See, Gawaine,' said Guenever, when her guests were come, 'how I have sent to the orchard for the best apples that are ripe, that you may not be without your favourite fruit this evening.' And Gawaine laughed and thanked her.

Now, one of the guests was a certain Sir Pinel, who hated Gawaine through envy of his prowess, and knowing his liking for apples, he had brought with him to the banquet several poisoned apples, and these he placed in the bowl when no one saw him.

But the Irish knight, Sir Patrice, was also fond of apples, though this Sir Pinel and the others did not know. And towards the end of the feasting, Sir Patrice took a poisoned apple and ate it, and immediately fell to the floor as though dead.

All the guests rose to their feet and there was consternation in the room; but when it was found that Sir Patrice was truly dead, and that nothing might avail him, the knights fell silent in horror. And in the silence Gawaine said slowly, 'That apple was meant for me.'

And they one and all thought how the feasting had been given by Guenever, and it seemed to them that she alone could have placed a poisoned apple in the bowl. They turned and looked at her but did not say a word, for they thought it too terrible a thing that their queen should be a murderess. And then after a time Gawaine spoke again, 'This feasting was yours, good queen, take care lest it bring you great shame.' But Guenever could find no words to answer him, and stood silent and afraid, so that her guilt seemed plain.

Then Sir Mador rose from where he had been kneeling by the body of Sir Patrice, and he was white with anger and grief. 'This shall not be the end of this matter,' he said. 'My kinsman has been foully slain and I will avenge his death.' And before them all he accused the queen of the death of his cousin. And there was no one there, not even Gawaine or Bors or Kay, who could in honesty protest her innocence, for they all believed her guilty.

Sir Mador went before King Arthur and again accused the queen, and in spite of Arthur's argument that Guenever could have no reason for wishing to poison Gawaine, Sir Mador held to his words. 'I believe the queen to be innocent,' said Arthur, 'and I would that I could prove it as her champion against Sir Mador, but in this matter I am the judge, and as judge I cannot do battle even for my own lady. Yet I have no doubt that among all my knights there are many who will be ready to defend her with their swords from being unjustly burnt.' But no one there spoke for the queen.

'Surely,' said Arthur, 'you other knights who were her guests at this unhappy banquet, surely you do not believe her guilty of this dreadful deed?' But they gave him no answer. 'Kay, Gawaine,' cried Arthur, 'surely you know she is innocent?'

'I would I were certain of it,' said Kay.

'What are we to think, my lord uncle, but that it was the queen?' asked Gawaine.

And Sir Mador demanded a day and a place when he might avenge his cousin's death. 'Fifteen days from now,' said Arthur, 'be ready and armed in the meadow by Westminster, there to meet with the queen's champion. And if at that time no knight will fight for her in this quarrel, then must she be burnt as a murderess.'

'I am satisfied,' said Sir Mador, and he went.

When they were alone, Arthur asked Guenever, 'How came this thing to happen?' And she wept and answered, 'I do not know.'

Arthur paced up and down the room. 'If Lancelot were here, you would have a knight to fight for you. Where is Sir Lancelot?'

Guenever wrung her hands, and said, 'I do not know, but I think that he is over the sea in his own land of Benwick, in France.'

'If he were here,' said Arthur, 'we should have no need

to fear, for you would have the best knight of all to defend you.' Then after a while he said, 'Sir Bors was at this feasting when Sir Patrice died, he is Lancelot's kinsman, perhaps for my sake and for Lancelot's, he will fight for you. You must ask it of him.'

So Guenever sent for Bors, and Arthur left her to speak with him. And because they were alone, and because Bors knew her love for Lancelot, she had no need for pretence. 'Since I have forbidden Lancelot the court,' she said, 'I have no one to fight for me. However unjustly jealous I may have been, and however harshly I have treated him, were Lancelot here he would not see me burnt. For Lancelot's sake, will you be my champion?'

'How can I?' asked Bors. 'For I was a guest at this feasting, and all men will think I had a hand in the slaying if I take up arms on your behalf.' And when she wept, he reproached her. 'You should not have sent Sir Lancelot away. Were it not for your groundless jealousy and spite, he would be here with you today.'

Guenever knelt before Sir Bors and implored him to fight for her. 'For the sake of Lancelot, your kinsman,' she pleaded.

Arthur returned and found her kneeling, and he said, 'Good Bors, I beg you, do this thing for me and for my queen, for though I do not know why your cousin, Sir Lancelot, has been gone so long from the court, I know that were he here he would not refuse us.'

And Bors raised the queen and said, 'For the sake of our good King Arthur and for the sake of Sir Lancelot, I will do this thing you ask, unless by the appointed day a better knight than I shall have offered himself as your champion.'

'You shall ever have my thanks,' said Arthur. But Guenever only wept.

Bors went from Camelot secretly, and rode to Windsor to the home of the hermit Sir Brasias, and told Lancelot all. For the first time in many weeks, Lancelot smiled. 'I have pity for Sir Patrice,' he said, 'yet save for my sorrow for him, this matter is not other than I would have it. Say no word of me, but only declare, as you have done, that unless a better knight is found, you will fight for Guenever. And when the appointed day is come I will be there to take your place.'

When the fifteen days were passed, King Arthur and all his court went to the meadow beside Westminster, where a great fire had been built around an iron stake, so that if Sir Mador won the day Guenever might be burnt. There was Sir Mador, waiting impatiently to avenge his cousin's death; and there was Sir Bors, awaiting a sight of Lancelot. And there too was the queen with a guard on either side of her, hiding her fear as well as she might.

Sir Mador came forward and took an oath before King Arthur that on a certain day the queen had caused the death of his cousin Patrice by means of a poisoned apple, and this he swore to prove against all men. Then came Sir Bors and cried aloud how the queen was innocent, and this he swore to prove with his sword, unless a better knight than he should come to take his place.

'Then make ready to fight upon this quarrel, good knights,' said Arthur, 'and may justice prevail.' And he turned and smiled at Guenever to comfort her, though in his heart he feared the strength of Sir Mador, who was a mighty fighter.

The Poisoned Apple

Sir Bors and Sir Mador went to their pavilions at opposite ends of the meadow, and there they were armed by their squires; and in his eagerness Sir Mador was ready long before Sir Bors. He rode from his pavilion and all about the field, calling out, 'Let the queen's champion come forth, if he dare.'

But Bors waited, since Lancelot had not yet come, and Sir Mador cried with scorn, 'Does the queen's champion fear the rightfulness of his cause, that he does not show himself?'

But still Bors tarried for Lancelot, until for very shame he mounted his horse and rode slowly into the lists. And then he saw how a knight all armed, with a shield whose device was known to no one there, suddenly came galloping from a wood near by the meadow, upon a white horse. And he guessed that it was Lancelot.

Lancelot called out to his cousin, 'Good knight, I pray you be not angered with me that I ask you this boon. Give to me the right to take the queen's quarrel on myself.'

Bors rode to where Arthur sat and told him of the strange knight's request. 'Who is this knight?' asked Arthur.

'That I cannot tell,' said Bors. 'But I know him to be a better knight than I.'

'Then if he is willing,' said Arthur, 'let him have this fight.'

So Lancelot and Sir Mador rode one to each end of the field and, holding their lances firmly, they charged. Sir Mador's lance broke with the force of their meeting, but Lancelot's held, and Mador was flung from his horse. Yet at once he arose and drew his sword. 'Dismount, stranger,' he said, 'and fight with me.'

Lancelot alighted from his horse and put his shield before him and drew his sword, and with great eagerness they fell upon each other. And because Sir Mador was a valiant knight, he withstood Sir Lancelot's great blows for almost an hour, and gave many in return. But at last, with a mighty stroke, Lancelot hurled Sir Mador to the ground, and stepping forward pulled off his helmet to cut off his head.

But Mador pleaded for his life, saying, 'Spare me, sir stranger, and I will declare the queen innocent in this matter.'

'If you will openly declare her innocence,' said Lancelot, 'and never again seek to do her harm, then will I give you your life.'

So Sir Mador swore to Guenever's innocence and promised loyalty to her and the ending of his quarrel; and Arthur went to Guenever where she stood between the guards and with happiness he kissed her and led her to sit beside him. 'Bring the strange knight to me,' he called, 'for I have thanks to offer him.'

When Lancelot was come before him, Arthur said, 'It is hard to give you thanks enough for what you have done for us this day.' He beckoned to a servant to bring wine that the strange knight might drink with him, and when Lancelot put off his helmet that he could drink, they all saw who he was, and Arthur embraced him in great joy.

'I need no thanks,' said Lancelot, 'for should I not be ever ready to fight for you, my lord king, since it was you who ordained me knight? And as for your queen, I am always her champion to fight for her in right or in wrong.' And Guenever wept for Lancelot's great love for her, which she felt she did not deserve.

And in the rejoicing that followed because the queen's innocence had been made good, Sir Pinel grew fearful and fled from the land, so that all men knew it was he who had sought to poison Gawaine. And Sir Mador pleaded for Guenever's forgiveness for his suspicions; and at Lancelot's request, she pardoned him, at which there was gladness, for Sir Mador was a brave knight, and much respected.

XXI

The Fair Maid of Astolat

ONCE, after King Arthur had been holding court in another place, as he was journeying back to Camelot, he proclaimed a great tourneying to be held there on his return. At that time Sir Lancelot was adventuring elsewhere, but when he heard the proclamation he thought how it would be a diversion to attend the tournament disguised and see if he were recognized or no. So he, too, rode towards Camelot, unknown to the king, and reached on the way the little town of Astolat, which is now called Guildford, just after Arthur and all his court had come to the castle there. And that he might not be known, he lodged at the house of an old knight named Sir Bernard.

But Sir Bernard's house stood close by the castle walls, and from a high window of the castle Arthur looked down and saw Lancelot walking in Sir Bernard's garden, and guessed why he was holding himself apart. He smiled. 'I have this moment seen one knight who will do great things at our tournament,' he said.

His companions crowded to the window to look out, but by that time Lancelot was once more within Sir Bernard's house, and they saw no one. 'Who was it?' they asked the king. Yet Arthur only laughed and said, 'You will all find out in time.'

Sir Bernard had two sons and a daughter. The two young men had but lately been knighted, and their sister was named Elaine, even as had been King Pelless' daughter, the mother of Galahad, but she was always called the Fair Maid of Astolat, for she was by far the loveliest damsel in the town.

Lancelot did not tell his name to Sir Bernard, but he told him of his intention to go to the tourneying at Camelot; and that he might be unknown there, he asked if his host could lend him a shield. 'For my own is too well known,' he said.

'Willingly,' replied Sir Bernard. 'My elder son, Tirre, was wounded on that day he was made knight, so he cannot go to the tourneying. His shield is known nowhere save here in Astolat, so you shall carry it and be unknown to your friends. And though you will not tell me your name, I am certain that you are a knight of great renown, and it would please me much if my younger son, Lavaine, might ride to Camelot with you.'

'I shall enjoy his company,' said Lancelot.

But Elaine, the Fair Maid of Astolat, looked at Lancelot and fell in love with him, and thought that there could be no greater joy in all the world than to have him for her knight. Shyly she came to him and asked him if he would wear her favour at the tournament.

'If I did that, lady,' said Lancelot kindly, 'it would be more than I have ever done for any other damsel.' For Lancelot ever fought secretly in honour of Queen Guenever, and never did he bear the tokens of any ladies. But when he saw how sad his words had made Elaine, he pitied her; and remembering that he was to go to Camelot disguised, he said, 'I will wear your favour, lady.' In great joy she gave to him a sleeve of hers, of scarlet silk sewn with pearls. And he gave her his own shield, wrapped in a cloth, to keep till he came again.

The next morning Lancelot and young Lavaine rode to Camelot, and there they were lodged with a rich merchant who was known to Sir Bernard; and Lancelot was recognized of none, for he kept himself from the company of all knights save Lavaine.

On the day of the tourneying Lancelot and Lavaine rode to the tourney-ground where the two parties already fought while Arthur watched with Gawaine to judge which was the better. And the party upon which were most of the knights of the Round Table was by far stronger than the other. Lancelot fastened the scarlet sleeve upon his helmet. 'Let us join the weaker side,' he said, and rode with Lavaine into the field.

With one lance he unhorsed five knights, and among them was Sir Kay the Seneschal; while Lavaine, for all his youth and inexperience, smote down both Sir Lucan and

Sir Bedivere his brother, old and well tried knights of Arthur. When his first lance was broken, with a second Sir Lancelot rode against three of Arthur's nephews, Gaheris, Agravine, and Mordred, and flung them to the ground. But against Sir Gareth he did not fight, for he knew that Gareth had sworn never to be against him at any time, since Gareth loved him above all other knights.

'See how my brothers are unhorsed,' said Gawaine to King Arthur. 'That knight who wears the scarlet sleeve upon his helm is indeed a mighty jouster. By his riding and his blows I would say him to be Sir Lancelot, were it not for the lady's favour that he carries.'

But Arthur guessed that it was indeed Lancelot, and he smiled. 'I have no doubt that when the tourneying is done the stranger will tell us his name. Till then, let him be.'

When they saw their own fellows of the Round Table worsted by two strange knights, Sir Lancelot's kinsmen came together in the tourney-ground and talked of it. 'If Lancelot were here,' they said, 'this would never be. But let it not be said of us that because we lack Lancelot there is no courage in us.' And Sir Bors and Sir Lionel and Sir Ector de Maris rode against Lancelot and Lavaine.

All three of them attacked together, so that Lancelot's horse was slain and he himself was wounded, for by mischance Sir Bors' lance passed right through Sir Tirre's shield at a place where Lancelot's armour was weakest, and the head of the lance pierced his side and broke off. When Lavaine saw how Lancelot was wounded and without a horse, he fell wildly upon another knight and flung him to the ground, then taking the fallen knight's horse he helped Lancelot to mount. And wounded though he was,

Sir Lancelot did great deeds against his own kinsmen, so that in the end they were discomfited. 'Whoever he is, this stranger knight,' they said, 'he would be a match for Lancelot himself.'

Then King Arthur ordered the trumpets to sound for the end of the tourneying, and with one accord the knight who wore the red sleeve on his helmet was declared to be the best of all, and he was called forth to receive the prize. 'Now,' said Arthur to Gawaine, 'shall we know who he is, this good knight.'

But Lancelot said to Lavaine, 'I am wounded and I must rest. Let us go from here.' And before they could be prevented, they were gone from the field and away to the near by forest. There Lancelot reined in his horse. 'My friend,' he said, 'the head of the lance which wounded me is yet in my side. I beg you take it out for me, for it gives me much pain.'

Lavaine took off Lancelot's armour and pulled out the head of the lance from the wound, which he bound as well as he might. Yet he was young and but lately made knight and he knew little of such things; and in the short time since he had first seen him he had grown fond of Lancelot. 'My good lord,' he said in distress, 'what shall I do now? If we do not find help and rest for you, in a little while you will be dead of this wound, alone in the forest.'

Lancelot smiled for all his pain. 'I would not wish to die of a wound from the lance of my cousin Bors; that would be an ill thing both for him and for me. Near here, in the forest, there dwells an old knight named Baldwin who was once a knight of the Round Table until he gave up the

222

world and came to the forest to live as a hermit. He had ever great skill in medicine. Help me to my horse, and I will show you the way to his house.'

With difficulty Lavaine helped Lancelot mount and together they rode as Lancelot directed; and after a time they came to Sir Baldwin's house. With one arm about Lancelot, so that he should not fall, Lavaine beat upon the gate with the shaft of his lance and cried for it to be opened. A serving-lad came running out, and after him Sir Baldwin. 'Who is it,' asked the old knight, 'who knocks upon my gate and shouts for me so loudly?'

'There is here a good knight,' said Lavaine, 'and he is wounded, it may be unto death. I pray you, save him with your skill, for today I saw him do great deeds in the tourneying at Camelot.'

'Of whose party was he,' asked Sir Baldwin, 'King Arthur's, or the other?'

'He was against the fellowship of the Round Table. Yet he won the prize.'

'Once,' said the old knight, 'I might have hated him for that, for I was of the company of King Arthur. Yet now all men in distress are the same to me. Let me help you bring him in.'

But when he saw Lancelot, Sir Baldwin thought that he knew him, though he could not be sure, for Lancelot's face was pale from his wound, and it was, besides, evening. 'What is your name?' asked Baldwin, as he helped him through the door.

'I am a stranger here,' said Lancelot. But when he was once in the house and the light was on his face, Baldwin knew him instantly. 'Why do you hide your name from me?' he said. 'For of all knights in this land you are the best. I am glad indeed that it has fallen to my lot to make you whole again.' And he saw Lancelot laid upon a bed, and he tended his wound and bound it with Lavaine to help him; and after, Lancelot slept. And Sir Baldwin turned to Lavaine and smiled to see him so white-faced. 'He will be well again,' he said. 'He will not die.'

When King Arthur found that the strange knight had gone wounded from the tourney-ground, he sent Gawaine to search for him. But though Gawaine and his squires rode all around Camelot, they found no trace of him; and after two days Arthur and all his court had to journey to London. On the way they passed through Astolat, and there Sir Bernard and his daughter the Fair Maid chanced to ask Gawaine, as one who had been present as a judge, for tidings of the tourneying at Camelot, for they had heard no word from either Lancelot or Lavaine.

'There was one knight at the tourneying who surpassed all others,' said Gawaine, 'and he wore upon his helmet a lady's sleeve, scarlet and sewn with pearls. Yet his name we do not know, nor that of his companion, who also showed himself a worthy knight.'

And the Fair Maid of Astolat cried out in her joy at his words, 'It was my sleeve that he was wearing, and his deeds were done in my honour.'

'And his companion was the younger of my sons, Lavaine,' said Sir Bernard proudly.

Gawaine turned to the damsel. 'What is the name of your knight?'

'Indeed,' she said, 'I do not know. But he is the only man whom I shall ever love.' And she told Gawaine how

Lancelot had taken her brother's shield and left his own with her until he should return from Camelot.

'Have you this shield still?' asked Gawaine. And she fetched it from her own room, and Gawaine saw that it was the red and silver shield of Lancelot, painted with his arms. 'Is this indeed the shield of the knight whom you love?' he asked.

She smiled happily. 'It is the shield of the only knight I shall ever love.'

And Gawaine pitied her, for he had never known Lancelot return the love of any lady. 'It is the shield of the best knight in all the land,' he said.

But she held up her head proudly. 'I was sure of that before you told me.'

'What is his name?' asked Sir Bernard.

'He is Lancelot of the Lake,' said Gawaine. And they were astonished.

'Where is he now?' asked the Fair Maid anxiously.

'That, lady, I wish I knew, for my own sake as well as yours.' And Gawaine told them of how Lancelot had been wounded and had ridden from the tourney-field with his companion; and the Fair Maid wept. 'I shall not rest,' she said, 'until he and my brother are found.'

Gawaine told King Arthur of all that he had learnt, of how the knight who had fought so well was Lancelot, and of how the Fair Maid of Astolat had a great love for him.

'I knew that it was Lancelot,' said Arthur. 'Yet since he wished to be unknown, I kept his secret. But I marvel that he wore this damsel's favour. Can it be that Lancelot has chosen a lady for himself at last? And I am much distressed at the thought of his wound; I would that we knew where he is.' But he could remain no longer in Astolat, for he was awaited in London.

In London Sir Gawaine told openly that it had been Lancelot who had worn the red sleeve at the tournament, and all his kinsmen were grieved when they knew how they had fought against him. And most grieved was Sir Bors, for it had been he who had wounded his cousin. But when Guenever heard of how Lancelot had worn a damsel's favour, she was angry and sent for Bors to question him further about the matter. 'I do not doubt, good queen, that it was for no other reason than that he might be well disguised,' he said.

Yet Guenever could not calm her jealousy. 'He is a false knight to do thus,' she said. 'And I am glad that for all his pride and boasting he was worsted and wounded by you.'

'Alas, good queen, that was by mischance, and you do him wrong to call him proud and boastful who is the most modest of men.' And Bors made ready to ride back to Camelot to seek his cousin.

When Guenever saw that he would leave the court, she asked him, 'Where do you go, Sir Bors?'

'To seek Lancelot, good queen.' And though she was glad in her heart, she shrugged her shoulders as though she did not care.

The Fair Maid of Astolat begged that her father would allow her to journey forth and seek Lancelot and her brother, and he gave her leave. So with a squire and two servants she went all about the country that lay round Camelot. And it chanced one morning when Lancelot was better that Sir Lavaine left him for an hour or two and rode out from the house of Sir Baldwin to exercise his horse, and the two of them met and greeted each other joyfully. 'Tell me, how is Sir Lancelot?' asked the Fair Maid.

'He is sorely wounded, but the good knight Sir Baldwin has promised that he will recover. Yet tell me, sister, how do you know his name? Is he really Lancelot of the Lake?'

And she told Lavaine of all that Sir Gawaine had told her, so that he was amazed.

When the Fair Maid saw how pale and weak Lancelot still was, she wept, but Lancelot smiled at her. 'Do not fret, lady, for I shall soon be well.' And she set herself to tend him until he should be recovered, never leaving his side; and no damsel could have done more for the knight she loved.

But Lavaine asked, 'Are you truly Lancelot of the Lake?'

'I am, my friend, but how did you come to know?'

Lavaine told him all his sister had said of Gawaine and the shield, and Lancelot thought to himself, 'Gawaine will have told Arthur and all the court of this, and so will Guenever know how I wore the damsel's sleeve, and she will be angered.' But aloud he said, 'When my kinsmen hear of how things are with me, one of them will ride forth to seek me, of that I am certain. I beg you, good Lavaine, look out for him that you may bring him to me when he comes to Camelot.' And he told him how he might know Sir Ector de Maris, Sir Bors, and Sir Lionel. 'Though I do not doubt that it will be Bors who seeks me,' said Lancelot, 'for it was he who wounded me.'

So Lavaine kept watch at Camelot until Sir Bors was come there, and he greeted him and told him that he was from Lancelot. And together they rode to Sir Baldwin's house.

'Forgive me for the hurt I did to you,' said Bors when he stood at Lancelot's bedside.

'How could you have known it was I?' asked Lancelot. He smiled. 'Do not grieve for it, good cousin. Let us forget it and talk of something else. Tell me, how does our lady, the queen?'

'She is angered because at the tournament you wore a favour given you by the Fair Maid of Astolat, and because she has heard of the great love which that damsel has for you.'

'I feared it would be so,' said Lancelot.

Bors looked at the Fair Maid where she moved about the room, setting things to rights. He said quietly, so that she should not hear, 'The damsel who brings your food and tends you, is she the Fair Maid of Astolat?'

'She is indeed, cousin.'

'She is truly fair,' said Bors. 'Good Lancelot, I would that you could love her, for she seems as sweet a damsel as a man could find, and would make a good wife for any lord.'

'You know, Bors, that there is only one lady whom I shall ever love.'

'This damsel,' urged Bors, 'it is plain she loves you well.'

Lancelot turned his head away and sighed. 'I would that she did not,' he said.

After that they talked of other things, and Bors told Lancelot how there was to be a great tourneying in London at All-Hallowmas, and Lancelot thought how, if he were well enough by that time, he would take part in it, that he might see the queen and perhaps by his prowess win her regard once again. 'If my wound is healed,' he said, 'I shall go to London with you for this tourneying.'

But when he told Sir Baldwin, the old knight would not hear of it. 'You shall not go from here until Christmas,' he said.

A few days before All-Hallowmas Sir Baldwin walked out in the forest to gather herbs for his simples, and he took the Fair Maid of Astolat with him, for she was ever eager to learn of healing that thereby she might help Lancelot. When they were gone, Lancelot sat up in his bed. 'Bring me my armour, Lavaine,' he said. 'And you, Bors, bid my horse be saddled, for I would see if I can ride. If all is well, I shall be able to go with you to London.'

So Sir Lavaine helped him arm himself, and he went out and mounted his horse and took up a lance and tilted at a tree. 'See,' he called to the others, 'I am well again, for all Sir Baldwin says.' And with that he thrust his lance mightily against the trunk of the tree. But such force there was in the blow that his wound was broken open with the strain of it, and he sank fainting from his horse to the ground.

Bors and Lavaine ran to him to raise him, and in that moment the Fair Maid returned. 'What have you done?' she cried to them. 'You have let him kill himself in your folly.' And she called to Sir Baldwin.

'This is a sorry thing to happen,' said the old knight. 'Why could he not have had patience?'

They carried Lancelot indoors and laid him in his bed, and he opened his eyes and smiled a little. 'I thought that I would have been strong enough to joust at London, but it seems I was mistaken.'

'If you are wise,' said Baldwin, 'you will do as I say. Let your cousin go to London and then return and tell you of the tournament.'

So Bors went to the tourneying, with many messages from Lancelot for Arthur and the knights of the Round Table, and a special word for the queen. But Guenever received it in scornful silence, as though she cared not for Lancelot. Yet in her heart she was thankful that he was recovering and she longed to see him once again.

At the tournament Sir Gareth did great deeds and won the prize, and when Bors returned to Sir Baldwin's house with the news from London, Lancelot was glad of it. 'Gareth is a good knight,' he said, 'and well deserves his victory. I would that I had been there to see him.'

At last a day came when Sir Baldwin declared Lancelot might travel, and with many thanks to the old knight he rode for Astolat in the company of Bors and Lavaine and the Fair Maid. Sir Bernard's joy was great to see his son and daughter home once more, and his elder son, Tirre, now healed of his wound, welcomed Lancelot. 'You have my gratitude for the shield you lent me,' said Lancelot. 'Though I fear that it was sadly battered in the fighting.'

'That matters not,' said Tirre, 'so long as it was of service to so famed a knight.'

Lancelot and Bors remained one night in Sir Bernard's house and in the morning they prepared to ride away. But when Lancelot would have taken his leave of Sir Bernard and his family, the Fair Maid of Astolat said, 'Have pity on me, Sir Lancelot, and do not let me die from love.'

'What is it that you want?' asked Lancelot.

'I would be your wife,' she said.

And Lancelot thanked her with courtesy, and said, 'I shall ever remember with gratitude all your great care of me. But forgive it, lady, for I have no mind to wed.'

'Then shall I die,' she said, and wept.

'This is indeed a grievous thing,' said Sir Bernard.

'I give you my word,' said Lancelot, 'I made her no promises. She is a good and sweet damsel, and beautiful, but I would she had never set eyes on me.'

'Father,' said Lavaine, 'he speaks the truth. He has never given her any hope that he loved her. This thing comes all from herself. Yet is it strange that she should love him? For is he not the best knight there is and the noblest man?'

Distressed, Sir Bernard bade Lancelot farewell and led his daughter away, and Sir Tirre followed them. Lancelot turned to Lavaine. 'God keep you, my friend. What will you do now?'

'With your leave,' said Lavaine, 'I will ride to Arthur's court with you, or wherever else you choose to go, for there is no lord whom I would rather serve.'

So Lancelot and Bors and Lavaine rode on to Westminster where Arthur was keeping court that winter, and a great welcome Arthur gave to Lancelot, as did all the knights of the Round Table. Yet Guenever would not speak with him save when, in company, she had to, and Lancelot was unhappy at her anger.

But the Fair Maid grew pale and weak, and nothing that her father or her brother Tirre might do could cheer her; and at last it was plain to all that she was dying. She called her father and her brother to her bedside. 'You are a scholar, Tirre, will you write a letter for me?'

'Willingly, sweet sister.' And he fetched pen and parchment.

'Write this,' she said. ' "To the most honoured knight, Sir Lancelot of the Lake. I was she whom men called the Fair Maid of Astolat, and when you read this I shall be dead, even as I told you when we parted. It is for love of you I shall have died, that you could not love me in return. Yet, I beg you, see me buried fittingly and say a prayer for me. It is but a little thing I ask." That is all, Tirre, that I would write. When I am dead, father, as I shall be very soon, lay me in a barge with this letter in my hand, and so let me be rowed along the river to Westminster. Promise me this thing.'

With tears Sir Bernard promised; and in a very little while she died. As she had asked, her father and her brother laid her body in a barge all hung about with black silk, with the letter in her hand, and a trusted servant was sent to steer the barge to Westminster.

It happened that King Arthur and Queen Guenever were standing together at a window of the castle at Westminster which overlooked the River Thames, and as they looked out they saw the barge. 'What can this mean?' asked Guenever.

Arthur called Kay to him and asked him concerning it. 'My lord king,' said Kay, 'I know nothing of this thing, but I will ask.' He went down to the river and spoke to the boatman. Yet not a word would the man give him in answer. Sir Kay returned to the king. 'In the barge,' he said, 'is the body of a fair young damsel clad in rich robes, but who she is the man who guards her will not say.'

'We must see this thing for ourselves,' said Arthur.

Together he and the queen went down to the river and entered the barge and saw the Fair Maid of Astolat. 'How lovely she is,' said Arthur. 'It is a great grief that she should have died so young.'

But Guenever saw the letter that was in the Fair Maid's hand. 'See, here is a letter,' she said. 'Perhaps it may tell us who she is.'

Arthur broke open the seal of the letter. 'It is for Sir Lancelot,' he said. He read the letter out to all those gathered there, and many wept for pity of the damsel who had died for love.

But Guenever thought, 'So Lancelot never loved her, and I have wronged him yet again.' And when she wept her tears were for herself and Lancelot, as much as for the death of the Fair Maid.

'Go, fetch Sir Lancelot,' said Arthur, 'for this matter is for him.'

And when Lancelot was come, and Sir Lavaine with him, Arthur handed him the letter. When he knew what was written there, Lancelot sighed. 'She was a sweet damsel and good and kind. I would that she had not died. It is a great sorrow to me that she loved me too well.'

'She could not have done otherwise,' said Sir Lavaine, 'for you are the best knight of all.'

'It is a pity,' said Arthur, 'that you could not have loved her in return, and so her life would not have been lost.'

'My lord king,' said Lancelot, 'love cannot be commanded to be where it is not, any more than it can be forbidden where it is.' And for a moment he looked at Guenever and she at him. And in that glance each knew from the other's eyes that their quarrel was ended.

Sir Lancelot, and Lavaine with him, saw that the Fair Maid of Astolat was buried fittingly, as she had asked, and Lancelot ever prayed for her soul, and regretted her death.

But young Sir Lavaine remained with Lancelot and proved himself in all manner of knightly feats, so that in time he was admitted to the fellowship of the Round Table.

XXII

How Guenever went a-Maying

ONE spring morning Queen Guenever had a mind
to go a-Maying in the woods near Westminster.
She took with her ten of her ladies and a little
page, and chose out ten knights to ride with her: among
them Sir Kay, Gawaine's young brother Sir Agravine, and
Sir Ironside who had once been known as the Red Knight
of the Red Plain and had been won for King Arthur by Sir
Gareth. Early in the morning they set out, all dressed
in green according to the queen's commandment, and
rode from Westminster across the bridge to the fields
beyond.

'What folly it is,' grumbled Sir Kay, 'to sit on the grass
and pick flowers when there are other deeds to be done.'
But after a time he forgot to complain, and he too enjoyed
the freshness of the morning and all the welcome sights
and sounds of spring, and rejoiced with the others that
winter was gone.

On the edge of the woods, Guenever sat upon a mossy
bank, and all about her, her ladies gathered primroses and
violets and twined them into wreaths; whilst the knights
plucked long sprays of hawthorn blossom and pink crab-
apple and laid them at her feet.

Now, in the woods, not far from that place, there was a
castle which belonged to Sir Meliagrance, the son of good
Sir Bagdemagus who was now dead. This Meliagrance
had long loved Queen Guenever unknown to any; and

with his love there had come upon him a great madness and he had sworn to himself that one day he would carry off the queen and keep her in his castle. Hearing that she had come a-Maying so near his lands, he called together his followers, and with a score of men-at-arms and a hundred archers he rode out from his castle.

As Guenever was sitting upon the bank, laughing with her damsels, one of them looked up and saw a knight ride out from the woods at the head of a band of well-armed men, and told the queen. 'What means this?' asked Guenever.

The knight rode straight to her. 'Lady,' he said, 'I am Meliagrance, and you are my prisoner.'

'Your father,' said Guenever, 'was a good knight and true to his king. It grieves me that I cannot say thus of his son.' And the ten knights cried out against Sir Meliagrance, calling him traitor.

'It would be best, lady, that you mounted your horse and rode with me before any blood is shed,' said Meliagrance.

'That shall she not,' said Kay, drawing his sword. And all those of the queen's ten knights who had thought to bring a sword with them did likewise; yet some of them were armed with no more than a dagger, and none of them wore armour, since it was not for fighting that they had ridden forth. And though the ten of them fought bravely, and none more bravely than Sir Ironside, they were no match for twenty men-at-arms and a hundred archers.

So that the knights should not be slain, Guenever cried out to Meliagrance, 'Call off your men and I will ride with you to your castle. But my ladies and these ten knights must come with me, for I will not be parted from them.'

'Let that be as you wish, lady,' said Meliagrance. He bade his men cease fighting and watch his prisoners carefully, while those of the knights who had been wounded were helped to their horses, and Guenever's terrified ladies were calmed.

But Guenever waited for a moment when no one saw her, and she beckoned to the little page, and taking a ring from her finger, bade him ride away as soon as he might and take it to Sir Lancelot. 'Tell him what has befallen me, and ask his instant aid,' she said.

As soon as they were all mounted on their horses and about to ride for the castle of Sir Meliagrance, the page on his palfrey slipped between the men-at-arms and galloped away across the fields. Meliagrance called out to his archers to shoot, but their arrows missed their mark and the page escaped. Angrily Meliagrance turned to the queen. 'I see that you would send for help, but it will not avail you. No doubt you hope that Sir Lancelot or another of King Arthur's knights will ride out when he hears of your plight. We shall be ready for him.' And he ordered thirty of his archers to lie in wait along the road to his castle, to kill any knight who rode that way to rescue the queen. 'But if he rides upon a white horse,' he said, 'it will surely be Sir Lancelot, and then beware of fighting with him, for he is the best knight of all in battle, and it will go ill with you.'

But Guenever laughed in scorn. 'Even thirty bowmen are no match for Lancelot.'

'We delay too long, lady,' said Meliagrance. 'Come.' And he caught at the bridle of her horse so that she had to ride with him; and her damsels and her ten knights came after, well guarded by Sir Meliagrance's men.

But the page galloped as hard as he might and at last he came to the court at Westminster, and there he sought out Sir Lancelot and gave him the queen's ring. Lancelot called for his sword and his armour, and for his horse to be saddled; while the page told how bravely Sir Kay and Sir Ironside and the others had fought. 'Why was I not there, that the queen might have been spared this?' exclaimed Lancelot.

He took up his shield and mounted his horse and was gone, galloping through the streets of Westminster and out through the city gates and over the bridge. In time he came to the place where the ten knights had fought to save their queen, and he saw how the grass was trampled underfoot and strewn with broken flowers as he rode on into the wood.

The thirty archers saw him come and said to one another, 'It is a knight come to the aid of the queen, and see, he rides a white horse. It will be Sir Lancelot, we must beware.' And they stepped forth and stood in his path and bade him turn back, each fitting an arrow to his bow. Yet they stood at a distance from him, for they heeded well their master's warning.

'I am a knight of King Arthur's Round Table,' said Lancelot, 'and I shall ride where I please.'

And the archers shot their arrows so that Lancelot's horse was killed, and in anger he drew his sword on them, and they were afraid. 'It is several miles yet to our master's castle,' they said, 'it will take him long enough on foot. We have done our duty.' And with that they fled.

Lancelot took up his shield and his weapons and walked on, fretting at the delay; but burdened though he was by his armour and his lance, he dared cast nothing aside, for he knew that he would need them if he had to fight with Meliagrance.

But there chanced that way with a cart a man who had come to fetch wood. 'Will you drive me in your cart some three miles to a castle where I would go?' asked Lancelot.

The carter refused. 'I have been sent into the woods to fetch faggots for the fires of my master, Sir Meliagrance,' he said. 'It is no part of my task to drive a strange knight about the countryside.'

'It is to your master's castle that I am bound. I bid you take me there.'

And though at first he would not, at last the man was afraid of an armed knight, and he consented. Lancelot climbed into the cart and the man urged on his horse, and so, in a creaking, jolting cart, they came to the castle.

One of the queen's ladies was looking out from a window that she might tell her mistress if she saw help come to them. 'What do you see?' asked Guenever.

'No more than a knight in armour, riding by in a cart. He must be a robber knight, riding by to his hanging, since for what other reason would a knight ride in a cart?'

Guenever rose and went to the window, and at once she knew Sir Lancelot. 'How happy I am,' she said, 'to have a friend whom I can ever trust. That is no robber knight, that is good Sir Lancelot.'

When Lancelot came to the gates of the castle, he found them locked against him, but he leapt down from the cart and hammered on the gates with the shaft of his lance and called out to Meliagrance to let him in. And Meliagrance, afraid, went to Guenever, and, falling at her feet, besought her pardon for his treason.

'Did you not guess,' she answered, 'that I should not lack a knight to save me?'

'I beg of you, good queen, speak for me to Sir Lancelot, or else I shall be killed.'

'Why should I speak for you?' asked Guenever. 'Have you not wronged me and my lord the king?'

But Meliagrance still pleaded. 'I have loved you many years,' he said, 'and my love has been as a madness upon me. Have mercy, good queen.'

And because she pitied him, Guenever forgave him. And Meliagrance ordered the gates to be opened. Lancelot came into the great hall of the castle, still calling for Meliagrance. 'Come forth, traitor knight, and fight with me.'

But it was Guenever who came down to him, and after her, her ladies, and Sir Agravine and those of the ten knights who were not so sorely wounded that they might not walk.

'Heaven be praised that you are safe,' said Lancelot. 'Where is Meliagrance, that I may kill him?'

'We have made peace together and I have forgiven him his treason,' said Guenever. 'Let you do likewise, Lancelot.'

But Lancelot was angered and would not hear of it. Guenever laid a hand upon his arm and spoke gently, 'He loves me, even as you do. Yet I love him not in return. Can you not pity him? Oh, Lancelot, we can well afford to show him mercy.'

And Lancelot smiled at her. 'Then, though I like it not, let it be as you say.'

There was great rejoicing among the ten knights and the queen's ladies that they were free to go when they would, and that no harm had come to any of them more than a few wounds which would quickly heal; for all that Sir Kay grumbled and said, 'Now do we see what comes of it, when one rides a-Maying.'

But Agravine, Gawaine's young brother, who had never liked Sir Lancelot, marked how the queen had greeted him with an even greater joy than a lady might show to a rescuer; and he watched carefully how she smiled when she spoke to him. And in his mind he considered it well and did not forget.

XXIII

The Healing of Urre

IN the days of King Arthur there was a good young knight of Hungary named Urre who ever loved tournaments and jousting and all manner of adventures. Since he could not find in the land of Hungary adventures enough to satisfy him, he wandered all about the world and achieved himself some fame.

Now, it happened that at one time he was in Spain where he encountered with a Spanish knight who had much renown in his own land, and at a tourneying they undertook to joust to the uttermost to prove who was the better. Mightily they met together and the battle lasted long, but in the end, though sorely wounded, Sir Urre was the victor, and the Spanish knight was slain.

Sir Urre gained much admiration for his skill; but the mother of the Spanish knight was a witch, and in her anger for the death of her son she laid a spell on Sir Urre that his wounds would never heal until they had been tended by the best knight in the world. Sir Urre had seven wounds, three on his head, three on his body, and one on his left hand, but though he sent to all those men and women in Spain who were the most famed for their knowledge of medicine and the cure of wounds, they could in no way help him, and always the wounds would be festering or bleeding afresh, so that Urre was ever in pain.

But someone heard the witch-mother boasting how she had avenged her son and went to Sir Urre and told him of

the spell that she had laid on him. 'There are good knights in Spain,' said Urre, 'let all of them who will, come here to me.' So one by one all the knights of any worth in Spain came to the bedside of Sir Urre and touched his wounds, but it brought him no relief. 'It seems,' said Urre, 'that the best knight in the world is not to be found in Spain. I will go back to my own land and seek help there.' So his squires laid him in a horse litter and they travelled back to Hungary.

The distress of Sir Urre's mother was very great when she saw him come home in such a plight, but at once she sent word through all the land that her son might only be healed by the best knight in the world, and she begged all knights in Hungary to come to her castle to see what they might achieve. Yet when all the knights in the land had tended Urre's wounds, he was in no better state than before.

And Sir Urre, who had ever lived for jousting and feats of arms, lay on his bed and sighed. 'My life is a burden to me, good mother,' he said. 'I would that I were dead.'

But his mother was a lady of courage and determination, and she made up her mind that Urre would be well. 'There are other lands in the world beside Hungary and Spain, my son. And you shall go to them all until you have found the best knight in the world.'

So once again Sir Urre was laid in a horse litter, and accompanied by his mother and his young sister he set out to travel from one land to another in quest of the best knight in the world. And from one land to another they went, from one king's court to another, until seven long years were passed, and still they had not found what they sought.

'There is no help for me, mother,' said Urre. 'We had best return home.'

'There yet remains for us to cross the sea to Scotland and to Britain,' said his mother.

'Somewhere,' said his sister, 'somewhere there must be a knight who is the best of all.'

So Sir Urre and his mother and his sister set sail and early in the spring they came to Scotland. They travelled from one end of Scotland to another, but all to no avail. 'Let us go home to Hungary, good mother,' said Urre, 'for you and my sister must be weary.'

'There is yet Britain and the court of King Arthur,' said his mother. 'There are many good knights in Arthur's court, I have heard.'

Now, King Arthur chanced that year to be keeping the feast of Whitsunday at Carlisle and as soon as she was come to that city, Sir Urre's mother sent a squire about the streets to tell of her son and his wounds and beg the help of all true knights. When Arthur heard of this, he said, 'Here may be a marvel for our Whitsun feasting.' And he sent for Sir Urre to be brought to the castle.

When Sir Urre and his mother and his sister were come Arthur made them welcome and asked all their story.

Then he looked at Sir Urre where he lay in his litter, and he saw that though weak and pale he was a fine young man. 'It would be a shame,' he said, 'if such a good knight were never to be made whole. But I have many noble knights in my fellowship, and one indeed whom I have ever considered the best in the world. If God wills, here in

Britain will your son find healing. Let him be taken from the litter and laid upon the ground, and I and all my knights will in turn lay our hands on him.'

So Sir Urre was laid upon a heap of cushions in the great hall of the castle at Carlisle and Arthur knelt by him. 'I will try first,' he said, 'that if I fail, my knights will not fear to risk failing after me.'

Sir Urre smiled wearily. 'I thank you, good king. May you not fail.' But in his heart he had little hope, for it had been thus for seven years, with kings, noblemen, and knights failing, one after another.

Gently King Arthur uncovered the wound on Urre's hand and touched it, while all the knights and Urre's mother and his sister watched. But the wound remained the same. 'It is not I,' said Arthur sadly. 'Yet though I may not help you, good Sir Urre, I have many knights. We must not despair.' And he rose to give place to another. 'King Uriens,' he said, 'let you try next.'

King Uriens who had married Morgan le Fay stepped forward. 'Where Arthur fails I shall fail also,' he said. But he knelt down beside Urre and touched the wound. Yet as he had said he would, he failed, and the wound remained the same. And the knights of the Round Table sighed, while Urre's sister began to weep.

'We must not despair,' said Arthur again. 'I have many good knights yet. Let them all try in turn.'

So one atter another all the knights of the Round Table laid their hands upon Urre's wounds; and there were gathered there in Carlisle for the Whitsun feasting the whole company of the Round Table save only Lancelot and Lavaine, who had ridden on an adventure some days before.

First came Gawaine and his brothers, Gaheris, Gareth, Agravine, and Mordred; and they, like their uncles, failed. And after them came Lancelot's kinsmen, Bors, Lionel, and Ector de Maris; and they too could not heal the wounds. 'How could we succeed?' they said to each other. 'We are not the best knights in the world, for Lancelot is a better knight than we.'

Then Sir Kay the Seneschal tried and failed; and Sir Lucan and Sir Bedivere his brother, both old and trusted friends of Arthur, and they also had no fortune. And after them came in turn all the other knights of the Round Table who still lived and had come safely back from the quest of the Grail: Sir Mador, Sir Tor, Sir Geraint, Sir Ironside, and all the knights to the full number of those gathered there.

And when they had all tried and failed, Arthur said, 'I would that Lancelot were with us today.' Then, sad though they were, Arthur offered all the cheer he might to Urre's mother and his sister and bade them celebrate the Whitsun feast with him; while many of the knights stood about Sir Urre and told him tales of their adventures; but for all their courtesy, his heart was heavy, since he might have no adventures of his own.

Then a servant hurried in and knelt before King Arthur. 'At this moment,' he said, 'Sir Lancelot of the Lake rides into the courtyard with Sir Lavaine.'

'Lancelot is returned to us,' said Arthur. And he looked up to see Lancelot come into the hall with Lavaine, and he rose joyfully to greet them.

After a minute or two, Sir Urre's sister ran to where he lay and knelt by him. 'There is another knight come, brother, and he seems to me worth all the rest.' And she helped him raise his head upon the pillows that he might look at Lancelot where he talked with Arthur. Urre smiled a little, and said, 'He is the finest knight that I have ever seen.' Then he sighed. 'Yet it would be too much to hope that he should be the best knight in all the world.' But after a little he looked again at Lancelot and whispered, 'Yet it could be.'

Arthur told Lancelot of the wounded knight from Hungary and how they had all sought to heal his wounds. 'Now must you do likewise, Lancelot.'

'When you, my lord king, have failed, and so many others, how should I presume to try?' asked Lancelot.

'You shall not presume,' said Arthur, 'for it will be by my commandment.'

And Lancelot remembered how for so long men had spoken of him as the best knight in the land, save while Galahad his son had been alive; and he remembered too how he had not been worthy to see the Holy Grail uncovered; and though he had ever been modest of his own achievements, in this one moment he felt that he could not face the shame of failing as he was sure he would. 'I beg you to excuse me from this thing,' he said.

'You cannot hold back, Lancelot,' said Arthur, 'for I have more hope in you than in any man.' And from where she sat, Queen Guenever watched anxiously, though she said nothing.

But Lancelot shook his head. 'I cannot, my lord king.' And he turned away.

Sir Urre saw him turn away and weakly he tried to raise himself and call to him; and Urre's sister ran forward and laid her hand on Lancelot's arm. 'Good knight, my brother would speak with you. Have pity on him.'

Lancelot stood beside Sir Urre and looked down at him. 'God keep you, stranger,' he said.

'It has seemed to me,' said Urre, 'that since you came into the hall my pain has been a little less. I implore you, try to heal my wounds.'

And in his pity and his courtesy, Lancelot could not refuse him. 'I shall fail,' he said, 'but I will try.' And he knelt down beside Sir Urre and with care unwrapped the cloths about his head, and touched gently the three wounds; and they bled a little and then straightway were healed, without a scar, as though they had never been there. Then Lancelot touched the wounds upon Urre's body, and lastly that upon his hand, and likewise they all were healed and left no mark.

Arthur came to Sir Urre and asked, 'How is it with you now, good knight?'

Wondering, Urre arose. 'My lord king, I have never in all my life felt better.'

And Arthur and Urre himself and all the knights and ladies knelt down and gave thanks that Sir Urre had been saved and that Lancelot had won great glory for them. But Lancelot was too moved to rejoice and he wept, for he had not failed and he was indeed the best knight in all the world.

And on the morrow King Arthur ordered a tournament in honour of Sir Urre, with a diamond as the prize, and he and Gawaine and Lancelot sat as judges to see who should do best. And Sir Urre, who for seven years had longed to joust again, took part in the fighting and excelled, together with Lavaine. And to them was given the prize.

When the time came for Urre to return to his land of Hungary, he would not go. 'I cannot leave my lord, Sir

Lancelot, to whom I owe so much,' he said. And so he remained in Britain at King Arthur's court, and in time he was made a knight of the Round Table. But ever his great love was for Lancelot and, like Lavaine, he would never leave his company.

XXIV

Lancelot and Guenever

THE two youngest brothers of Sir Gawaine, Agravine and Mordred, were in many ways quite unlike
Gaheris, Gareth, and Gawaine himself, being bitter
and envious and greatly ambitious. Mordred had little
love for his uncle, King Arthur, and he longed that he too
might be a king and rule over a kingdom; while Agravine
longed to be a knight skilled above all others and renowned
throughout the land, and he envied Gawaine and Sir
Lancelot. Yet since Gawaine was his own brother, he
could not hate him, and all his hatred he spent on Lancelot.
And because the two of them dissembled, Lancelot had
no knowledge of Agravine's envy; and Arthur loved all
the five sons of his sister Margawse, though none so well
as Gawaine.

It was by chance one day that Agravine saw how, at
a moment when she thought herself to be unobserved,
Queen Guenever smiled at Lancelot with a smile that was
more than common courtesy, and he marked, too, how
Lancelot returned her smile. 'The queen and Sir Lancelot
love one another,' he thought, and considered how this
knowledge might one day serve him well. He told his
brother Mordred of it. 'Let us watch the two of them until
we are sure of it,' said Mordred. 'Then we will tell our
uncle the king and thus be rid of Sir Lancelot and maybe
gain favour for ourselves.'

So whenever they could, Agravine and Mordred

watched Guenever and Lancelot and spied upon them until they thought they knew enough to go to Arthur. 'Yet it were best if in this thing we had the approval of our brothers, if it may be won,' said Agravine.

So when the five brothers were together one day, at a time when Arthur's court was at Carlisle, Agravine said, 'It seems to me a shame and a reproach how our good uncle is deceived in his queen, for she loves not her lord but Sir Lancelot. Well would it be if the king were to know this thing.' And he told how he and Mordred had watched Guenever and Lancelot until they were certain of their love.

'If that is true, brother,' said Gawaine, 'you need not think to have me stand by you when you tell our uncle of it. I will not meddle in such matters.'

'Nor I,' said Gaheris. 'And more, I have already forgotten what I have this moment heard you say, for I will have no part in such knowledge.'

But Gareth rose, clenching his great fists. 'Lancelot is the best knight in all the world,' he said. 'And were you any man but my brother, you would die for speaking thus of him. I will no longer listen to your base lies.' And he turned and left the room in anger.

Mordred laughed. 'So our good brother Gareth is not with us in this thing,' he said. 'The more fool he.'

'And neither am I with you,' said Gawaine. 'Would you stir up strife and trouble?'

'Are you afraid that even your gentle speaking, Gawaine, may not be able to smooth over this ugly matter?' sneered Agravine.

'Lancelot once saved me from the cruelty of Sir Turquine,' said Gaheris. 'I will not be against him.'

Agravine turned to Mordred. 'Then it seems that we must do this thing alone, brother.'

Gawaine and Gaheris would have reasoned with them longer, but by mischance King Arthur came that moment into the room and greeted his nephews kindly.

'Let us do it now,' said Mordred.

'If you have any love for our uncle,' said Gawaine in a low voice, 'you will keep silent on this matter.' But Mordred only laughed at him.

Agravine stepped forward. 'My lord uncle,' he said, 'may I speak with you?'

Arthur smiled. 'What is it you would say, good nephew?'

'May heaven forgive the two of you,' said Gawaine. And he and Gaheris hastily took leave of Arthur and went from the room.

'I hope this is no quarrel,' said Arthur. He smiled again at Agravine. 'What is it you would say?'

'My lord uncle, it is to me the greatest grief in the world that I must tell you this thing. Yet I can keep silent no longer.'

'What thing is this?' asked Arthur.

'The queen, my lord uncle, is guilty of treason, in that she loves not you, her lord the king, but Sir Lancelot. And he is a traitor, for he loves her in return.'

'That cannot be true,' said Arthur, 'and I will not believe it.'

But they told him of how they had watched Guenever and Lancelot, and of all that they had seen and heard; and at the end of their telling Arthur sat pale and stricken, staring at the floor. And after a long silence he spoke. 'She was the only damsel in all my land of Britain whom I would have as a wife. Merlin told me that great sorrow would come of it. And Lancelot, he is the one whom I love best of all my knights.' Arthur rose. 'He is a true friend to me and the best knight in the world. I will not believe this thing on no more proof than your words, for all you are my sister's sons and dear to me.'

'When she knows you are from the court,' said Agravine, 'the queen ever sends for Lancelot that they may speak alone. Ride out hunting tomorrow, my lord uncle, and tell the queen that you will be gone for two days. Then shall we show you proof enough.'

'I do not care for this spying and this trickery,' said Arthur. 'They are not my way. But I will do as you say, and may you be proved wrong.' And he left them.

Agravine laughed. 'Soon there will be an end of Lancelot, whom fools have called the best knight in the world.'

But Mordred did not answer, for he was thinking, 'My uncle and the queen have no children. When I have done this service for him, might he not in gratitude make me his heir?'

So the next day Arthur rode a-hunting by Tarn Wadling in the forest of Inglewood where he had once met the ugly lady, saying that he would not return until two days were passed; and Agravine and Mordred waited.

That evening, after she had supped, the queen left the great hall and went to her apartments and sent for Sir Lancelot. And as he went to her, from a dark corner of the corridor, Mordred watched him.

A waiting-woman opened the door to Lancelot and the queen rose to greet him. 'We shall have a little time together,' she said. He kissed her and they sat beside the fire and talked.

But barely half an hour had passed before Agravine and Mordred and twelve knights of the Round Table who were their friends came fully armed and knocked upon the door, crying out, 'Come forth, Sir Lancelot, if you dare, for all your treason is known.'

Guenever rose, pale and fearful. 'It is Agravine and Mordred, I know their voices. What shall we do, Lancelot?' But Lancelot only stared at the door where the knocking had not ceased. 'They have guessed our love and they will kill you for a traitor, and I shall be burnt,' said Guenever, and she began to weep.

'I have my sword,' said Lancelot. 'Is there in your rooms any armour I may wear?'

'There is no armour, nor even a shield, and they are many against us. If only you could escape alive, Lancelot, we both should be safe. For I know that you would rescue me from the fire.'

They stood waiting, wondering what they might do, and ever Agravine shouted, 'Come out, Lancelot, you coward, and fight with us.'

And at last Lancelot said, 'I can bear it no longer. Even death is better than this. I must go out to them. Dear Guenever, if I am slain, you must not fear, for my kinsmen, Ector de Maris, Bors, and Lionel, and my good friends Urre and Lavaine, will never see you burnt. They will find a way to save you, whatever becomes of me. They will take you to my castle, Joyous Gard, and there you shall rule as a queen. And if you should be driven forth from Joyous Gard, why, there are yet my lands of Benwick, in France.'

'If you are dead,' said Guenever, 'I shall not want to live.'

Outside, the knights brought a bench from the hall, that they might batter down the door with it.

'If I had my armour,' said Lancelot, 'men should speak with admiration of my last fight. But remember, my kinsmen will always protect you.'

'If only my life could buy your freedom, I should die happily,' she sobbed.

He took her in his arms and kissed her. 'If they kill me, Guenever, pray for my soul.' He picked up his sword, wrapped his cloak around his arm, and went to the door. 'Cease your hammering,' he said. 'Would you break down the king's castle? I am coming out to you.' And he unbarred the door and held it open a little way.

Yet before he had time to step forth, a knight who was one of Mordred's friends thrust his way eagerly into the room and struck at Lancelot with his sword. But Lancelot stepped behind the opened door and so avoided the blow; and before the knight could attack again, he had raised his own sword and given him such a stroke upon the head that his helmet was split open and he fell dead inside the room. 'Quickly,' said Lancelot, 'close the door.' And before Agravine or Mordred or any of the others could follow him into the room, Lancelot had dragged the dead knight from the doorway and Guenever and her ladies had barred it once again. Lancelot smiled a little. 'See, I have won myself armour and a shield.'

Guenever helped him arm himself, and all the while Agravine called to him to come forth and fight. When he was ready, Lancelot answered him. 'If you will stand aside and let me go free, I give you my word that I shall come before the king when he returns and answer the charge you would bring upon me, and I will prove against you all that I am no traitor.'

Agravine laughed. 'Come out, Sir Lancelot, for we would kill you now, lest the king should pardon you.'

'Then take care for yourselves,' said Lancelot, and he opened the door and went out. With his first blow he struck down Agravine and killed him. The other twelve knights all rushed on him at once, but he fought so mightily that they could in no way withstand him; and many of them were wounded, and among them Mordred. And Mordred struggled to his feet and fled, for he had no mind to die before he had been a king. Seeing his flight, his friends followed after, and the way was free for Lancelot to go. He turned to Guenever where she watched from the doorway. 'I have killed Agravine,' he said. 'Arthur will find it hard to forgive me that. Will you come with me now while we may go, or will you chance his anger when he returns?'

'I will chance his anger,' she said. 'For neither Gawaine nor Gaheris were here with their brothers, and perhaps Arthur may be persuaded by them. If I find no mercy, I know you will save me from death.' She kissed him. 'Now hurry, for there is little time to lose.'

Lancelot went at once to his cousin Bors and woke him and told him what had befallen. 'I must ride from Carlisle at once,' he said, 'for tomorrow the queen may have need of me. Good cousin, are you with me in this thing?'

'I am with you always, Lancelot, and I am not the only one.' Bors rose and dressed himself and roused his brother Lionel, Sir Ector de Maris, Sir Urre from Hungary, and

257

young Sir Lavaine, and certain other knights who were their friends, and told them of how Lancelot and Guenever were named for traitors. 'We hold with Sir Lancelot,' they said, 'no matter the outcome of this.'

'My friends,' said Lancelot, 'would you be against our lord King Arthur?'

'We care not whom we are against, so long as we are for you,' they answered. Then each of them armed himself, and together they rode forth from Carlisle before dawn and waited in a wood near by the town.

And while it was yet dark, as soon as his wounds were bound, Mordred rode as fast as he might to the forest around Tarn Wadling, and there, in a hunting lodge, he found Arthur with Gawaine and told him how they had trapped Lancelot and Guenever. 'But we could not take Lancelot,' he said, 'for he armed himself and came upon us, and though we were fourteen many of us were slain; and there died Agravine my brother, and so the traitor escaped.'

And Arthur smiled a very little, as though for a second he forgot his grief. 'So he escaped from fourteen of you. He is a very brave knight, my Lancelot, and there is no other like him.' Then he sighed. 'And the queen, what of her?'

'The queen is in the castle at Carlisle, my uncle, and though Lancelot has escaped, she may die for her treason.'

And Arthur thought, 'I would that Lancelot had taken her with him, my sweet lady Guenever, that thus she might be saved.' But aloud he said, 'So shall it be, for such is the law.' And he bowed his head.

But Gawaine pleaded with him. 'I beg you, good uncle,

do not be rash in this matter. The queen might have sent for Lancelot for any other reason than that she wished to speak words of love to him. Consider how well you have loved and honoured her for many years. And remember how faithfully Lancelot has served you both, fighting in your cause whenever you needed him.'

'Have you no shame, Gawaine?' cried Mordred. 'He slew our brother Agravine, yet you can speak soft words for him.'

'I grieve for Agravine, brother, but he brought his own death on himself. I bade him not meddle in this matter.'

Arthur hesitated, torn between their counsels, and in his heart he longed to do as Gawaine advised, whether it were right or wrong. But Mordred flung himself at his feet and wept, saying, 'Agravine your nephew, who loved and admired you, is dead, and it was for you he died. Shall his slaying go unpunished? Shall one of your own blood be unavenged? Oh, my good uncle, what will you say to Margawse our mother when she asks after Agravine her son?'

Arthur covered his face with his hands, and after a time he said, 'Guenever shall be burnt tomorrow, and if I take Lancelot, he too shall die.'

'May God have pity on us all,' said Gawaine. 'And may he keep Sir Lancelot.'

Arthur rode back to Carlisle in the morning, and there he spoke to Gawaine, Gaheris, and Gareth. 'Go, put on your armour and fetch the queen, that she may be judged and burnt.'

'My lord uncle,' said Gawaine, 'since the day you made

me knight I have respected and obeyed you in all things. But this thing I will not do. I beg you hold me excused.' And without waiting for Arthur's reply, he turned and went from him.

Arthur looked at Gaheris and Gareth. 'What say you?' he asked.

'Since it is your commandment, and you are the king and our uncle,' said Gaheris, 'we must obey, though it is against our will. But our armour we shall not wear, for it is no knightly deed to fetch a lady to her death.'

But Gareth said nothing, for he was thinking of Lancelot.

So Gaheris and Gareth brought Guenever outside the walls of Carlisle, where a great fire had been built, and sentence was passed upon her that she should be burnt. And there, before all those gathered in that place, her rich robes were taken from her and she was led to the stake and bound; and in that moment Lancelot and his friends and kinsmen rode down upon the crowd, crying out for the queen. And Gareth, guessing that Lancelot was come to save her, was glad.

Many of the knights there drew their swords to fight for Arthur, and some were struck down by those who followed Lancelot; and in that way Sir Tor was slain. But Lancelot, riding at the head of his friends, saw nothing but the queen. He rode straight to the stake where she was bound, striking down with his sword all who sought to prevent him or who stood in his way. And it was thus that Gareth and Gaheris died, for they were without armour. But Lancelot did not know that he had killed them, nor had he even seen them there, for he had eyes only for Guenever. With his sword he cut the bonds which held her and lifted her upon his horse where she clung to him, weeping. 'I knew that you would come,' she said. 'I had no fear, save only for your life.'

And Lancelot cried out to his friends to follow him for the queen was saved, and with great speed they rode away from Carlisle and were not pursued, for Arthur gave no orders to ride after them.

They came to Lancelot's own castle of Joyous Gard. 'This shall be your home for as long as you need it,' said Lancelot to Guenever. And she dwelt there among his kinsmen and his friends in great honour.

But when Arthur heard of how Gaheris and Gareth had died, struck down unwittingly by Lancelot, he wept. 'My three good nephews are slain, my queen is gone from me, and I have lost out of my company the best knight in the world and the man whom I loved most. My knights are set one against the other, and the fellowship of the Round Table is broken. May God have mercy on the soul of Agravine, that he stirred up all this strife.'

And Gawaine's lady, who had once been so ugly and now was so beautiful, went to her lord where he sat alone in the castle of Carlisle, grieving for the queen and Lancelot, and she told him how they had escaped. Gawaine smiled. 'I am glad of it. I did not believe that he would leave her to be burnt, but I feared that if he came to save her, he too would be slain.' He took her hand and smiled again. 'He did as a true knight should have done. Had I been he, I would have done the same for my lady.'

She knelt by him and put her arms about him. 'Your brothers, Gaheris and Gareth, were slain in the fighting, Gawaine.'

For a long time Gawaine said nothing, and then he asked, 'Who killed them?'

'It was Sir Lancelot.'

'Never will I believe that Lancelot slew Gareth, for it was Lancelot made him a knight, and Gareth held him dearer than his own brothers; and had Lancelot bidden him, he would have gone with him last night and been against our uncle the king and against the rest of us. No, it was not Lancelot who slew him.'

'My lord, it was Lancelot, for he was seen by many men. Both Gaheris and Gareth were slain by him as they stood beside the queen.'

And Gawaine rose crying, 'Oh, that was basely done. They were unarmed. Gaheris was a good knight and never harmed any man. I remember well how first we came to Arthur's court together and rode on our first adventure. And Gareth: Gareth loved Lancelot above all other knights, and now is he slain by him. Never can I forgive Lancelot for this.'

'It is said, my lord, that in the press of battle Lancelot did not see whom he slew, or else he would have held his hand.'

But Gawaine would not hear her. 'Shamefully has Lancelot slain my brothers, my good brothers whom I shall not see again, and with God's help I will avenge their deaths.' And he wept, while his lady sought in vain to comfort him.

XXV

The Siege of Joyous Gard

AFTER the deaths of Gaheris and Gareth, Sir Gawaine
went to King Arthur and urged him to make
war on Lancelot. All his wonted gentle speaking
utterly forgotten, he talked to Arthur of nothing but
revenge, for he could not believe that Lancelot had not
intended to slay his brothers. 'I shall not rest,' he said, 'until
I have avenged their deaths. I shall seek out Lancelot and
meet with him and either he or I shall die. And it would be
great shame to you, my uncle, if you were not to fetch
back the queen from Lancelot who has stolen her away.'

At first King Arthur would not. 'Lancelot was my
friend,' he said, 'and the best knight in the world. I cannot
hate him, even now.'

Yet ever the Lady Linette whom Gaheris had married,

and fair Lionesse who had been Gareth's lady, knelt before him with tears and implored him to avenge the deaths of their lords; and ever Gawaine persuaded him, saying, 'If you will not do this thing, my lord uncle, I must withdraw myself from your court for ever, for I will not have part in your dishonour.'

So that at last Arthur sighed and said, 'I have lost Guenever and I have lost Lancelot, and I have lost three nephews already in this matter. I cannot lose you also, Gawaine. I will do as you ask.'

Arthur called his knights and his men together, and with an army he marched in the spring to Joyous Gard, and laid siege to it. But Lancelot would permit no one to go forth from the castle to fight with him. 'He is my lord King Arthur,' he said, 'and I will not bear arms against him.' And thus they remained all the summer, until it was harvest time.

And then one day Lancelot went upon the walls of Joyous Gard and spoke to Arthur where he was encamped below. 'My lord king,' he said, 'call off your siege, for this war will bring no glory to either of us.'

Arthur looked up. 'Come down if you dare, Sir Lancelot, and you and I will meet alone and fight together for Guenever my queen.'

'It was you who made me a knight, good king, I will never fight with you.'

Arthur smiled bitterly. 'Your words are fine and noble, I would that your deeds matched them. Where is Queen Guenever?'

'Here, where she is safe from burning,' replied Lancelot. 'She is a true and noble lady, guilty of no treason, and that

I am ready to prove with my sword against any man who denies it, save only yourself and Gawaine.'

Gawaine came and stood beside his uncle. 'Far be it from me to speak evil of the queen, for I have ever held her in honour. She is a good and loyal lady, and the king will win her from you once again.'

'I do not hold her here by force,' said Lancelot, 'but only for her safety. If you would give me your word, my lord king, that she should come to no harm, she might go freely from my castle if she would.'

But before Arthur could reply to him, Gawaine had spoken once more. 'For all your boasting, Lancelot, my uncle the king shall have his queen again and upon his own terms, and he shall take your life if it pleases him. And if he does not kill you, then I shall, for you slew my brother Gaheris who never did you harm, and Gareth who loved you well.'

For a moment Lancelot did not answer him, remembering Gareth. Then he said, 'Bitterly have I regretted their slaying since first I learnt of it, but I never willed that they should die. I would as soon have slain my own cousin Bors, as Gareth your brother.'

'You lie,' cried Gawaine. 'And I shall one day avenge their cruel murder. Never say I have not warned you of it, false Lancelot.'

'I know well', said Lancelot quietly, 'that if ever you take me captive I can expect no mercy. But I will not fight with you.'

Then, at the order of Gawaine, many men called out upon Lancelot, naming him traitor and coward that dared not take up a sword. When Sir Bors and Sir Lionel and Sir

Ector de Maris could bear it no longer, they pleaded with Lancelot to give them leave to go out and fight. Lancelot went once more upon the walls and spoke to Arthur and Gawaine. 'I and my friends will come forth and fight with you, but I beg that you, my lord king, and you, Sir Gawaine, will hold you from the battle, for I wish no harm to come to you from me.'

'If you are afraid of me and of my lord uncle the king,' jeered Gawaine, 'that is nothing to us. Do you think that we should hold from the battle when it is in our own cause that we have come against you?'

'Then I see that it must be as you will,' sighed Lancelot.

In the morning Lancelot bade all his friends and their men be ready to fight for him and the queen that day, and they were glad. 'But I would not have our lord King Arthur or his nephew, good Sir Gawaine, come to any harm,' he said, 'and I forbid you to seek to kill them.' They rode out from the three gates of Joyous Gard with Lancelot at the head of those who came through the middle gate and Bors and Lionel leading those on either side. And King Arthur's army was drawn up ready to meet them.

Immediately Gawaine rode forth into the midst of the field and challenged to single combat any who would fight against him, for he hoped thereby to shame Lancelot into doing battle with him. But it was Sir Lionel who rode to meet Gawaine. Yet, for all that Lionel was a good knight and brave, he was no match for Gawaine, and with a mighty blow Gawaine thrust him through the body with his lance, so that Lionel fell to the ground senseless, and Sir Ector de Maris and his squires carried him back to Joyous Gard, where he was in time healed of his wound.

Then Arthur gave word for the battle to begin, and the armies fell upon each other, and many great deeds were done by either side. But ever Lancelot tried to avoid King Arthur, though Arthur sought him out and attacked him; yet never would Lancelot strike at him in return, and ever Lancelot watched to see that Arthur and Gawaine came to no harm.

Once when Arthur would have provoked Lancelot to fight with him and Lancelot did no more to defend himself than to take as many as he might of Arthur's heavy blows upon his shield, Sir Bors rode forward, and with a great thrust of his lance flung Arthur from his horse. He dismounted and drew his sword and stood above Arthur and called out to Lancelot, 'Shall I make an end of this battle, cousin?'

But Lancelot leapt from his horse. 'If you value your own life, Bors, you will not touch him, for never will I see the good king who made me knight either slain or shamed.' And he raised King Arthur from the ground and helped him to mount his horse once more. 'My lord king,' he said, 'might we not be accorded?'

And looking on his friend, Arthur wept and rode away without a word, thinking, 'In courtesy there is no one like him.'

Soon after that it was evening, and fighting ceased until the morning. When it was light, as on the day before, Gawaine rode alone on to the field and challenged any who would to single combat; and thinking to avenge his brother Lionel, Bors rode to meet him. With the great force of their charge they were both flung to the ground, but though Gawaine rose to his feet and drew his sword,

Bors lay still and had to be carried by his squires into Joyous Gard. Then once again the battle started.

But because Lancelot had no heart in the fighting and would not strike down without mercy those who fought for his king, his men were hard pressed and many were like to have been slain. And Sir Urre, the knight of Hungary, came to him and said, 'The day will be lost for us, Sir Lancelot, if you do not fight your best, for our men lack courage seeing you spare those who do not spare you.'

And from pity for his friends Lancelot fought mightily, and all his men with him, so that King Arthur's army was worsted and would have been defeated, but that Lancelot bade the battle cease until the morrow, that Arthur and his men might have time to recover.

But the next day there came to the king the good bishop of Rochester. 'My lord king,' he said, 'this is no way for Christian knights to fight together, slaying one another as though they had not all once belonged to the noblest fellowship of knights in the world, your own Round Table.' And he bade the king in the name of God take back Queen Guenever and be accorded with Sir Lancelot.

Arthur would have been glad and willing to do both, but Gawaine would not hear of any friendship with Lancelot. 'It will be a happy day, lord uncle, when our good lady the queen is restored to you, but you will be shamed for ever if you forgive Sir Lancelot.'

So sadly Arthur replied to the bishop, 'If Lancelot will give her up, I will take back my queen and she shall have all respect and honour. But with Lancelot I cannot be accorded.'

The bishop went to Joyous Gard with word of the king's decision; and Lancelot told Guenever of the offer. 'What would you that I should answer him?' he asked.

After she had thought, Guenever said, 'For both our sakes, and for the sake of Arthur whom we two love and honour, it is best that I should go back to him and that this war may be over.'

'If the king will give his word,' said Lancelot to the bishop, 'that good Queen Guenever will be received with honour and kindness, and that never will any man speak against her or call her traitress, then I will give her into his hands.'

'I myself will be her surety,' replied the bishop.

'I have ever trusted King Arthur,' said Lancelot. 'I shall trust him in this. Go you to him, my lord bishop, and tell him to be ready, in eight days, to receive the queen.'

Arthur withdrew his army and returned to his castle at Carlisle; and when eight days were passed, Lancelot and Guenever rode forth from Joyous Gard. Guenever was all in white and gold, and never had she looked more fair, though her heart was breaking for all the sorrow that had come to the land through her, even as Merlin had prophesied. And thus they rode through the city of Carlisle where the townsfolk wept in joy to see their queen once more.

When they had come to the courtyard of the castle, Lancelot took Guenever by the hand, and led her into the great hall where Arthur sat upon his throne, and going to the foot of the dais they knelt before the king. But Arthur looked at them and said nothing, for he loved them both too much to trust himself not to speak kindly to Lancelot.

When Lancelot saw how the king would not speak, he stood up and raised Guenever to stand beside him, and quietly he said to Arthur, 'My lord king, as you commanded, I have brought to you Queen Guenever, and if there is any here, save only yourself, who would call her other than a most true and noble lady, he will have to answer to me for it.' He waited, but no one spoke against her. 'My lord king,' said Lancelot, 'there was a time when you were glad enough of my sword to defend the queen. When I proved her innocence against Sir Mador's accusations, you had only praise for me. Remembering that, do you think I could have done other than saved her from your anger when you would have burnt her, knowing that when it was done you would have regretted it? Yet Sir Agravine and Sir Mordred called me traitor.'

'And they spoke truly,' cried Gawaine. While Mordred smiled, thinking, 'Gawaine is with me now.'

'Sir Agravine and Sir Mordred called me traitor,' repeated Lancelot, 'but I have ever been a loyal knight to you and served you faithfully.'

'I have never given you reason to be otherwise,' said Arthur sadly. 'For of all my knights I have loved and honoured you the most.'

But Gawaine, from where he stood beside the throne, thinking that Arthur might yet be accorded with Lancelot, said, 'My uncle our king may do as he pleases in this matter, yet I will never call Sir Lancelot my friend, for he slew my brothers, and one day I shall be avenged on him for that.'

'Have you forgotten, Gawaine,' said Lancelot gently, 'the great grief you had when your cousin Uwaine died at your hands? Even so did I feel when I heard how I had slain Gareth and Gaheris. I ever pray for their souls, and if it is pleasing to you, I will build an abbey in memory of them.'

But Gawaine was a brave and honourable knight, and to him it was a terrible thing that one man should slay another who was unarmed and his friend; and because he could not believe that Lancelot had not seen Gaheris and Gareth when they stood close by the queen on that day when she was to have been burnt, he could not forgive him. 'Your offers will avail you nothing, Sir Lancelot, yet since you have come here to Carlisle in peace today, we may not fight. I may only say that I can never again call you my friend, and I can only ask that our lord the king will forbid you his realm and banish you for ever.' And he bent his head and spoke apart with Arthur, urging him to send Lancelot away.

Arthur feared for the lives of both Gawaine and Lancelot if they were not parted, and though he longed to keep Lancelot about him, he said, 'It shall be as Sir Gawaine wishes, and you, Sir Lancelot, must go for ever from my land of Britain upon pain of death if you return.' And he turned away and would not look at Lancelot.

After a time Lancelot answered him. 'Though this is not my own land, I have ever thought of it as my home, and for me, in all the world, there has been no other king than King Arthur. And since he is my lord, I obey him in all things, even in this last and hardest command of all.'

Arthur bowed his head and wept, but Gawaine said, 'Have done with talking, Lancelot. Give up the queen and go.'

271

Lancelot turned to Guenever, and taking her hands in his, spoke to her before all those gathered there. 'Good queen, I must go from you and from my lord the king and from the brave and noble fellowship of the Round Table for ever or be put to death. I beg you, remember me with kindness and pray for me. But if ever at any time any man should wrong you or speak false words of you, or if ever you need a true knight to serve you, send me word of it, and I will come to you, no matter who would prevent me.'

But she could not answer him for her tears. He kissed her hand and led her to King Arthur. 'Here is my lady your queen,' he said, 'and may no man dare to speak ill of her.' And he put her hand in Arthur's and turned and went from the hall. And there was no one there who did not weep, save only Gawaine.

Lancelot rode from Carlisle and came for the last time to Joyous Gard, and there he called his kinsmen and his friends together. 'I must leave this land,' he said, 'never to return, and I go with neither honour nor good name, for I am banished. So must I bid you all farewell.'

Young Sir Lavaine leapt to his feet. 'My good lord, if you would stay in Britain, I for one will be ready to defend you against the king. And I do not doubt that there are others would do likewise.' And all Lancelot's kinsmen and his friends cried out in agreement.

Lancelot shook his head. 'You have my thanks for that, good friends and kinsmen. But I have ever loved our lord King Arthur, and I would not rebel against his commands. I shall go, and since my lands in Britain are left to me, I give them all to you, that you may never want, even when I am gone.'

Yet they all cried out at once, 'If you go, you do not go alone, for we shall all go with you.'

'My friends, I can only thank you,' said Lancelot.

So Lancelot set sail from Britain, together with his brother and his cousins and his friends Lavaine and Urre, and all those others who loved and honoured him. And so he came to his own lands of Benwick in France, where his father had been a king.

XXVI

Lancelot and Gawaine

AFTER Sir Lancelot had gone from Britain there was little happiness for King Arthur or Queen Guenever, with the fellowship of the Round Table broken and divided and so many good knights gone with Lancelot.

Now that of the five sons of Arthur's sister Margawse he and Gawaine alone remained, Mordred had an even greater part in the counsels of the king. But his ambition was in no way content, nor would be until he wore the crown. Lest at any time he might find their services useful to his ends, he gathered to himself secretly a number ot traitor knights, promising them great rewards if ever he achieved his aim. And he thought to himself, 'If my uncle and Gawaine went into France, I should be left to rule the kingdom in their absence. And who knows what I might not do then.'

So he set himself to persuade Gawaine afresh against Sir Lancelot. 'Here we sit idly, brother, while Lancelot lords it in his castle in Benwick and laughs when he remembers how he slew our three brothers. For shame, have you forgotten all the ill he has done to us and to our uncle the king? Shall it be left to me to avenge Gaheris, Gareth, and good Agravine? I who was the youngest of us all and the least experienced in knightly deeds; I whose proud boast it has ever been that my eldest brother is a knight unsurpassed in skill, honourable and courteous above all others?

Why, Gawaine, soon men will forget your past glories and say that you are afraid of Lancelot.'

'I have not forgotten, brother,' said Gawaine. 'I shall go to Benwick and seek out Lancelot.'

'Do not go alone, Gawaine. Let us persuade our uncle the king to go with you and take an army, that all those traitors who hold with Lancelot may reap a just reward. For who knows, they may even now be plotting against the king.'

So without respite, Mordred and Gawaine urged Arthur against Lancelot, warning him how Lancelot and his friends might one day do great harm to Britain; so that in the end he half believed them and was persuaded by Gawaine's sincerity and Mordred's cunning arguments. He sighed. 'I will take an army into France, lest Lancelot's friends seek to avenge his banishment, though Lancelot himself would give them no encouragement in such designs, of that I am certain.'

So Arthur and Gawaine sailed with an army over the sea to Benwick, while Guenever wept unceasingly and Mordred was left to govern Britain until they should return. 'I will see that all things are ordered as you would wish them to be ordered, my lord uncle,' he said, and smiled.

Arthur and Gawaine laid waste all the country round about the city of Benwick and besieged the city; yet Lancelot did not come out to meet them, and forbade his knights to do otherwise.

And one by one Lancelot's kinsmen and his friends came to him, beseeching him to let them fight. 'Are we cowards that we should hide in the city? Give us leave to go out and join battle.' But Lancelot would not. 'I do not wish this war,' he said. 'I will send to our lord King Arthur and ask for peace.' So he sent forth a young damsel on a palfrey to speak with the king, and she rode to Arthur's camp. There she was received by good Sir Lucan. 'Do you come with offers from Sir Lancelot?' he asked.

'He offers peace,' said the damsel.

Sir Lucan sighed. 'I think that my lord the king would be accorded with Sir Lancelot were it not for Sir Gawaine.' He helped the damsel from her palfrey and led her into Arthur's pavilion.

When Arthur heard how Lancelot asked for peace he did not answer, but sat silent, remembering the old days.

'Let us return to Britain, my lord king,' said Sir Lucan, 'for there is no glory to be won in warring on Sir Lancelot.'

But Gawaine knelt before his uncle. 'Will you turn back now, with my brothers unavenged? All men will speak of your cowardice and shame.'

'Let it be as you wish,' said Arthur. 'For I have little joy left in life now, save only you, who were ever my best loved nephew. Give you the answer to the damsel, for I cannot.'

Gawaine rose and turned to the damsel. 'Lady, tell Sir Lancelot that it is too late to ask for peace. And tell him too that I have come here to meet with him, to avenge my brothers or be slain.' And with courtesy he went to her and took her by the hand and led her to Sir Lucan. 'See the lady safely on her way, I pray you.'

When Lancelot heard the answer to his offer, he said, 'There can be no honour to us in fighting against our lord the king.' And he went apart from his friends.

276

The next morning Gawaine rode up to the main gate of the city, carrying his lance. 'Is there one within who dares come forth and fight with me?' he called.

'Allow me to go, good cousin,' said Bors to Lancelot.

'As you will,' replied Lancelot.

So Bors armed himself and mounted his horse and the gate was opened and he rode forth; and at Gawaine's first stroke he was hurled to the ground, so that his squires had to make haste and carry him into the city.

The next day Gawaine came again and called out his challenge, and Lionel rode forth to him, and fared even as his brother. And after that Gawaine came each day, and each day one knight or another rode out of the city to fight with him; but no one of them could withstand him. Ector de Maris, Lavaine, Urre, and all the others, they were overcome and wounded, so great a jouster was Gawaine.

And at last there came a morning when Gawaine rode to the main gate of the city and called out, 'Where are you, Lancelot, you coward? I have met with all your knights and worsted them, do you lack their courage? Are you ashamed of your evil deeds that you do not show your face? Come out, traitor and murderer, and fight.'

And Lancelot's kinsmen and his friends all looked at him and asked, 'What will you do now?'

'I would avoid this thing,' said Lancelot. 'Three of his brothers have I killed, I would not risk killing Gawaine.'

'He has called you murderer and coward, the shame is ours as much as yours if you do not go out to him.'

'I will go out,' said Lancelot, 'and may God have pity on us both.'

So Lancelot armed himself and took up his lance and

rode forth on a white horse. 'I have waited a long time for this day,' said Gawaine. 'We fight to the uttermost.'

A great crowd of Lancelot's friends and followers came out from the city and stood below the walls to watch; while from the pavilions of Arthur's camp the knights hurried to see this greatest fight of all between two matchless foes.

But Arthur turned away and would not watch. 'They are both too dear to me, and today one of them must die,' he said to Sir Kay. And Kay had no comfort to offer him.

Lancelot and Gawaine faced one another and charged. The force of their meeting was so great, as the lances of each of them struck on the other's shield, that their horses fell beneath them. They drew their swords and fought on foot, and many mighty blows they gave each other. Yet at first neither gained the advantage, so well matched they were. And then, after an hour or two, it seemed as though Gawaine were the stronger, and Lancelot did little more than defend himself.

'How goes the battle?' asked Arthur of Sir Kay.

And from where he stood in the opening of the king's pavilion Kay answered, 'It seems as though the victory will be Gawaine's.'

Arthur covered his face with his hands. 'May God defend them both,' he said.

But when they had been fighting for three hours Gawaine grew tired and, seeing this, Lancelot increased his blows and put forth all his strength, and with one mighty stroke upon the helmet he felled Gawaine to the ground.

'How goes the battle?' asked Arthur.

'Gawaine is fallen, but Lancelot still stands,' said Kay.

'It is the end,' said Arthur. 'I have now but one nephew left to me.' And he wept.

But Lancelot, leaning on his sword, watched Gawaine for a moment, and then he walked away a little distance to give Gawaine a chance to rise. Gawaine raised himself on his elbow. 'Why do you fly from me, traitor? Come back and kill me, for if you leave me my life I shall fight you again one day.'

'I shall be ready for you,' said Lancelot.

'We swore to fight to the uttermost, Lancelot. Come back and finish this fight.'

'I will not kill you while you cannot stand, Gawaine. And I will not insult you by asking you to yield.'

Gawaine struggled to rise, but he could not, and he fell back upon the ground and lay still. And when he saw that their battle was over for that day, Lancelot turned and went to his friends. And Arthur's knights took up Gawaine and carried him towards Arthur's pavilion.

'Is the battle over, Kay?' asked Arthur.

'It is over,' replied Kay, 'and both Lancelot and Gawaine are yet alive.' Arthur came and looked at Gawaine as he was laid upon a couch, and he saw that he was indeed alive. 'How did it happen?' he asked Kay. And when Kay had told him, Arthur said, 'Lancelot is not only the best knight in the world, he is also the noblest enemy.'

'Enemy?' said Kay. 'You might call him friend, for well has he shown his friendship this day for you and yours.'

But Gawaine lay on his bed and thought with bitterness of Lancelot. For though he would have honoured and admired such mercy in any other knight, he held it a shame to himself that he should have taken his life as a gift from one whom he believed had murdered his brothers, and he waited only until he might meet with Lancelot again.

When three weeks were passed and he was healed of his wounds, he armed himself and rode to the main gate of Benwick. 'Come forth, Lancelot,' he called. 'Come forth, that we may finish our fight.'

Lancelot went upon the city walls and Gawaine looked up at him. 'Come down,' he called. 'Last time we met you had the better of me. This time it is you who will lie upon the ground.'

'May heaven protect me from being at your mercy even as you were at mine,' thought Lancelot. 'For then would I be dead indeed.' He sighed and came down from the walls and armed himself and rode out through the city gate upon a white horse. And once again, on either side, the knights and men came forth to see the fight.

At their first charge Gawaine's lance shattered, but Lancelot's held, and with the force of his blow Gawaine's horse rose with its forefeet in the air, and Gawaine was flung backwards over the saddle bow. He drew his sword and held his shield firmly. 'My horse has failed me, Lancelot, but I shall not fail myself. Dismount and fight.'

So they fought together on foot, and once again never had such a battle been seen. For three hours and more they fought, until at last the advantage lay with Lancelot, and he gave Gawaine such a mighty stroke upon the helmet, over the old wound, that with the force of it and the pain Gawaine dropped his sword and fell, while all there watched with held breath, wondering if Lancelot would spare him yet again. And Lancelot stepped away from Gawaine and waited for him to rise.

Gawaine raised himself upon one hand and fumbled for his sword on the grass and took hold of it and looked at Lancelot. 'You have slain three of King Lot's sons, come now and slay a fourth,' he taunted.

'I will not slay you while you cannot stand,' said Lancelot. And though Gawaine called to him and mocked him, he did no more than wait. And when he saw that Gawaine was too far spent to rise, he went again into the city.

It was a month before Gawaine was healed of his wound; and each day Lancelot went upon the city walls to watch for him, for he knew that he would return to finish the fight. But one day, when he looked out, he saw that the siege was lifted and Arthur was striking camp.

'What can it mean?' asked Lavaine, as they watched the baggage horses hastily loaded and the pavilions taken down. 'Would they lure us forth by a trick?'

'That is not King Arthur's way,' said Lancelot.

'Perhaps they are afraid of our might,' said Urre.

'Our lord the king fears nothing,' said Lancelot.

'Perhaps Gawaine has abandoned his quarrel at last,' suggested Lionel.

'Gawaine has sworn to avenge his brothers. He has never yet broken an oath,' said Lancelot.

Together Lancelot and the others watched the knights mounted upon their horses and waiting before the city walls; and then Arthur himself appeared with Gawaine at his side, and they rode at the head of their men, away from Benwick towards the sea and Britain. Yet still no one could guess why they had gone.

XXVII

The End of Arthur

WHEN Sir Mordred was left to govern the land of Britain, he thought how at last the crown was almost in his grasp. First he sent word to all those traitor knights whom he had won to him, bidding them be ready to come when he needed them. Then, while Arthur laid siege to Benwick, Mordred sent men about the country to speak subtly against the king: how he waged an unjust war on Lancelot and yet did no more than lay waste his lands, fearing in his weakness to meet him face to face. Many of the simple folk believed these things, as did many of those who had loved Lancelot and to whom he ever stood as the pattern of all knighthood, and they were angered at the king.

Then, when he thought the time had come, Mordred called out his knights and their men, and marched upon Camelot where Queen Guenever was. 'You are greatly loved by the people, good queen,' he said, 'and your voice speaking for me would bring me much support against the king.' Angry and appalled, Guenever called him a traitor, but Mordred only smiled and said, 'Why should you show any duty to him, does he not war against your Lancelot?'

'Were either Lancelot or Arthur here, you would not live long to speak thus,' said Guenever.

'But they are far away, good queen, and I am here, so it were best for you that you did as I say.'

And Guenever thought how it is only by guile that guile can be met, and she pretended to be ready to give him her support against the king, and she was thus allowed to go freely about Camelot. And when she saw her chance, she fled by night to London, with a few of her ladies; and going to the Tower of London, she called to her all knights who were faithful to Arthur, that they might oppose Sir Mordred. And she sent a message over the sea to Benwick, bidding Arthur return.

Mordred, angry at having been tricked so easily, led his army to London and besieged the Tower, calling upon Guenever to surrender. But she waited for Arthur to come home and save his land, and answered Mordred with defiance.

When her message was brought to Arthur, he sent for Gawaine and told him of it. Gawaine, not yet healed of the wound he had received from Lancelot, wept and knelt at Arthur's feet, pleading for his uncle's forgiveness that it was his own brother who had shown himself a traitor. 'It is not your fault nor is it your shame that Mordred has done thus,' said Arthur. 'And though I have now lost four of my five nephews who were the sons of my sister Margawse, three in death, and one in treason which is worse by far than death, I have still the one I have ever loved the best. Come, cease your tears, Gawaine, we must return to Britain with no delay.'

At once they abandoned the siege of Benwick and withdrew from Lancelot's lands, making with all haste for the coast of France, and from there they set sail for Britain, reaching shore at Dover. But Mordred had word of their coming, and he was there to meet them with his army.

Mordred fell upon Arthur and his men as they disembarked, and there was a great battle on the shore. But though Mordred had the greater numbers, he had not the same just cause; and though Arthur lost many of his good knights, he won the day, and Mordred retreated to Canterbury.

When Arthur looked about him in the evening to see how many of his knights had been slain, he saw Gawaine lying on the beach. He knelt beside him and put an arm beneath his shoulders and tried to comfort him.

Gawaine's voice was weak when he spoke. 'I was hurt upon the old wound which Lancelot gave me, and I am dying, my uncle. But if I must die, I am glad that it is from a wound given me by Lancelot, and not by the hand of a lesser man. Good uncle, had Lancelot and his kinsmen and his friends been here with us today, my traitor brother would be dead and the land would be yours again. And I am to blame that he was not here, for when you would have made peace with him I would not hear of it. I beg of you, my uncle, before it is too late, find me a man who will go swiftly over the sea to Benwick and carry a message to Lancelot.' And when a knight had been found to do the deed, Gawaine said to him, 'Go to the city of Benwick and greet Sir Lancelot of the Lake from me. Tell him that my brother Mordred has taken up arms against our lord the king, and bid him come to Britain with all speed. Tell him that I am dying of the wound which he gave to me, and that it is all through my own fault. And bid him pray for my soul.' When the knight was gone, Gawaine smiled a little. 'Do not weep, my lord uncle, for though you have lost me, soon will you have Lancelot again. But do not, I beg you, trust Mordred, and do not meet him in battle again until you have Lancelot with you.'

'I shall remember,' said Arthur. And in a little while Gawaine was dead.

Arthur sent for Sir Lucan and Sir Bedivere his brother, and said to them, 'In a month Sir Lancelot should be with us, but until that day we are not strong enough to fight again with Mordred. Go to him and make peace with him for one month from this day. He also has lost men in this battle, so he will agree to my proposal.'

Sir Lucan and Sir Bedivere went to Mordred and told him of Arthur's offer, and Mordred was glad, for it gave him longer to increase his strength; and a place was appointed where Arthur and Mordred might meet on the morrow to set their seals upon the treaty.

The next day the two armies were drawn up on a broad plain, and on the open ground between them it was agreed that Arthur should meet Mordred. But Arthur remembered Gawaine's warning and he did not trust his nephew. He left word with the leaders of his men, bidding them, 'If you see any man draw a sword, it will be treachery, and come in to the attack immediately.'

Arthur and Mordred met between the armies and each had fourteen knights with him. And Arthur forebore to speak as he wished to Mordred, as they laid their seals to the treaty, and when a cask of wine was brought, they drank together.

But one of the knights who followed Mordred trod upon an adder which was hidden beneath a clump of heather and it bit him. Feeling the bite, he looked down and saw the snake, and drew his sword to kill it. And when those with Arthur's army saw the blade flash in the sunlight, they cried, 'Treachery! To arms!' and charged. And Mordred's men, seeing the attack, did likewise; and instantly there was confusion, and the battle was joined.

Arthur mounted his horse and galloped back to his men. 'Of all my misfortunes,' he said, 'surely this must be the last.'

In the fighting on the plain died the king's best and noblest knights: Sir Geraint, Sir Mador, Sir Ironside, and many others. And there, too, was slain sharp-tongued Sir Kay the Seneschal who had been Arthur's first friend, striving bravely and railing against all traitors until he was struck down.

All day the battle lasted and on to the day's end, until on both sides there were but few left alive. And at sunset, Arthur, wearied from his fighting, looked about him and found that of all his knights of the Round Table only his old friends Sir Lucan and Sir Bedivere remained alive, and they both were wounded, Lucan grievously.

'Are there but we three left?' asked Arthur.

'No more than that, my lord king,' said Lucan.

Then Arthur saw where Mordred stood, spent and worn, leaning on his sword, a short way off, among his own slain men. 'The traitor still lives,' he said. 'Give me your lance, Sir Lucan, for mine is broken.'

'He is all that is left of his great army,' said Lucan wearily, 'and he is most wretched. Let him be. The day is ours, though we are but three, for he is one alone.'

'Shall I let my brave knights go unavenged, and good Sir Kay who was my foster-brother? Give me your lance, Lucan.'

Sir Lucan held out his lance and Arthur took it; and Sir Bedivere looked up from where he sat upon the ground. 'God be with you, my lord king,' he said.

Arthur went to where Mordred stood, and Mordred lifted his head and saw him come. 'Now shall you die, Mordred my nephew,' said Arthur.

'I tried for a crown and I failed, but I do not ask for mercy,' said Mordred. 'I am ready.' And he raised up his sword with both his hands. Arthur thrust forward with the lance and drove it right through Mordred's body; but the sword came down upon his head, cutting through his helmet, and at the same moment that Mordred fell dead, Arthur fell senseless beside him.

Sir Bedivere and Sir Lucan came to Arthur and stood by him. Arthur opened his eyes and looked about. 'Oh, Lancelot,' he said, 'had you been here with me, I should not now be dying.' He held out his hand to Bedivere. 'Help me up, good friends. There is a lake in the valley below this plain, it is even that same lake where Merlin once led me. I would go to it again.'

But when they bent to raise him, Sir Lucan's wounds

broke out afresh, and he fell to the ground and so died. 'Good Lucan,' said Arthur, 'he would have helped me, but he had more need for help than I.' Bedivere wept for his brother. 'All my old friends are gone, save only you,' said Arthur.

Sir Bedivere helped Arthur to his feet and laid Arthur's arm about his shoulders, and so they went together towards the lake. And when they were within a little distance of it, Arthur said, 'Leave me here and take my sword and carry it to the water's edge and throw it in; then return and tell me what you see.' And he gave Excalibur to Bedivere.

'I will do as you ask, my lord king,' said Bedivere. But on his way to the lake he looked at the sword and thought how it would be a shame to cast away such a fine weapon and one which had served his king so well. 'Besides,' he thought, 'my lord King Arthur may not die, and then he will have need of it again.' And he hid Excalibur beneath a tree and returned to Arthur.

'Is it done?' asked Arthur.

'It is done,' replied Bedivere.

'And what did you see?' asked Arthur.

'My good lord, I saw no more than the water.'

'Then you have not done as I commanded you. Go back and do as I bid.'

So Bedivere returned to where he had left Excalibur, but as he took it up he thought, 'The king is sorely wounded, he is not in his right mind. If he comes to himself again, he will blame me for this.' And he replaced Excalibur beneath the tree.

'Is it done?' asked Arthur when he returned.

'It is done,' said Bedivere.

'And what did you see?'

'I saw no more than the ripples on the water, my lord king.'

'Then you are lying and you did not throw it in,' said Arthur. 'You are the only knight I have left to me, and I have ever trusted you, and now you would betray me and have the sword for yourself, because it has a golden hilt.'

And Bedivere went to where he had hidden Excalibur and brought it out and carried it to the water's edge and flung it in. And he saw how a hand clothed in white silk interwoven with threads of gold came out of the lake and caught the sword as it fell, shook it three times, and vanished below the water. Marvelling, he returned to where Arthur awaited him.

'Is it done?' asked Arthur.

'It is done,' said Bedivere. And he told Arthur of what he had seen.

Arthur smiled. 'It is even as I thought it would be,' he said. 'Now take me to the lake.'

So Bedivere helped him down to the shore of the lake, and when they were there a barge came out of the dusk to the water's edge, and in the barge were four damsels wearing cloaks with black hoods. 'Lay me in the barge,' said Arthur.

Sir Bedivere laid him gently in the barge and the four damsels knelt about him, and one of them was the Lady of the Lake who had once given him Excalibur. 'My good lord king,' said Bedivere, 'would you leave me?'

'There is no more that I can do for you or for any man,' said Arthur. 'I go perchance to be healed of my wound;

and if I am healed maybe I shall return, or maybe I shall never come again. So farewell, my last remaining friend.'

The barge moved away from the shore and slowly out into the darkness of the lake, while Bedivere wept.

And thus Sir Bedivere remained all night; and in the morning he wandered away, and came at last to a hermitage, and there he dwelt with the good hermit for the rest of the days of his life.

And that was how King Arthur ended, and no man since has ever known whether he died or whether, somewhere, he still lives.

When Gawaine's message was brought to Sir Lancelot, he said, 'Pity was it that I did not kill Mordred on that night he escaped from me.' Then he sent for his kinsmen and friends. 'Our lord the king has need of us,' he said. 'We must leave at once for Britain.'

So with all the speed they might they left Benwick and sailed once more to Britain; but when they were come there it was too late and the great battle between Arthur and Mordred was over. 'If only I had been by his side,' said Lancelot, 'he would still be with us.' And he wept.

'What will you do now, good cousin?' asked Bors.

'I will go find my lady the queen,' said Lancelot. And he rode to Almesbury where Guenever had taken refuge in a nunnery. When they saw each other once again they wept as though they could not cease.

'Through us,' said Guenever, 'came all this sorrow upon our lord King Arthur and upon the land of Britain and upon so many noble knights.'

And though now at last they might have married, they had no heart for it, for they knew that ever between them would be the memory of Arthur, whom they both had loved and honoured, and who had held them both so dear. And there in the nunnery at Almesbury they parted for the last time, and Guenever became a nun, while Lancelot rode about the land until he came by chance to the hermitage where Sir Bedivere dwelt, and there he remained; and there he was one day joined by Sir Bors.

And in time Guenever died, and, soon after, Lancelot, and so they were at peace.